CW00868066

A Criccieth Lore

Mansell Williams

New Generation Publishing

Other novels by the author:

Echoes and Ashes

The Estuary

The Bowler Hat

Pasticcio

The Square Patio

The Profiteers

Pretence

Discord

Rustic Riddles

Couriers

Riffs

Designer Deeds

Furtive Fates

Images

Watersheds

A55. J18

This is for the people who know me.

Acknowledgement:

A sincere Thank You to Gillian for her support and guidance during the editing.

Passages from the poem *Welsh Incident* by Robert Graves (1895- 1985) are quoted in the novel.

The book's front cover was designed by the author.

1

Thursday evening, on the 26th October 2017, the small coastal town of Criccieth, situated on the southern edge of the Snowdonia National Park in north Wales, was pitch black. The temperature was tumbling and storm force south-westerly winds, plus torrential rain, were pummelling the dwellings near the town's foreshore.

Twenty-nine-year-old, married Mancunian, Kelly Glover, alone in the roomy lounge of the spacious state-of-the-art top flat in a two-storey Victorian-style detached house, with views over the bay, was waiting for news from her husband, Ray, who was travelling from Manchester to join her.

The handsome six-foot plus tall, thirty-four-year old Ray, also a native of Manchester, had shoulder-length black hair crowning blue eyes and a silky skin face. A consultant anaesthetist in a Greater Manchester hospital, he was a fitness fanatic, cycled and ran on his off-duty days. His parents, both retired professional people, lived in a two-bedroom bungalow in the town of Bury.

Tall and well covered, without being overweight, Kelly was dressed in a cream shirt under a grey crew neck thick woollen jumper, blue jeans and well-worn white trainers. Shining shoulder-length black hair, flanking an attractive unblemished face, highlighted pristine teeth and lively blue eyes. She was an only child; her father had died four years previously, and her mother, Laura, a building society manager, lived alone in a first floor flat in Bolton.

Warmth from the gas central heating countered the icy storm beating against the double-glazed window of the roomy lounge, plus those in the two en-suite bedrooms and the designer-kitchen window. These rooms, plus a shower room and a separate toilet faced south.

The nearby 13th century Criccieth castle's ruins, perched on the craggy peninsula was visible from the kitchen. Harlech castle, also visible from that room, was situated on coastal hills above the south banks of the expansive estuary that divided the two fortresses that had provided vistas for the Romantic painter, JWM Turner.

Close to the side door of the single garage that housed a tumble dryer, a covered flight of slip-resistant iron stairs, lit by a sensor-controlled floodlight, provided the only access to the flat.

A gravel and grassy track, running alongside the garage's other side wall, linked the main road to a concrete parking area at the rear of the building. Kelly's two-year-old white Vauxhall Astra was parked there, company for the nearby unemployed rotary washing line.

The flat, owned by Josie Harold, an attractive forty-five-year-old widow, who lived in Greater Manchester, was Kelly's aunt.

Josie had no children. She'd bought the property five years ago as a bolt hole, a two and a half hour car journey from bustling Manchester. She was travelling to Criccieth on Monday, staying a week to lock up the flat until the following March. The property was used only for about four months in each year, during the warmer seasons, so Josie, despite the temperamental mobile phone signal in this part of Wales, had discontinued the landline.

The ground floor apartment was empty; the owner, a retired banker, like many other second home owners in the area, was wintering in warmer climes. November was only a few days away and Criccieth's population had returned to its customary three thousand inhabitants.

A steep, tortuous climb through narrow terraced streets with their small shops and a restaurant sprinkled between small colourful dwellings, crossed the Cambrian Coast Railway line to the coastal arterial gateway to the Lleyn Peninsula.

A lecturer in the history of English Literature at a teacher training college in Manchester, Kelly had completed the first of a two-day lecturers' seminar in the

North Wales Teacher Training College, ten miles away. She was returning to Manchester on Monday morning.

She twisted her fleshy lips into a wry smile as she considered the English establishment's educational philosophy, and how her attraction for such was lodged in the history of north Wales and its legends.

Kelly shivered; the weather depicting her mood: no walking along the foreshore for several days, but her husband's company-celebrating their first anniversary on Saturday night in a local restaurant-might offset that. Reading poetry and analysing authors' minds would re-enter her life again next week, and she'd return to her hobby of amateur dramatics, rehearsing for a Christmas play.

Kelly went into the small sitting room at the front of the flat and peered through the window: the relentless torrential rain intensified the gloom and her despondency. Light from the only streetlamp was an anaemic glow, struggling to penetrate the moisture, powerless to reach the narrow pavement. Nature's ferocious anger always frightened her; she felt vulnerable in the lonely environment. Shivering again from her increasing despair, she tugged on two nylon cords at the inside of the window frame and secured the exterior Louvre shutters. Afterwards, she secured the ones that protected the lounge plus the bedrooms' windows, and then she entered the kitchen.

She opened the freezer; instant meals were plentiful. Her eyes focused on chicken curry and rice-the ideal hot meal helped down with red wine was the correct decision on such an evening.

Meal cooked, Kelly took it into the large lounge, switched on the wall-mounted plasma television and ate the spicy dish while watching the early evening news.

The plate and utensils cleaned and stacked in their respective places, she checked the tide timetable that Josie had pinned to the back of the kitchen door. Spring tides tonight and over the weekend, their magnitude reducing on Wednesday of next week. Tonight's high water was a few minutes before midnight. Kelly thought of Ray's journey: it could be long and tiring or, he might travel by train to Bangor.

She returned to the lounge, updated her laptop with what she'd gleaned at today's lecturers' training session, then slipped a Chris Rea CD into the music centre. A soft, slight Mancunian accent tinged her clear pleasing voice as she sang along with *On The Beach*-her preferred track when she was in Criccieth.

The strengthening wind, and the roar from the spring tide's rolling waves crashing against the seawall and the peninsula on which the castle sat, added to her anxiety. She shivered again but, recalling what she had seen on the beaches during her numerous visits to Criccieth and, now Halloween's Welsh influences, lessened her unease.

She poured herself another glass of red wine, ambled from the lounge into the flat's small front sitting room that was shielded from the foul weather, switched on the television, sat on the sofa and sipped the drink while watching an Agatha Christie whodunit.

The mystery solved, she switched off the set, placed the empty wine glass on the coffee table and checked her mobile phone. No text or messages, the signal struggling between poor and non-existent.

Kelly picked up the empty wine glass and returned to the kitchen. The rain, whipping against its window, disturbed her again. She looked out: lights in nearby houses and cottages were indistinct orange and yellow blurry dots in the wild night.

She returned to the lounge, thought about the first year of marriage: her lips' muscles in a fascicular condition, and her wide-open eyes didn't flicker as she focused on the wall. A pained expression. She recalled the events of the past year: because of their different professions she and Ray had tracked down different paths. The Saturday evening anniversary meal could ease the anguish. She rose from the sofa, ambled to the drinks' cabinet, poured out a large gin and tonic, reckoning that it, plus the previous drinks of red wine, would be soporific, cancel out the tempest's noises.

Fifteen minutes later she placed the empty glass on the coffee table and went into the bedroom. She switched on the bedside lamp, undressed, swilled her face, cleaned her teeth and then switched off the bedside light as she got into bed. Ten minutes later she was asleep.

2

Kelly Glover turned over in her bed, yawned: and listened; no sound in the flat or from the adjacent bedroom. Probably Ray had arrived in the early hours, exhausted.

She rubbed her eyes and aimed her hazy vision at the shuttered window: no morning light showing in between the overlapping wooden staves. She released the shutters, the rain and wind still battering the south-west facing window, and switched on the bedside light. The clock was showing eight-ten. She ambled back to the window, looked out at the rainy blackness, reckoned dawn was about twenty minutes late.

Head buzzing, hair dishevelled, still bleary-eyed and her mouth dry, she switched on the bedroom's main light and ambled to the room's wash basin. She swilled her face, then drank a tumbler of cold water and decided she wouldn't disturb Ray, he'd probably struggled against the elements while driving along the A55 from the border. Let him sleep.

She lifted her wool dressing gown off the hook at the back of the bedroom's door and walked, barefoot, into the lounge, switched on the main light, released the shutters and looked through the window: wind and rain, although neither matched last night's ferocity, continued to pummel it.

She went into the front room peered out of the window: the street lamp glow remained a weak orange tint as did the poorly-lit street and the pavement; small broken tree branches littered both. She sighed, then looked down at the parking space below the flat. Ray's one-year-old light grey B Class Mercedes wasn't there. She shouted: 'Ray.'

No answer.

She hurried back to her bedroom and looked out: weak daylight was penetrating the low clouds. She shivered, stood, looked for several seconds at the angry scene and then turned and trotted into the other bedroom.

The room was empty, no signs that the bed had been slept in.

A nervy Kelly shouted again: 'Ray.'

No response.

Heart pounding, she hurried into the kitchen and switched on the neon light; no signs of anyone having been there. Next the bathroom; it hadn't been used.

Panicking, she ran to the flat's main door, opened it and activated her mobile phone again. Despite a poor signal, she managed to check for texts and messages; there were neither.

Sweating, hyperventilating and fingers tingling, she returned to the kitchen, made a mug of unsweetened black coffee and sat at the table.

Her senses in a whirl, she pondered: maybe the driving conditions along the north Wales expressway in last night's weather were too hazardous.

Kelly drank the coffee, put on her hooded anorak collected her mobile phone, then went outside the flat again and dialled her home landline in Bury.

No answer

She dialled Ray's mobile; no response.

She dialled a further three times without a reply. Despondent, she hurried into the bathroom, swilled her face with cold water and returned to the kitchen, stood at the basin, head in her hands and thought: What the hell has happened to Ray?

She dashed back to the bedroom, opened her handbag, fished out her address book, opened the flat's door once more, stood on the top step and turned her back on the weather. Despite sweaty and trembling fingers, she managed to dial the Manchester hospital's anaesthetic department.

Diane, the Anaesthetics Department's senior secretary, answered her query: 'The surgical session finished early; Ray deposited his notes in the office soon afterwards.' A sigh, then a supple Lancashire lilt danced through each syllable as she continued: 'He left around six, anxious to start his journey to north Wales.'

A thinking Kelly considered Diane's words: if Ray left Manchester at six-thirty he should have arrived around nine, maybe a bit later in that weather. She dialled Ray's parents, described the situation.

He hadn't contacted them; they weren't expecting him to phone while he travelled in the ghastly weather.

Kelly returned to the bedroom, sat on the edge of the bed, gave out a long, loud sigh and   reflected: there has to be a simple, logical explanation for Ray's absence. Don't overreact, be calm and wait, today's seminar doesn't start until one o'clock.

She removed her damp clothes and underwear from her cold body and showered. Afterwards, wearing fresh warm garments and moccasin slippers. She went into the kitchen, placed the soiled clothes in the washing machine and programmed it for a quick wash and efficient spin dry, clothes would be nearly dry, and then she'd give them a final warm blast in the tumble dryer in the garage.

A cooked breakfast was not considered, waves of anxiety-induced nausea suppressing her appetite. She made another mug of black coffee, switched on the radio, sat at the kitchen table and waited for the nine o'clock local news and traffic update.

The news bulletin was unhelpful: this weather, tempestuous at times, would continue until early Monday morning but, apart from localised flooding on short sections of some main roads, there were no reports of accidents or delays on the A55 expressway.

No one had phoned, which didn't surprise her; no text message and the weather remained ghastly. Confused and alarmed at the situation, she looked out of the lounge window again. No traffic, the area deserted of people, the town was still asleep. .She felt trapped.

What could she do? What should she do? Her husband hadn't arrived, no news from him, no contact between him and his family. According to the adage: *no news is good news,* but one questions this when alone and worrying in this ghastly environment.

Kelly mused: be active, clean the flat.

She looked at the kitchen clock: a few minutes after nine. The washing would be finished in forty minutes; ample time to reconsider her thoughts and actions.

Cleaning completed, she made a mug of sweetened black coffee and listened to the ten o'clock news, nothing of note was reported.

Kelly drank her coffee, put on her hooded anorak, changed her slippers for leather shoes, then collected the washing, placed it in a large black plastic bag and opened the flat's door. Grabbing the steps' handrail with one hand; she shut the door with the other, then lifted the bag and, with her back turned to the atrocious weather, descended slowly.

She unlocked the garage's side door, switched on the neon light, and then saw a man on the concrete floor, face down, a few feet in front of the tumble dryer. Petrified, she stared at him: he was dressed in a plain white polo shirt, blue jeans and white trainers on bare feet.

She gasped, dropped the bulging plastic bag at the side of the tumble dryer and walked slowly towards the body. Recognising the man's wristwatch, she screamed, then rushed to the front of the garage, unlocked its main door and continued screaming.

3

Thirty-year-old Huw Davey, wearing a hooded long anorak and carrying a small knapsack on his back, struggled uphill from his housel, battling the wind and the rain from a moving ceiling of scudding black clouds, as he hurried to his workplace.

Loud high-pitched screams, defying nature's furore, stopped his haste. Although unable to see anyone through the sodden gloom, he stopped. Sensing that the cries came from the direction of the castle he ran in that direction.

A shaking and sobbing Kelly, leaning against the garage door's concrete pillar, saw Huw approaching and then she pointed with a trembling arm to the inside of the garage.

A panting Huw walked towards her, said nothing, went into the garage, saw the body, opened his anorak's pocket, fished out his mobile phone, ran downhill towards the lifeboat station for a decent signal and dialled triple nine.

Five minutes later, a blue lights flashing First Response paramedic ambulance and a police car arrived.

PC Roger Young, the police car driver, and Sergeant Iwan Drew plus WPC Helen Manning, all Welsh speaking officers, hurried out of the vehicle, approached Kelly and Huw and showed their ID cards as they introduced themselves.

Iwan Drew advised his colleagues: 'We conduct the inquiry in English except when we discuss the evidence in private.' He then advised the two-man paramedic team to remain in the vehicle.

Huw Davey, standing outside the garage's door gestured with a shaky side nod of his head to the inside of the structure and, his north Wales lilt evident in his trembling voice, said, 'There's a dead person, a man, on the floor.'

The thirty-two-year old, tall, muscular non-smoking Iwan Drew had short brown hair under his peaked police cap. Weather-beaten facial features, the result of regular rambling in the mountains and the occasional fishing stint on the foreshore near his house, highlighted glistening blue eyes. Once a week he met his friend in a local pub for a chat and an occasional game of snooker.

Married to Eileen, a pharmacist, they had one child, an eight-year-old daughter, Delyth. Iwan's strong voice carried a marked north-west Wales accent. Home was a terraced house near Criccieth rail station, a five minute walk along the coastal road to the castle. Transport was a three-year-old five-door blue Honda Civic.

Iwan Drew nodded to Huw then approached the First Response team again and told them: 'The police will enter the garage, carry out a cursory view of the body and then we wait for forensics.'

The paramedics nodded and then, Iwan raising his hand to affirm his authority, turned to a colleague and they entered the garage. They looked at the body; didn't touch it. There were no signs of violence or obvious cause of death, and then they returned to the garage's main entrance.

Iwan approached a sobbing Kelly and, compassion coursing through in his voice, asked her: 'You are?'

Shaking, she blabbered: 'Kelly Glover,' and, pointing with a quivering hand at the steps, stammered: 'I...I'm staying up there, in the first-floor flat, it belongs to my aunt.'

'I understand your distress, Miss or Mrs?'

A shivering cold Kelly shook her head several times before answering in a trembling soft Mancunian accent: 'Mrs Glover.'

'Are you on vacation?'

Kelly, whimpering between sentences, described the past few days.

The understanding Iwan Drew said, 'Ended with an unpleasant experience, Mrs Glover; we'll check the garage again before forensics arrive.'

Kelly nodded.

Iwan advised WPC Helen Manning to take Kelly up to the flat.

'That is my husband in the garage,' a panicking and sobbing Kelly screamed as she clambered up the wet steps to the flat.

Born in north Wales, the tall, slim and attractive twenty-five-year-old Helen Manning was single. Shoulder length blonde hair and blue eyes highlighted her pale face. She lived in a two bedroom flat in Criccieth near a farm where she kept a horse. Her private transport was a three-year-old cream Mini. Her parents lived in Bangor and she had one brother, a student in Chester Art College She followed the shivering Kelly into the lounge, then guided her onto the sofa and sat next to her.

Despair coursing through her restive body, Kelly; her head shaking, tissues in her clenched fist and eyes red, rose from the sofa and walked around the room.

Helen Manning asked routine questions as she tried to side-track Kelly's torment and explained that the Sergeant would question her and then contact the CID.

Iwan Drew phoned the local constabulary in Madogton, a small town three miles away, and asked for more men to attend the scene. 'Tell them to wear warm wet weather clothes and boots; it's one hell of a cold, wet and dark morning.'

Three police officers arrived within ten minutes, then PC Roger Young arranged for them to cordon off the dwelling, the garage and nearby roads.

Iwan Drew took a shivering Huw Davey to the side of the garage in the lee of the weather and told him: 'Please lower the anorak's hood, I want to see the person with whom I'm speaking,' then said, 'I want your full name, address and story.'

Huw slipped the anorak's hood off his head. Five-eight tall and lean with short black hair topping a thin pale face and blue eyes, he said, 'Huw Davey.' He gave his address then: 'I'm a bachelor, live with my widowed mother,' he pointed, 'it's a terraced house about a hundred yards down the road, near the lifeboat house. I was on my way to work; start at eleven.'

'What time was it when you heard the screaming?'

'I usually leave the house about an hour before I begin work, so I guess it was a few minutes after ten.' Tense and frightened, Huw's nasal syllables commanding his rapid, nervous speech, explained: 'I'm a chef in the Seaside Hotel; I'm cooking the lunches today, finish at five, and then the evening chef takes over.' He pointed. 'The hotel is on the other side of the castle, above the north beach.'

Iwan wrote in his notepad and then told him: 'Go on.'

A trembling Huw considered for a few moments and then said, 'The screeching became louder; the rain intensified, the wind strengthened and visibility was minimal; so I ran towards the castle and saw the woman,' he paused, sighing and exhaling, then continued: 'she was pointing to the inside of the garage.' He stammered: 'I …I…….I saw the man; he was lying, face downwards, on the concrete floor. I then rushed away from the garage, ran down the hill until I obtained a decent signal on my mobile and then I phoned the emergency number.'

Iwan Drew, placing a hand on the distressed Huw's shoulder, told him: 'Tell your employee what's happened. I will want a statement from you later; report to Madogton's police station after you've finished work.'

Huw thanked Iwan and then placed the anorak's hood over his head and hurried past the castle to the hotel.

4

Iwan Drew turned to Roger Young. 'Is the dwelling and immediate area cordoned off?'

'Access only for nearby residents and commercial vehicles.'

'We'll look at the body again,' Iwan Drew said, his nasal voice gaining strength as he considered the incident: 'I'm getting wary signals.'

They put on rubber gloves and advised the First Response paramedics' team: 'We'll all go inside and we'll take photographs.'

The operation took ten minutes.

Iwan thanked the paramedics, advised them to return to their vehicle and that he'd advise them about the removal of the body soon.

Following a cursory examination of the body, Iwan Drew declared: 'It is still warm, Roger; no blood, nothing to suggest a struggle or violence.' He checked the neck: 'Carotid pulse is absent,' and then said, 'no injuries to the neck or face.' He pointed to the eyes. 'Pupils are dilated,' and then he told Roger Young: 'check his pockets.'

A few minutes later Roger Young stood, shook his head and announced: 'No ID documents, no wallet, no cash, each pocket is empty.'

A bemused Iwan Drew told him: 'Take more photos of the body plus adjacent surroundings; forensics might want to check them and the paramedics' shots later.'

That completed, Iwan Drew gazed at the scene again, opening his arms as he asked: 'What strikes you when you view this space, Roger?'

The twenty-seven-year-old, observant and ambitious Roger Young said, 'Considering the incessant copious rain and the fierce winds, Sarge, why the body and clothes are dry?'

Roger, an only child, was a bachelor, lived alone in a small cottage in a village between Madogton and Criccieth. Playing soccer for the local team kept his lean six foot body fit and trim   Collar length black hair capped a thin face, blue eyes and strong facial contours. A non-smoker, he drank lager occasionally and transport was a two-year-old Ford Focus. Out of choice, girls were absent from his life; his priority was ascending the police ladder.

'Indeed,' Iwan confirmed, 'he's wearing warm-weather clothes;' a snigger, then: 'not suitable for these violent conditions.'

Roger stared at the body for several moments and then, a high-pitched local accent commanding his resolute voice, commented: 'Young man, good physique, no sign of violence, and his well-manicured hands are clean.'

Iwan, walking slowly around the body, said to Roger: 'Why are his hair, shirt, jeans and trainers dry?' He considered for a few seconds, then remarked: 'He, plus clothes would have been soaked, his trainers possibly muddy; yet there are no footprints on the garage floor;' a shake of his head as he confirmed: 'the floor is dry.... intriguing' He paused, looked at the man's face and pointed out: 'Bland expression, no cyanotic hue on the lips, face or extremities....what's happened?'

Roger didn't reply.

Iwan checked that the garage's main door was unlocked, then he found a thin piece of wood at one corner at the back of the building, placed it under the garage door and told Roger: 'Nosy locals we do not need.'

The two officers left the garage through the side door, then Iwan shone his torch around the immediate vicinity and noticed an iron ladder with hand rails fixed to the garage wall leading up to the building's roof. He shook his head and, in Welsh, asked Roger to climb it and photograph the roof.

A shivering, wet and cold Roger clambered up the ladder, looked around the roof, took a few snaps and returned to the ground. 'Nothing there, Sarge,' he said, 'I took a few shots of the roof.'

Iwan nodded and said, 'Deploy uniform while I ask Kathy Glover about the ladder,' and then he scrambled up the steps to the flat.

Two of the newly-arrived constables guarded the garage.

Non-residents were denied entry to the street. Residents in nearby streets who had heard and seen the police cars, gathered outside their doors, exchanged wide-eyed glances; incredulity sketching their faces, as they watched the intense police activity. What has happened? This degree of police presence in the town was unknown.

Helen Manning, trying to comfort the distressed, shivering Kelly Glover, asked her if she wanted medical help when Iwan Drew arrived.

She refused.

A cold and wet Iwan explained the inquiry's procedure to Kelly and then said, 'I noticed a ladder fixed to the garage wall.'

Kelly whispered: 'My aunt Josie decided the roof would be an ideal spot for sunbathing.'

Iwan didn't comment; said, 'WPC Manning will stay here until we decide on future plans. CID and forensics will need to question you.' He looked at Helen.

Helen, her mild north Wales cadence straddling each syllable in her gentle voice, said, 'Kelly has changed her clothes; she's now wearing warmer ones, and she's had a strong coffee, Sarge.'

Iwan nodded. 'Good,' then he asked Kelly: 'what make of car did your husband drive?'

After a few seconds of incomprehensive garbled words, she said, 'One-year-old light grey B Class Mercedes,' and gave Iwan the car's registration number.

Iwan thanked her and then asked: 'Do you have additional keys for the garage's main and side doors?'

'There are two sets here, each on a key ring.' She opened a wall-mounted glass cabinet, took out a set of keys, handed it to Iwan and said, 'My aunt also, has duplicates.'

Iwan thanked her and then advised: 'Officers will carry out house-to-house inquires and check all cars in the immediate area.'

He left the flat and, after struggling in the rain-soaked wind as he descended the steps, he walked to the First Response paramedic team's ambulance. 'Thank you for your help and patience; PC Young and I are returning to the station now. Follow us, have your meal break, then print the photos you took inside of the garage and put them on my desk.' He added: 'I'll contact the North Wales CID when we return, and we'll all follow their instructions.'

5

A native of Liverpool, forty-year-old DCI Eric Bolton had been head of the West Division of the north Wales CID for over three years, promotion followed a two-year illustrious period as a DS in the Merseyside CID.

He'd been in his office since eight-thirty poring over the details of a recent robbery in the area. An arrest was imminent. The six-foot tall Eric had short black hair, a resilient bony face, brown eyes and an athletic build from swimming regularly in the local sports centre. A non-smoker, he enjoyed a lager when off duty and followed Everton FC.

Eric lived in a detached house in Conwy with his thirty-seven-year-old wife, Ella and their one child, David, an athletic fourteen-year-old, who attended the local comprehensive school.

Twenty minutes after midday on Friday, Eric Bolton and his colleague, thirty-four -year-old Detective Sergeant James Elson, known as Jimmy, had just finished a snack lunch in Eric's office in Bangor's CID complex, when the phone rang.

Eric lifted it, gave his rank and listened. It was his friend, Sergeant Iwan Drew, from Madogton police station.

They exchanged pleasantries, then Eric gestured to Jimmy to pick up the extension line. 'I've asked Jimmy Elson to listen in.'

'Good morning, Jimmy,' Iwan said and then described the events: 'Cold, stormy night, sweeping black rain-filled clouds,' then: 'not much better today. Kelly Glover was waiting for her doctor husband, who was driving from Manchester, to arrive. He didn't, then she thought he'd decided not to travel in the night's adverse weather conditions. She discovered his body in the garage this morning but no sign of his car.' Iwan described the scene inside the garage. 'Bizarre situation, eerie,' he declared, 'uncanny; we haven't touched the body but the man's pockets, all empty, no ID.'

'The property's address and the directions to it please,' Eric said.

Iwan said, 'I'll fax them to you after this call. Advice for you: the weather here remains foul, no respite forecast until Monday.'

Eric commented: 'Noted,' then: 'I'll contact the forensics team in Bangor, arrange for them to follow us,' he looked at the wall clock, 'considering the poor driving conditions, we'll meet you in Criccieth around two-thirty.'

'Thanks, Eric,' and Iwan ended the call.

Iwan replaced the receiver in its cradle, faxed Eric the address plus a map, then stared at the ceiling, gave out a long sigh and looked at Roger Young.

'Food, Sarge?' Roger hinted.

Iwan smirked. 'Take money out of the petty cash fund and get two microwave meals, we return to Criccieth by two-thirty.'

Eric Bolton, looking at a frowning Jimmy Elson, remarked: 'Strange story,' then he picked up his notepad and checked who the on-duty forensics adviser was. 'It's Dr Lucy Grange in HQ; I'll phone her soon.' He turned to Jimmy. 'Phone DC Glyn Salmon and tell him to bring waterproofs.'

The five-ten, broad, thirty-four-year old bachelor, Jimmy, stood and then left the room, walked to his office, contacted Glyn Salmon on the internal phone and, a slight

Merseyside accent flowing through his strong voice, gave him the news. A native of Chester, Jimmy was promoted to Detective Sergeant in the past twelve months after spending two years as a Detective Constable in the Cheshire Police Force.

Glyn Salmon said, 'The weather in Caernarfon was horrid when I left home this morning; my wet weather outfit is there, Sarge. Perhaps, on the way to Criccieth, we can call at my flat to collect it.'

Jimmy told him: 'Yes, you'll need it.'

'I'll be with you in five minutes, Sarge,' Glyn declared, a strong north Wales accent oscillating in his clear voice.

'Two minutes,' Jimmy said and ended the call.

Eric Bolton phoned Eifion Pask, the fifty- year-old South Gwynedd coroner at his office in Caernarfon. Tall and thin, fit, with black thick hair crowning blue eyes and-tanned face, he was the senior partner of a law practice, eight miles away in Bangor. Married to forty five year old Gwyneth, they had one adult daughter, a lawyer and working in Liverpool.

Eric informed him of the situation.

Eifion Pask sanctioned a post mortem examination.

Eric replaced the phone in its cradle and then dialled the North Wales Forensics HQ.

It was answered on the third ring: 'Dr Lucy Grange, North Wales Forensics.'

Eric Bolton described the circumstances, then: 'the coroner has given permission for an autopsy.'

A hint of a mixed Cumbria and Lancashire accent trickling through Lucy's voice, the forty-two-year-old, five-seven, slim and married Lucy said, 'I've got the gist, Eric. Where is the body?'

Eric told her: then: 'I have directions.'

Lucy said, 'I'll .advise the Bangor team that you'll contact them,' and ended the call.

Iwan Drew and his team returned to a cold Criccieth soon after two o'clock, the rain had lessened but the forceful wind hindered the ebbing tide.

'I'll stay in the car,' Iwan told Roger Young, 'check the officers' house-to house info.' He gave out a loud sigh. 'I'm not hopeful, last night's weather conditions weren't conducive to viewing the outside world; sensible people were watching television. The officers can go off duty once you've spoken with them.

Ten minutes later, Roger Young returned to the car; shook his head as he sat in the driver's seat and, speaking in Welsh, said there was no joy; people neither heard nor saw anything of note in that storm.

A thinking Iwan Drew reverted to English: 'What's the CCTV coverage in the town?'

'I know of one camera in the High Street, Sarge; maybe there's one at or near the castle.'

Iwan thought for a few seconds and then said, 'I doubt if we'll see anything of note during last night's weather, but it's worth a look. Phone the local council in the morning.'

Roger Young wrote a memo in his notepad.

Iwan said, 'We'll visit Kelly Glover and Helen Manning while we wait for the CID team.'

The newly-acquired purpose-built forensic department near Bangor Hospital boasted views of the Menai Starts and Snowdonia. The chief forensic officer, Dr Tim Wilding, took the details from Eric Bolton and, in a soft Manchester accent said, 'Dr Lucy Grange has briefed me;

my team will meet you in Madogton police station within the hour.

Kelly Glover and WPC Manning were sitting in the flat's front siting room when Iwan Drew and Roger arrived.

A fraught Kelly Glover, sitting in an armchair, gestured to Iwan and Roger to sit on the sofa next to Helen Manning and then whispered to Iwan: 'I need a member of the family with me.' She looked at him. 'Perhaps someone could contact my aunt, Josie Harold; she owns this property, she's due here on Monday, staying a week to check the flat before the arrival of real winter. In view of the circumstances perhaps -'

Iwan nodded once. 'Her address and phone number please, Mrs Glover.'

Kelly handed him a printed card with Josie's details.

'I'll phone Greater Manchester Police with the details later.' Iwan then looked at Helen Manning and asked her: 'How are you fixed for food?'

The weary WPC, faking tiredness, said, 'I'm fine, not hungry, there's bread and ham here. I can make a sandwich, and there's plenty of tea and coffee.'

'Good.' He glanced at his watch, 'two twenty-five, CID should arrive soon. Once I know their plans I'll arrange for someone to take over from you.'

'Okay, Sarge; thank you, I'm -'

Roger Young announced: 'I can hear a vehicle arriving.' He looked out of the window and declared: 'The CID officers are here.'

Iwan and Roger thanked Helen, explained the CID's presence to Kelly Glover and then he left the flat.

6

DCI Eric Bolton, DS Jimmy Elson and DC Glyn Salmon, arrived.

The three, dressed in appropriate clothes and footwear, were greeted by Iwan and Gareth. They exchanged pleasantries and then hurried to the side of the garage, sheltering from the icy wind and rain.

Iwan described the situation again, then pointed. 'The wife is in the upstairs flat; WPC Helen Manning is with her. I'll inform Greater Manchester Police that you've arrived.'

Eric told him: 'Do that now, Iwan.'

The call took five minutes.

Eric Bolton wrote in his pad and said, 'We'll wait for forensics before we view the body.' He checked his watch, then: 'They'll be arriving soon; we met up with them in Madogton police station.'

Within a few minutes the white purpose-built forensic van arrived.

The forensic team: Dr Tim Wilding, the Chief Forensics Officer, and his colleagues, Dr Edward Brown plus photographer Tony Simpson, all known to Eric Bolton and his colleagues, stepped out of the van.

Dr Tim Wilding, on seeing the ambulance, advised the two paramedics to remain in the vehicle; hoped their wait wouldn't be a long one in the foul weather and then he and his colleagues walked up to Eric Bolton and his team and exchange pleasantries.

A native of the town of Flint, forty-four-year old Dr Tim Wilding was married and had one adult son, a student in Lancashire College. The slim, tall six-one pathologist had short fair hair crowning active hazel eyes and a rugged face, the latter from sailing in the Menai Straits waters in a range of conditions varying from a tranquil waltz to a boisterous jive. His garb consisted of a water-proof heavy navy anorak, polo cream woollen polo shirt, brown cord trousers and ankle-high durable boots. An astute medical analyst, he was promoted to chief forensics officer in Wales's Gwynedd region two years previously after a commendable five -year stint in the North Manchester forensic division. He looked at Eric Bolton and, in a soft north Manchester accent, asked him for a summary of events.

Eric directed him to Iwan. 'Sergeant Drew has the details.'

Iwan described the developments then added: the covered steps at the side of the building is the only access to the flat.'

'Nothing's been touched or moved since the body was discovered?' was Tim's rhetorical question.

Iwan nodded. 'Correct.'

'Okay.' Tim turned to his colleagues. 'We'll don our forensic gear in the van,' then shouted to the paramedics: 'we won't be long.'

Ten minutes later Tim and his associates, Wilmslow born, thirty-one-year-old six-foot bachelor Edward Brown sporting crew-cut brown hair, plus third member of the team, five-ten, broad and strong thirty-year-old, recently married, photographer, Tony Simpson, returned to the front of the garage.

Tim said, 'Somebody please open the garage door for us.'

Iwan's nodded-a tacit affirmative.

Tim said, 'Everybody gloved please,' then to Iwan: 'open it up, please,' and then to Tony Simpson: 'Take the usual photos before we examine the body.'

Anglesey-born Tony, his short thick black hair topping a strong face, brown eyes and a perpetual smiling expression highlighting pristine white teeth, covered his hair with the uniform's hood, walked up to Iwan and, in a broad north Wales accent, said, 'I'm ready.'

Iwan lifted the garage door and switched on the neon light.

Tony Simpson entered, looked around and declared aloud: 'I can't see a body.'

A stunned Eric Bolton and DS Jimmy Elson hurried inside, looked around the garage, no dead body, only a black plastic bag alongside the tumble dryer.

Eric Bolton commented: 'The footprints you see on the garage floor probably belong to Kelly Glover and the police.'

Tim asked Iwan Drew and Roger Young: 'You confirm a body was here?'

Iwan coughed once, then said, 'We looked at it for several moments -'

'And?'

'It was warm, no colour change on the skin. The clothes: shirt, jeans and trainers, were dry, not suitable gear for last night's weather.' Iwan flicked Roger a side nod. 'PC Young took numerous photos of the scene.'

Tim sucked in his cheeks for a few seconds, then asked Roger to show Tony Simpson the spots from where he'd taken the shots. 'As near as possible please, PC Young, then we can compare them with the ones Tony takes.'

Roger said, 'Will do.'

Tony Simpson completed the exercise in ten minutes and thanked Roger.

Tim Wilding looked at Edward Brown. 'What do you make of this?'

Edward shook his head several times, his wide-open blue eyes staring at the empty floor. He then lobbed Tim a white-tooth smile and said, 'I'll take samples from the floor, the side door.' and, producing a small, but powerful torch from inside his large firm leather case, added: 'I'll scan the floor in front of the tumble dryer for human hairs.'

The two CID officers, plus Iwan Drew and Roger Young, looked at one another before Iwan, incredulity in his hushed voice, said. 'I don't understand; the body was there when we shut the garage door.'

Tim Wilding asked Tony Simpson to speed-process the photos when they returned to the lab.

Tony nodded.

Tin Wilding asked Roger Young: 'Do you have your digital camera?'

'Yes, sir.'

'Please,' he said, holding out his hand.

Roger handed it to him.

Tim passed it to Tony. 'Compare the two sets of photos.'

Tim Wilding then asked Edward Brown: 'How the sample collecting progressing?'

'Just finishing, Tim.' He rose from the floor, placed several plastic specimen containers in his case and then walked to the black plastic bag. 'I'll check its contents.' He picked it up and carried it, plus his case, out of the garage and walked to the forensics van.

The CID officers and the local police remained silent until the forensic team had completed their investigation.

Tim said, 'I doubt if we'll be able to ascertain a DNA profile of the man from swabs we've taken off the garage floor.' He sighed and declared: 'Apart from taking a buccal swab from the wife for DNA profiling, we're finished here, Chief,' then Tim added quickly: 'I won't mention what we didn't find.'

They all left the garage.

Iwan shut it.

One of the police constables who had been on house to house work told Iwan that no residents had noticed any activity in the street and there was no sign of the Mercedes car.

Iwan said, 'Officers will be stationed outside the property throughout the night.' Pointing up to the flat he asked Eric Bolton and Tim Wilding: 'Do you want to speak with Mrs Glover?'

Eric said, 'Lead the way.'

Eric and Tim introduced themselves to Kelly Glover and Helen Manning.

Helen Manning continued to comfort Kelly while the police explained the procedure, and then Tim explained why he wanted a swab from the inside of Kelly's mouth. 'Routine check for our records, please, Mrs Glover.'

Kelly obliged.

Tim thanked her, turned to Eric Bolton and said, 'You'll have a report tomorrow on our findings, plus comments on the two sets of photos,' and then he hurried down the steps, informed the paramedics and then said, 'back to base.'

The forensics van and the paramedics left. .

7

Eric Bolton and Jimmy Elson stood several feet away from a tearful Kelly Glover: her head bowed, her sweaty hands grasping paper issues.

A compassionate Eric spoke in a low, soft voice: 'We want to ask you some questions, Mrs Glover; it's important that we form a picture of what might have happened. I am aware that you provided Sergeant Drew with information. Is there anything you wish to add?'

Kelly, wiping away tears, raised her head slowly and looked at Helen Manning, but didn't speak.

Helen, appreciating Kelly's distress, said to her: 'Now is the time to tell the Chief Inspector of anything you neglected to tell the local police.'

Kelly sniffled, looked at Eric and then, in a fractured moist voice, told him: 'I told Sergeant Drew all I can remember.'

Eric changed tack: 'I believe you're a lecturer on English literature in a teachers' training college, your hobby is amateur dramatics and that you will have been married twelve months tomorrow.'

Kelly wiped her soggy nose and, nodding nervously, said, 'I booked a table for us in a local, family-owned, restaurant…..a quiet celebration on Saturday evening.' She cried.

Helen Manning wrapped an arm around Kelly's shoulder.

A silent Eric turned and looked at Jimmy Elson.

Jimmy twitched his lips and then, in a considerate soft voice, said, 'Mrs Glover, I'm Detective Sergeant Elson; I advise you that, during the inquiry, you remain in Criccieth until we advise you otherwise.'

'I understand, Mr Elson.'

Jimmy splayed the fingers of both hands and then asked her: 'Do you have a copy of this building's plans, the flat, and the garage?'

The tearful Kelly threw him a curious look, then: 'No, sir.'

Jimmy asked: 'Who can we contact to explain the circumstances for your absence from Manchester?'

'My aunt Josie is driving here on Monday, she'll advise the department.' She opened her handbag and gave Jimmy Elson an address book. 'Her name is Josephine Harold; address and phone numbers are in there;' a short pause, then: 'she'll probably have the plans of the building.'

Jimmy recorded the details and returned the book to Kelly.

Eric said, 'Contact Mrs Harold on the radio phone, Jimmy; no landline here and mobile signal is poor, then phone and inform the Greater Manchester Police.'

Jimmy said, 'I'll do that now,' then to Kelly: 'excuse me, Mrs Glover -'

'That reminds me,' Iwan Drew interjected, 'I need to phone the local station and arrange for another WPC to take over from Miss Manning this morning.'

Eric nodded.

Iwan Drew and Jimmy Elson left the flat.

Eric Bolton walked slowly around the room several times and then stood in front of Kelly: 'Did you speak with your husband last evening?'

'No, sir; I went out onto the side stairway, managed to get a signal; the family, no one have had no contact with him. I then contacted the hospital. The Anaesthetic Department's secretary told me that Ray had left the hospital around five-twenty, having told her that he was driving to north Wales. I thought he'd arrive around nine,' she stopped speaking for a moment and then said, 'I didn't tell Sergeant Drew that, I thought Ray might have changed his mind and travel by train, so I anticipated I'd be driving to Bangor rail station.'

'What time was that?'

'Early evening, then I watched an Agatha Christie whodunit on television that started at eight o'clock.'

'What time did you go to bed?'

'After eleven, following a stiff drink; I heard nothing.'

Eric closed his notepad and said, 'that will be all for now, we will need a statement later, Mrs Glover. I'll arrange for a WPC to escort you to Madogton Police Station tomorrow -' Iwan Drew returned.

Eric greeted and updated him, then: 'we'll use your station as the inquiry's HQ. Mrs Glover will make her statement there.'

Iwan nodded and then said that a WPC was on the way to take over duties from Helen Manning.

Seconds later Jimmy Elson returned: 'Mrs Harold is driving to Criccieth this evening. I've informed Manchester Police.'

Eric Bolton told Kelly: 'The WPC will stay with you until your aunt arrives. I won't meet Mrs Harold this evening,' then an afterthought: 'how close are you to her?'

A tearful Kelly snivelled, wiped her nose, and said, 'She is my late father's sister, a widow; I'm her only relative. We're close, a dear aunt. This flat has been her holiday home for several years.'

Eric thanked her, then: 'We'll leave now,' he then added: 'I'll ask your aunt if she has a plan of the whole of this building,' and then he and the officers left.

An anxious Kelly waited until the CID officers left, then she rose from her chair, sighed, exhaled and wobbled a few times before getting upright.

Iwan Drew and Helen Manning helped her to another chair, then Helen asked her if she needed a drink of water.

Hyperventilating, her moist hands clasped, the agitated Kelly shook her head, rose from the chai, walked to the window and looked out at the bay's active sky and waters and whispered: 'How unpredictable temperaments insult nature's varied elements: anger, then change dramatically to embrace the environment with benign and harmonious splendour.' Kelly dwelled over the situation, thoughts of the past few months: Ray's behaviour, his changing attitude towards his work and social life. Although the marriage was twelve months old, they had gone their separate professional ways, hence this Saturday evening was to be a romantic event, an attempt to heal rifts. Yet there had been no known physical acrimony. Mental? Maybe? She considered her husband's behaviour: was he trying to frighten her, attempting a system of constant mental turmoil where she'd alienate him? A manipulative ploy? Why? What has gone wrong? She trembled. Perhaps nothing. She shivered again, realising she was in denial. Should she be worried about the present situation? Did she give the impression she was? That was important, show alarm, disbelief, she was convinced she portrayed a distressed wife, emotionally drained. Where was Ray? She'd told the police of the possible scenarios in the severe weather, no contact from him, a mobile phone signal was non-existent here, especially in the atrocious weather. Ray, as far as she knew, hadn't phoned his family. She tried to think logically, no news is good news? She switched the radio on, tuned into the local station and waited for the traffic report: there were no serious accidents or hold-ups on the north Wales roads and the A55 Expressway was problem free. She turned off the radio; the news lessened her near-panic state: the hyperventilation diminished, the nausea disappeared and she became controlled. She walked to the drinks' cabinet, looked at it, decided on a large gin and tonic.

Kelly was silent.

Iwan Drew and Helen Manning didn't speak, then Iwan said to Kelly: 'Confirming what Chief Bolton told you, WPC Manning will remain here until her colleague WPC Norma Taylor attends; she will then stay with you until Mrs Harold arrives from Manchester.'

A silent Kelly nodded and sipped her drink.

Iwan left the flat, met the well-formed WPC Norma Taylor, who was clad in appropriate clothes for the weather, at the bottom of the steps and briefed her.

She thanked him, then climbed the steps and entered the flat.

Helen introduced Norma to Kelly, then: 'I'll update you, Norma,' and ended with: 'Josie Harold is on her from Manchester; once she arrives you can go off duty.'

The CID officers, plus Iwan Drew and Roger Young sheltered from the weather at the side of the garage,

Eric Bolton said, 'Darkness is not far away; nothing more to do here tonight. We meet in Madogton station tomorrow morning at nine to discuss our m.o.'

The CID officers left the locality.

Before leaving the scene, Iwan Drew spoke in Welsh to his officers, pointed to a late night café in the direction of the town's centre, told his team that he'd forewarned the owner of the police presence. A positive response: the establishment would stay open until ten-thirty, then re-open at six in the morning and that the outside toilet door would remain unlocked. Iwan, smiling at his last directive, said, 'I've arranged for a changeover of officers at ten tonight, then at four and then at eight in the morning.'

At eight-twenty a nervous and tearful Josie Harold arrived at the flat, dumped her holdall on the lounge floor and hugged Kelly. Both women sobbed.

Norma Taylor introduced herself to Josie and then, in a firm local accent, said, 'The main street below is cordoned off; where did you park?'

'In a side street, near the Lifeboat Station.' Josie said, her Lancashire accent bouncing in her hurried speech. She added: 'I showed a police officer my driving licence, described my car, it's a two-year-old five-door white BMW, then gave the car's registration number and told him that I'd collect the rest of my luggage later.'

Despite her distress and ruffled shoulder-length blonde hair, the tall, lithe widow, wearing a white anorak, a grey polo shirt under a V-neck maroon woollen sweater, blue jeans and white trainers, looked attractive.

Norma Taylor briefed Josie and added: 'either I or WPC Manning will call in the morning to escort Kelly to the local police station for her statement.' She gave Josie a card. 'The police Sergeant's name, the station's address and contact phone numbers. I'll wait here until you've collected the rest of your luggage.'

Ten minutes later, a windswept and wet Josie, carrying the remainder of her luggage, returned to the flat.

A relieved Norma then patted Kelly on her back and said, 'I'll leave you in your aunt's capable hands. Good night,' and she left.

8

Saturday morning in Madogton was cold, wet, windy and dark, daylight struggling to penetrate dense clouds. Nature's unrelenting capricious elements established when Iwan Drew drove into the police station's car park at eight forty–five.

He put on his hooded anorak, grabbed brief case and, as he began walking towards the main entrance, press and media reporters fired salvos of questions at him.

He told them that he had no news at present and that he was waiting for the CID team to arrive at the station. He looked at his wristwatch. 'Chief Inspector Eric Bolton and his colleagues will be here around nine o'clock, then we'll discuss the events and issue a statement later.' He pointed towards the town centre. 'A café, fifty yards up the hill, is open; return here in an hour.'

The group left.

Iwan entered the station, greeted the duty officer and described the encounter with the press. 'Anyone else arrived?'

The duty officer shook his head and handed Iwan some mail.

Iwan thanked him, then asked: 'What's the stage of progress on the incident room?'

The young duty officer told him: 'The back room was converted overnight; it has several phone lines, numerous computers and a portable evidence board.'

'Good,' was Iwan's unemotional remark, then walked into his office, removed his hooded anorak, hung it on the back of the door and sat at his desk. Photographs taken by the First Response paramedic team and Huw Davey's statement were on his desk. He checked both and placed them in his case file.

Ten minutes later, the cold, windswept and wet trio of Roger Young, Helen Manning and Norma Taylor entered Iwan's room.

Iwan Drew stated the obvious: 'It's hell out there again today; get out of those wet clothes, make coffee and return here; Chief Bolton and his team will be along soon.'

Ten minutes later the three officers, each holding a mug of steaming coffee, sat in chairs arranged in front of Iwan's desk. They drank the coffee while Iwan reminded them of yesterday's events. He then updated them of the morning's meeting with the press and the media. 'They are returning in about an hour.' He gestured with his hand to the rear of the building. 'The incident room is set up,' then, in a frank tone, declared: 'we need more manpower to search the castle's grounds, the beaches, the shoreline's inlets and inside the nearby caves.'

Roger Young agreed and added: 'I'll check the CCTV Company now.'

'On reflection,' Iwan said, 'CCTV coverage of this area is monitored in Caernarfon police station.'

Roger left and met the CID team outside. He explained his mission and then opened the door for them.

Iwan rose from his chair, greeted the team, then: 'Coffee everyone? The incident room is operational.'

'That will be welcomed by the team,' was Chief Eric Bolton's grateful reply.

Helen Manning rose, smiled and declared: 'Five minutes.'

'We'll be in the incident room,' Eric Bolton told her, and then to Iwan: 'Take us there.'

Iwan described the station's other rooms as they walked to the incident room and then updated the CID officers. 'State of the art technology, sir.'

Eric looked at the equipment 'Ideal, spacious, numerous chairs, good lighting, a small fridge and tea and coffee-making facilities.'

The CID officers removed their heavy duty anoraks and hung them on the back of the chairs.

Eric sat at the long desk and asked Iwan if there were any overnight developments.

'No, sir; I require more men,' and then said, 'the tides' levels are decreasing, but the flooding and ebbing offshore currents remain formidable. They will remain in this mode until next Wednesday. So, we need to scour the lengthy shore and hinterland as soon as possible. High water today is twelve-forty.'

Helen, carrying a tray with the coffees, entered and placed it on the desk. 'Milk and sugar if you need them,' and sat in a chair.

Eric drank his coffee quickly, then walked to the evidence board, wrote Ray and Kelly Glover on it and then the group discussed and were unable to interpret anything of note from the events.

A despondent Eric looked at everybody then, as he lifted the phone, said, 'I'll update the coroner.'

Eifion Pask was in his office; he listened to Eric and then said, 'No arrangements until I hear from you again,' and ended the call.

Eric replaced the phone in its cradle, then looked at everybody and asked: 'Any ideas?'

Iwan said, 'If, somehow, Ray was dragged into the sea he could be in the bay now, maybe in the Irish Sea, but if the tide was flooding at that time there's an outside chance he could be lodged in a rocky inlet.'

Eric nodded. 'Indeed,' then he said, 'We are looking for a well-built scantily-clad male. You are familiar with the area, Sergeant, organise a search party before the tide snookers you.'

Iwan lifted the internal phone and told the duty officer: 'All the off duty officers, yes, all of them, to be outside the station within the next thirty minutes.'

Glyn Salmon declared: 'We should interview Kelly Glover again.' He'd deliberated over the enigmatic situation and declared: 'any tangible info on this woman's true history? Answer is no. Any witnesses to the events? No again. What of her emotional state? Were her histrionics an act? He paused for a second, then affirmed: 'Bizarre; unimaginable story.'

Eric looked at Helen Manning. 'I want Kelly's statement this morning, and bring the aunt here.'

Helen nodded. 'I'll call for them at ten,' and she left.

Roger Young entered the room, 'The CCTV monitoring centre in Caernarfon recorded no nil of note in Criccieth on Thursday or Friday.'

Eric sighed. 'Thanks Roger,' then he told Iwan: 'Get to Criccieth with your team.'

'Understood,' Iwan acknowledged, then told him: 'Chief, the press and media will be back soon.'

A resolute Eric told Roger and Iwan: 'Leave; I'll deal with them.'

9

Eric Bolton and his colleagues returned to the incident room once the press and the media had left.

Eric Bolton had a drink of water and said, 'That session, despite the lack of positive info, will keep the reporters busy,' and then he asked Jimmy Elson and Glyn Salmon: 'What are your feelings on the situation, gentlemen?'

Jimmy Elson, after considering the insubstantial info, said, 'I repeat the obvious description again…weird.' Grinning, and then, a strong Cheshire accent toning his voice, he remarked: 'Halloween is approaching so, it could be a related prank.'

Glyn Salmon grunted before he admitted: 'If the situation is what you think it to be, Jimmy, the couple is wasting valuable police and forensic scientists' time,' a grimace, then: 'and that irks me. If only the garage could speak,' he sighed, considered for a moment and then, looked at Jimmy and challenged him: 'Are you suggesting the couple plotted a sick All Saints joke?'

Eric leapt in: 'A theory to be considered,' then he asked Glyn Salmon: 'What's your take on the meagre evidence?'

Glyn, his voice oscillating between aggression and anger, said, 'I've considered questions and answers to what we've discovered, sir: One: has a crime been committed? The answer is no. We have no evidence as to how Ray Glover faked his death and,' he stressed: 'question two: do we know if the man,' he paused momentarily, 'is Kathy's husband? Answer is no. She, according to Sergeant Iwan Drew's account, identified him. Question three: Did she look at the body, did she see his face? The answer is no; identification was established by a wristwatch.' Exasperated, Glyn raised his voice and declared: 'Roger Young's digital photos are pivotal.'

A tense silence pervaded the room while his words were considered.

Eric Bolton left his chair, ambled to the evidence board, picked up a black marker pen, wrote **Means** in bold letters on it and then said, 'Glyn has suggested several options. A question central to the quandary: who had the means to achieve this disappearance act? I believe that Ray Glover, did -'

'Maybe with another person,' an impatient Glyn said, 'he might have had an accomplice.'

'Interesting hypothesis, Glyn,' and then Eric wrote **Opportunity** on the board. 'Did Ray Glover act alone? As to another person being involved? I have no idea.' He sighed, then wrote **Motive** on the board and asked: 'Who had a motive for this charade? Perhaps there are dire personal circumstances of which we are not aware. We are without evidence to discuss motives or a third party's involvement.' Eric turned away from the board, shook his head and, gloom trawling through his uncharacteristic monotone, conceded: 'Zilch information; the photos might produce answers. Indeed, Dr Tim Wilding and his colleagues will be interested in PC Young's shots -' the ringing phone interrupted him.

He lifted it.

The officer at the front desk told him that the press and media had retuned.

'Okay,' Eric said, 'take them into interview room one; they'll appreciate the refuge. I'll be with them soon.' He then jotted notes on a piece of paper and asked Jimmy Elson to check them.

'Shall I speak with them, sir?' Jimmy asked, 'give them minimal info, usual spiel?'

Eric nodded. 'Okay. Glyn and I will accompany you.'

Jimmy Elson introduced himself and his colleagues.

Eric and Glyn and summarised the events, emphasising that the police were not certain of the man's identity and that he had disappeared. Jimmy then conceded: 'Conundrum is a mild adjective to describe the incidents. In view of the inclement weather, the inquiry is now concentrating on the town's foreshore and the area around the castle. The man's car has not been found, we are seeking help from the Greater Manchester Police. Forensics are looking at evidence.'

One reporter asked if dogs would be deployed.

Jimmy shook his head. 'We have no garments for the dogs to sniff and their ability to detect a human scent in these wet conditions are nil.' He splayed his hands and said, 'In your coverage and reporting please ask the local people to be observant, especially if they walk their dogs along the beaches. That is all we have for you at the moment; our press officer will update you. Thank you.'

The reporting units left and then the three officers returned to the incident room.

Eric Bolton, glancing at the wall clock, said, 'It's coming up to eleven, time for a coffee. WPC Manning should be arriving soon with Kelly and her aunt, Josie Harold.'

The three CID officers were discussing the dearth of evidence again when Helen Manning arrived with a tired-looking Kelly Glover and a sallow-faced Josie Harold. Despite wearing heavy thigh-length waterproof anoraks over warm woollen garments, both women shivered.

Helen Manning ushered them to chairs opposite the desk, then helped them to remove their anoraks and then placed the garments on hooks on the back of the door.

Eric offered the two women a drink but they declined.

'We had a coffee before we left the flat,' Josie said, her Manchester lilt fluctuating in her shaky voice. 'No sleep last night, thought a slug of strong caffeine this morning would counter effects of insomnia.'

40

Grasping paper tissues in one hand, a trembling Kelly, wearing a pale blue woollen shirt under a light grey weighty V-neck sweater and navy cord trousers, plus heavy duty brown walking shoes, wriggled in her chair.

Josie Harold, despite dull eyes depicting sleep deprivation, sat upright in the chair. The sheen of her below shoulder length blonde hair setting off a maroon shirt and navy trouser-suit, portrayed a confident personality. Durable black leather shoes completed her smart outfit.

Eric wondered why she was without a male friend. Cynicism entered his thoughts: why did she avoid male company? He reckoned the astute, wealthy woman felt most men were unemotional predators, an extreme thought maybe, but he suspected she was self-sufficient and, despite her obvious weariness, her eyes possessed an analytical gaze.

Eric told Kelly that he required a statement of the events and afterwards he wanted to see her and Josie Harold. He then told Helen Manning: 'I want to chat with you while Kelly writes her account. Ask another WPC to stay with the women in the interview room.'

Helen escorted the women out of the room.

Jimmy switched on the kettle, put instant coffee in four mugs and waited for Helen to return.

Jimmy Elson made the drinks.

Helen said, 'WPC Norma Taylor is with Kelly and the aunt,' then: 'what do you want to know, Chief?'

Eric handed her, Glyn Salmon and Jimmy Elson a coffee, then he sipped at his for a few seconds and then told Helen: 'For many hours you were company for Kelly,' another few sips before he added: 'What is your impression of her,' more coffee, then: 'I'm interested in your female perspective.'

'Difficult, sir; she's agitated, couldn't sit for any length of time on the sofa, tearful, yet,' a pause -

'Yes?' the attentive Eric asked.

'She seemed concerned about the worsening weather, looked out of the window at the garage, then at the castle and the foreshore. She seemed preoccupied with what she saw of that window;' a shrug of her shoulders, then: 'although panoramic views were absent in that weather, was she reacting to the circumstances?'

Jimmy came in with: 'Was she focusing on a predetermined spot or specific place, Helen?'

She didn't respond.

Eric remains silent, wrote in his pad then, raising his eyebrows, glanced at Helen.

Compassion in her lively voice, Helen responded immediately to Eric's unstated signal with: 'In view of the context, they were plausible reactions.'

Eric came back: 'Was it Kelly's husband in the garage? We have no evidence for a death. What do we know? Severe wet weather and a body, clothes and the garage floor dry. During the hours between the ID and the arrival of the forensics team the man has vanished.' He looked at Jimmy, then walked to the evidence board, wrote a summary of what he'd just said and told him: 'I'm following your lines of thought for now.' He stopped speaking, glanced at the wall clock and then told Helen: 'Check what's happening in the interview room.'

Helen left.

Eric looked at the evidence board again, then addressed Jimmy and Glyn: 'Can you evaluate anything from the sequence of events?'

Glyn remarked: 'I'm unable to apply any rationality to the info,' a sneer, 'I should say the lack of it,' then he added: 'hence my suggestion that this was a planned operation. Cynical maybe, but it won't be the first time people have tried to dupe the police -' a knock on the door stopped him.

Eric called out: 'Come in.'

Helen and Norma brought Kelly and her aunt into the room. Both, nervous-looking women, were dressed in thigh-length anoraks, polo shirts, woollen sweaters, jeans and hard-wearing shoes.

10

The two women were invited to sit.

Helen Manning handed Kelly's statement to Eric.

Eric thanked her, then he looked at Kelly and Josie. 'Coffee?'

Both shook their heads; then a fretful Kelly asked him how long it would be before she was allowed to return to the flat.

Eric Bolton manufactured a sympathetic smile and said, 'I'll read your statement Mrs Glover, I may need clarification on parts of it; I won't keep you any longer than required on my part; you must be tired.'

'Exhausted, Chief Inspector.'

'Indeed,' an understanding Eric concurred and then he read the statement.

Josie Harold placed an arm around the tense Kathy's shoulders and, in the surreal silence, whispered to her: 'You'll be back in the flat soon.'

Eric read the statement, then passed it to Jimmy Elson and, in a soft and courteous voice, told Kelly: 'I've studied your words and I am aware that emotional turmoil might have affected your description of what you actually witnessed. Before I ask a question I wish to remind you that your husband's car has not been found in the locality and that the body you discovered was wearing unsuitable clothes for the atrocious weather,' he paused for a second then, staring at her, added: 'but he and his clothes were not wet.' He stopped speaking, clasped his hands, looked at Kelly and then said, 'to state the obvious: it's an inexplicable picture.'

Kelly's body language remained one of profound agitation; she didn't comment, then clenched her teeth and wiped her clammy hands and tearful eyes with paper tissues.

Jimmy Elson, handing Kelly's statement to Glyn Salmon, asked Eric: 'May I ask Mrs Glover to clarify parts of her report, Chief?'

Eric nodded.

Jimmy Elson manufactured a tight-lipped smile and then told Kelly: 'My concern surrounds the time the police and the forensics team entered the garage; the door had been closed to prevent the public peering at or photographing the scene.'

The still emotional non-responsive Kelly looked at Jimmy.

The up-to-now patient Josie Harold chipped in with a feisty question: 'What's the reason for that question, Sergeant?'

'It involves the identification of the body,' a short pause, then: 'when forensics and the CID teams entered the garage the body had disappeared. We only have,' he stopped speaking, threw Josie a cynical smile and said, 'Mrs Glover's word that it was her husband.'

Josie looked at her flustered niece and adopted self-restrain.

Kelly, scraping the tops of the fingernails of one hand with the thumbnail of the other said, 'I don't understand, Sergeant.'

Jimmy Elson, sensing Josie's pique, decided not to pursue his questioning and said, 'Please continue, Chief.'

Eric glanced through his notepad and documents, then raised his head and, after observing the women's body languages again for several moments, addressed Kelly: 'I apologise for returning to the situation in the garage but,' he stressed: 'I'm confused by the scenes.' He stared at her as he spoke: 'Try and recall that moment when you discovered the body.'

Kelly told him, then said, 'Mr Davey phoned you soon afterwards.'

Eric scraped one side of his neck with a forefinger and then asked: Kelly: 'When you first saw the person were you aware that he was your husband?'

A trembling Kelly shook her head and answered in a quivering quiet voice: 'No.'

Eric, not allowing her to ponder, asked: 'Did you look at the man's face?'

A hesitant 'No, sir; it was against the floor.'

'Why are you certain the man was your husband?'

'The wristwatch; Chief Inspector; it was Ray's.'

'Did you hear or see any untoward activity or noises during the time the garage door was shut?'

Kelly shook her head. 'No sir, the police were busy, couldn't hear them in the howling wind.'

Eric turned to Josie. 'You checked with the family and the college?'

'Yes, Chief Inspector, no one has heard from Ray, no sign of his car at the home address,' a hint of emotion as she added: 'it's perplexing.'

Eric nodded. 'Absolutely, Mrs Harold.'

Eric looked at Glyn. 'Any questions for the ladies?'

'None for now, sir.'

Eric looked at Josie Harold and asked her: 'Do you have photocopies of the plans for this whole dwelling, your flat and the garage?'

She nodded. 'I keep them in the flat, Chief Inspector.'

'My colleagues and I would like to see them.'

Josie agreed.

Eric thanked the two women. 'You may leave now,' and then he turned to Helen Manning. 'Please take Mrs Glover and Mrs Harold back to Criccieth,' then to Josie 'Please give WPC Manning the plans, and do not leave the flat. If you need to go shopping please inform us. One of our WPCs will accompany you.'

11

Eric Bolton leaned back in his chair, sighed and, despondency coating his voice, declared: 'Kelly Glover did not see her husband's face. I'm none the wiser.'

Glyn Salmon, a contemplative tone in his unusually quiet voice, asked: 'Do you believe her?'

Eric thought for several seconds, then said, 'I'm keeping an open mind. Glyn, what's your take on it?' He smiled then: 'your tone of voice suggests you have one.'

'I believe Kelly Glover knows what happened, and is aware of subsequent events,' Glyn hesitated, pondered for several seconds and, in a quiet, measured and incisive voice, said, 'speculation on my part: was that man dead?'

Eric said with conviction: 'According to the officers who saw the body originally, despite it being warm, there was no sign of life.' He glanced at the wall clock, returned to his natural sitting position, fished out a twenty-pound note from his wallet and handed it to Jimmy. 'Pick up food from the local supermarket. We'll have a break, the carbs and caffeine might kick-start rational thinking while we review the paltry evidence.'

The three CID officers finished their snack lunches before one-thirty and, once everyone had deposited the meals' plastic packaging plus cardboard coffee mugs in a bin, Eric leaned back in his chair, spent a minute glancing through a summary of his notes and returned to an upright sitting position. A sigh, and then he sauntered to the evidence board.

A few moments of concentration followed as he evaluated the evidence, then he turned, looked at his colleagues and, tedium in his voice, said, 'What are we missing -'

Glyn cut in: 'Nothing, Chief, because we are without anything of note,' then, realising he'd interrupted Eric, he stopped speaking.

'Please continue, Glyn; hone on to my dulled brain cells.'

'We have no evidence that the person in the garage was actually dead. I repeat: consider what wasn't found: a wet body, wet clothes and signs of wet footprints relating to the body. The garage door was shut.' Glyn stopped speaking and looked at Eric and Jimmy.

Eric said, 'Carry on.'

'About four later the body has disappeared. So, we consider the following: was the man dead? No, there was insufficient time for him to be moved from there, no police officer saw anything suspicious, the garage door remained shut,' then, shrugging his shoulders, Glyn asked: 'What happened to the body?' He smiled. 'We know that most crimes are committed by people associated with the victim -' the door opened and Helen Manning handed Eric the plans he'd requested from Josie Harold.

'Thanks.' Eric pointed to a chair. 'Please stay, we're discussing the meagre evidence.'

Helen sat.

The phone rang.

Eric picked it up, then waved to the extension lines.

Jimmy and Glyn picked up the phones.

'Chief Inspector Bolton.'

The officer in reception said, 'Dr Tim Wilding is on the line.'

'OK', Eric said, 'put him through.'

A click on the phone and then Eric spoke: 'Hi, Tim, any encouraging news for me?'

A downcast-sounding Tim said, 'Sorry to disappoint you, Eric; no joy yet from samples taken off the garage floor or from the clothing in the tumble dryer, it'll take a few days before we get DNA prints. Tony Simpson is still checking the photographs-'

Eric interjected: 'So?'

'The digital photos your PC took might be instructive,' Tim said, 'Tony will drive me to the incident room on Monday morning; you'll receive my report then and afterwards, we'll view the shots. Eleven o'clock?'

'See you then,' Eric said and ended the call. He glanced at the wall clock, then handed Helen the plans of Josie's property. 'Photocopy them, then I'll inform Sarge Drew and ask him to arrange transport for you to return the originals to Mrs Harold.'

Helen nodded and left the room.

Eric rose from his chair, then told his colleagues: 'We'll leave it there; grab your coats; we'll call on Sergeant Iwan on the way back to HQ.'

Night had arrived; the wind had moderated slightly and it was still raining when Eric and his colleagues arrived in Criccieth.

Iwan Drew was chatting to members of his team outside the garage.

Eric told him about his conversation with Tim Wilding, then: 'an update please, Iwan.'

A morose-looking Iwan answered in a pessimistic monotone: 'No new developments, Chief, searched for that car again, zilch. The castle grounds were empty, and the foreshores have revealed nothing of interest.'

Eric, looking up at the flat, asked: 'Any movement from there?'

Iwan shook his head. 'Officers will monitor the street until tomorrow morning, then I'll reviews the picture, maybe ask local fishermen to search the bay. Weather forecast remains grim, they wouldn't be out in these conditions and, certainly not searching for a body. We wait until Monday morning, the sea should be boat-friendly by then,' a pause, then: 'a futile exercise but -'

'It has to be done, Sergeant,' Eric said. He made a note and then, looking at Jimmy Elson and Glyn Salmon, asked them: 'Anything else?'

Jimmy suggested that the police cordon should be removed in the morning and that police presence should be reduced but, with the improving weather, continue checking the beaches twice a day after high tide.

Eric agreed, then told Iwan that Helen Manning was photocopying the plans of the dwelling, 'She can now return the originals to Mrs Harold.'

Iwan responded instantly: 'It'll be arranged this evening.'

'Good,' Eric said, 'we'll reconvene in the incident room at nine on Monday morning.' He grinned and declared: 'The weather is reminding us that summertime ends tonight,' and then he and his colleagues left.

Eric Bolton, sitting at his desk in his CID office, finished reading through his notes, then checked the time and phoned his wife, Ella.

Her contribution to the one-sided conversation was a monosyllabic drone.

Eric, striving to continue the strained dialogue, explained that the investigation would continue on Monday; he had one phone call to make before he drove home. He told his wife: 'I should be with you by six-thirty.'

Ella reminded him that she was collecting their son, David, from a gym class at seven, she'd pick up an Indian takeaway on the way home.'

'That sounds good,' Eric remarked with enthusiasm following the understanding positive response from Ella. He ended the call and then lifted the receiver.

12

Eric Bolton's phone call to Wrexham was answered on the fourth ring.

'Howard Baker.'

'Good evening.'

'I know that voice.'

'Eric Bolton.'

'A blast from the past,' the sixty-six-year-old Howard Baker proclaimed, then paused for a moment before continuing, his Manchester accent skipping along the surface of his quiet voice: 'it's many years since we worked in Manchester, Eric. By the way, it's remiss of me, I should have phoned you; congratulations on your promotion to the North Wales CID.'

Eric coughed and then said, 'I'm here because of the help and advice you gave me when I was a young inexperienced PC. I reaped a great deal from the tactics of a competent investigative journalist. You taught me how to become street-wise.'

'Cut the sickly verbal shit, Eric; what do you want?'

'Your help.'

'I'm listening, the wife is out, visiting our married daughter Pamela. She also, lives in Wrexham, a mile from us. You know the area, you came to my unofficial retirement party five years ago.'

'Two questions before I begin asking for favours: do you still write a weekly article for the local press and do you still have contacts in Manchester?'

'Yes to both, and as to your first, I produce an article on Friday for the *Deeshore Courier*, describing and analysing the area's news during the previous five days.in the area. As to your second question, I meet up with old friends and colleagues in Manchester on the last Friday of each month.' He laughed, then said, 'Gave up the fags four years ago, only drink a glass of wine and a few cans most evenings. I feel good, I'm slimmer and no longer wheeze -'

Eric remarked immediately: 'And saved money.' He remembered Howard Baker as a perceptive investigative journalist: tall, thin, in his late forties, long black uncombed greasy hair with long wayward strands escaping from the mane, flying across his eyes. Dress was a coloured cheque shirt, top button undone and an incomplete knotted self-patterned necktie. A beige and brown patterned sports coat and navy trousers, plus black leather slip-on shoes completed the unfashionable picture. His delightful wife, Joan, notwithstanding years advising Howard on sartorial elegance, accepted that metamorphosis was impossible. The quick thought completed, Eric said, 'Do you have a computer, Howard?'

'A laptop.' He gave Eric his e-mail address, then: 'an essential implement for my kind of work, Eric.'

Eric said, 'I'll outline the problem now, send you the details via e-mail after this call and, once you've read them, you might be able to help.' He sighed and added: 'I haven't told my team of this phone call.'

'Fire away.'

Eric, having described the people involved, the events and the findings, voiced his concerns: 'I'm without a detailed family history, they've only been married twelve months, celebrating their first anniversary in north Wales.' He continued: 'The weather, appalling at times, has hampered our inquiry and the forensic investigations. Immediate questions: how did this, apparently, dead man disappear? Was he Kelly's husband? I emphasise: we only have her word on the vanished person's ID.'

Howard, speaking in a calming voice, asked: 'What do you want from me, Eric?'

'Check the man, he is as an anaesthetist in the Manchester group of hospitals, and then Kelly Glover: she teaches English literature in a teacher training college in Manchester. Try and suss out the state of the marriage,' he paused, then: 'as you are aware, Howard, most crimes are committed by family or friends.'

'Send me the bumph, Eric. How soon do you want answers?'

'Contact me after nine on Monday morning.' He gave Howard his email address, his mobile phone number, the incident's room direct phone number and the police's computer email address. He ended the call and drove home.

13

Daybreak in Madogton on Monday was bright, dry and tranquil, the hostile storm clouds replaced by high, woolly, white and grey benign thin strata. A south-westerly zephyr and an ambient temperature of five-degree Celsius welcomed Eric Bolton and his two colleagues when arrived in Madogton police station at eight-thirty.

No news for them at the front desk and, when they entered the incident room, Eric noticed that the evidence board hadn't been updated.

Iwan Drew updated his team in his office, then picked up a folder containing the plans of Josie Harold's dwelling and told WPCs Helen Manning, Norma Taylor and PC Roger Young: 'It's time we greeted our colleagues; incident room next stop.'

Iwan reported to Eric: 'The local police haven't attended any major incidents during the weekend's horrible weather. The early Halloween celebrations were ruined and there were no reports of accidents or incidents.' He stopped speaking and waited for a response from Eric.

'Carry on,' Eric said.

'Tomorrow is Halloween, then it's Guy Fawkes Night next Sunday. I've checked the tide times and, weather permitting, we might have a few bonfires and firework displays on the local beaches- both evenings. The local schools, however, are on a week's half term break, families might be away....lessening any revelries.'

'Thank you,' Eric said and, pointing to the window, declared: 'The weather is friendlier today.' He looked at Iwan. 'Anything new on Kelly and Josie?'

Iwan shook his head. 'The two women went to a local supermarket, WPC Norma Taylor accompanied them.' He added: 'As to my other colleagues, nothing of note was discovered along the beaches.' He shrugged his shoulders and handed Eric the folder. 'The plans of Josie Harold's flat and the main dwelling, sir.'

A frowning Eric said, 'We'll view the plans now.' He put on his reading glasses, reiterated the reason for viewing the documents and, after thirty minutes of concentrated discussion, all agreed that there was no underground access to the foreshore from the dwelling or from the garage.

Eric opened his case file; looked at Jimmy Elson and said, 'Phone our Greater Manchester colleagues again; ask them to inform Ray's parents Kelly's mother of the situation.'

Jimmy nodded, wrote a memo.

Eric carried on: 'We are struggling, grasping at straws, Jimmy; ask our Manchester colleagues to check if Ray Glover's car is in the hospital car park.' He paused, then added: 'I'm sure the family would have contacted the police if they had news. Anyway, please confirm.'

Jimmy Elson left.

Eric, pressing his hands against his waist, looked at Iwan, Helen, Norma and Roger and admitted: 'I'm in need of suggestions as to what we do next.'

A concerted silence was the answer.

Sounding dismal, Eric said, 'Dr Tim Wilding and photographer, Tony Simpson, will be here around eleven.' He then told Roger the gist of his conversation with Tim. 'Forensics want to discuss, with you, the photos you took inside the garage.'

'Yes, sir '

Eric Bolton sighed. 'Forensics are without useful pathological or photographic evidence that might be useful to us.' He outstretched both arms and emphasised: 'Roger, your photos could prove pivotal; print copies for our colleagues' files.'

Roger nodded and left.

Eric, running the fingers of one hand through is hair, addressed Glyn Salmon and Norma Taylor. 'Use an unmarked police car to call on Kelly Glover and Josie Harold at eleven; explain that the forensics team is meeting the police here this morning to view and deliberate over the photos PC Roger Young took inside the garage.' He smiled, then: 'While you're in the flat, confirm Dr Ray Glover and Kathy's mobile phone numbers and service providers,' he scratched the side of one cheek with a forefinger and added: 'plus Mrs Harold's home number, her mobile phone number and service provider.'

'What if they refuse?' Norma asked, her strong accent dominating each syllable.

Glyn Salmon answered: 'They provide our requested info voluntary,' a cynical leer, then added: 'or we obtain warrants.'

Eric smiled, agreed with Glyn's sentiments and then told him and Norma: 'Have a coffee before you go. Use an unmarked police car. Once you return trace recent weeks' calls to and from Mrs Harold's Manchester landline and mobile.'

Glyn Salmon and Norma Taylor left.

Eric scribbled a note, then looked at the evidence board again, sighed and, pointing his pencil to it, looked at Iwan Drew and Helen Manning and admitted: 'Can't make sense from what's written there.'

Iwan concurred: 'No pattern; lack of positive evidence-all unhelpful,' then to Helen, 'any ideas?'

Helen looked at the board then, attempting to evaluate the contents, spoke in a thoughtful voice:: 'I wouldn't expect anyone to hear anything or notice suspicious incidents in that horrible weather,' a momentary pause and then, in a hurried voice, added: 'to repeat what we already know are significant observations: Neither the man's clothes nor his hair were wet,' a nod and a pause, 'but -'

The attentive Eric interjected: 'Yes?'

'The black plastic bag Kelly Glover brought to the tumble dryer -'

Eric interupt6ed her again: 'Explain.'

'Apparently it only had her personal washing, Chief.'

'Maybe, Helen,' Eric said, a short pause as he gazed at the ceiling, his eyes full of the distracted air of a thinker and then said, 'such bags can vary in size, irrespective of what is, usually, wet contents. Forensics admit that they've found nothing of note, as yet, from their examination of the contents. We'll view PC Young's photos of the body and the inside of the garage later.' He checked the wall clock then told Iwan and Helen: 'That's all for now; finish outstanding reports on the local policing, then get a coffee and return by eleven. I want you both to be present during the viewing.'

Iwan and Helen left the room.'

Eric Bolton, alone in the incident room, wrote more notes in his desk pad, then made a coffee, returned to his chair and sipped the drink while he stared at the evidence board.

The phone rang.

He lifted the receiver. 'Chief Inspector -'

'My return call as promised, Eric.'

'Good morning, Howard. Thank you. Any news?'

'Made a few inquiries, contacted old friends -'

'Cut the overture; have you any news for me, Howard?'

'Ray Glover is not popular at the hospital, staff regard him as an overambitious individual and, at times, an uncompromising person, a loner. He attends the obligatory staff meetings, otherwise spends little time in the hospital's social life.'

'Meaning?'

'Since attaining consultant status, he's become more attached to a lucrative private branch of medicine, has a consulting room in one of the private medical institutions. Now why should an anaesthetist have a private consulting room?'

'That is interesting, Howard; and I'm sure you'll investigate.'

'I sure will,' Howard said, relishing the prospect. 'I'll confirm his qualifications, seek the consulting room's address and phone number and obtain a brochure of his services.'

'What of the marriage?'

'It's a rolling tempestuous journey,' a sigh then: 'that's all I have at the moment. Call you with further news on Wednesday morning.'

14

Eric Bolton, alone in the incident room, considering Howard Baker's phone call, was interrupted by a firm rap on the door. He shouted: 'Come in,'

A stern-looking Roger Young, carrying an A4 pocket folder in one hand, entered.

Eric gestured to a chair with a flick of his a pencil. 'Sit, Roger, you've been busy?'

Roger opened the file, took out two large envelopes, then a smaller one and handed them to Eric. 'One of the large envelopes contain enlarged copies of the photos that were taken inside the garage and the area surrounding the flat and garage. Weather conditions outside the garage and the dark night weren't conducive conditions for photography.' He pointed to the other large envelope. 'I transferred all my material into the computer's document section and printed them, thought it might improve the photographic definition.'

Eric smiled, turned the computer's screen a hundred and eighty degrees and said, 'Everybody can see the screen now,' and added: 'help me arrange chairs in front of the desk.'

Eric thanked him, then he looked at the photocopies. 'You've captured an uninhabitable stormy scene,' he grinned as he advised: 'but this morning we concentrate on the images you took inside the garage.'

Roger, pointing to the small envelope, said, 'That contains a computer memory stick for Dr Tim Wilding and his team.'

'Good,' Eric said then, glancing at the wall clock, declared: 'Forensics should be here in about fifteen minutes; snatch a coffee before they arrive.'

'Thank you, sir,' Roger said, smiled and left the room.

Eric Bolton, using a magnifying glass, was poring over Roger Young's photos of the inside of the garage when Jimmy Elson entered.

'I'm studying the shots Roger Young took inside and outside the garage, Jimmy.' He showed him the photos, explained the prints' sequence and then placed the glass on the desktop.

'Met him as he was entering the main office,' Jimmy said, 'told me you'd received them.'

Eric pointed to the arranged chairs. 'We'll look at the shots on the computer screen with Tim Wilding and photographer Tony.' He checked the time. 'It's approaching eleven, so please summarise your news before they arrive.'

Jimmy nodded. 'I had numerous discussions with the Greater Manchester Police: Ray Glover's family have had no contact with him, ditto the hospital, and there's no sign of his car.' He handed Eric an envelope. 'Details of the calls and conversations with the police, easier for us to discuss -' a knock on the door interrupted Jimmy.

'Thanks, Jimmy, we'll discuss this later,' Eric said, and then shouted: 'Come in.'

Tim Wilding, Tony Simpson and Roger Young entered.

Eric greeted the forensics duo, then rang Iwan Drew and Helen Manning, told them to attend and, while waiting for their arrival, described his news to the forensic scientists. He looked at Tony Simpson. 'You are the expert in this exercise, so you sit on the central chair in front of the screen.' He handed Tony the small envelope. 'PC Young has transferred all his photos on to a memory stick; please view it on your lab's sophisticated computers.'

Iwan and Helen entered, greeted everyone and sat.

Tony Simpson, dressed in a check blue shirt, cream crew neck woollen sweater, navy cords and black slip-on shoes, placed his rigid plastic black case on the desk, thanked Eric, then slipped the envelope into his case and looked at his boss.

Tim Wilding smiled at him and, in a soft voice, said, 'I agree with Chief Bolton, you are central to the inquiry.' He then handed Eric an envelope. 'My current forensic report.'

Eric leaned back in his chair and said, 'DS Glyn Salmon and WPC Norma Taylor have travelled to Criccieth and will bring Ray Glover's wife and her aunt Josie Harold here. I want these two persons to be aware, I stress, of only a part of our deliberations,' and then he added: 'I suggest a coffee before we start.'

He received a united positive response.

Eric turned and eyed Helen Manning-a tacit request.

She made the drinks.

Eric pointed to the computers screen and announced: 'Time we viewed the photos.' He handed Tony Simpson the mouse. 'Trawl through the images.' He switched on a tape recorder. 'To record your observations.'

Numerous minutes later, Tony, having considered all the photography, jotted down his observations and opinions in his notepad and looked at Eric.

'Well?' Eric asked.

Tony took out an A4 pocket folder containing a bundle of prints from his document case. 'The photos I took, sir.' He selected several shots and declared: 'These are the important comprehensive photos I took inside the garage from where an alleged dead person vanished.' He placed them on the desk. 'I've compared these with PC Roger Young's snaps. Both reveal interesting features.'

'I'm listening, Tony,' was Eric's response.

'PC Young's original pictures show a male body lying face downwards on the garage's concrete floor. Considering the weather conditions, the clothes he's wearing are unseasonal and inappropriate. His body, clothes and shoes appear to be dry; no footprints on the garage floor.' He pointed at one photo. 'Note the black plastic bag near the tumble dryer.' He looked at Tim Wilding.

'Its contents have not revealed any significant info yet, they are still undergoing extensive forensic examination.'

Tim said, 'Back to you, Tony.'

Tony enlarged a particular picture. 'The garage, excluding the tumble dryer, is empty. Look at the black plastic bag,' a sigh, then: 'it may be my imagination. A question: has the bag moved, changed position since the body was inside the garage? I can superimpose the images, sir.'

'Please,' Eric said.

'OK.' Seconds later they appeared on the screen.

A pregnant silent stillness filled the room while everybody concentrated on them.

Tim Wilding ended the hush. 'Print copies of that image please, Tony, then hand everybody one.'

Tony, having completed his task, looked at his audience and then probed: 'What is apparent when we compare the two prints? One: the garage floor is dry, evidence of a body having been on the floor is absent, and the black plastic bag's contour has altered -'

Iwan Drew claimed: 'Somebody's tampered with it.'

Tony turned once more to Tim Wilding.

Tim spoke in a dour monotone: 'We've seen the evidence, or lack of it,' then to Eric: 'questions for your team, Chief: how did a dry body get into the garage during such adverse weather?' Then: 'How did it disappear without leaving any evidence? How many doors has the garage?'

Eric, staring at the desk top, said, 'A bizarre series of events is my obvious unhelpful reply, Tim; the incredible scenario defies common sense and prudence.'

The inquisitive Tim Wilding's flashing eyes stared at Etic, challenging him to reveal his perceptive thoughts.

Struggling to find answers, Eric ran a forefinger slowly along the inside of the back of his collar and said, 'As far as I'm aware the garage has only two entrances, the main door to the road and the other at the bottom of the iron steps up to the flat.'

'I believe we should leave it there, Chief,' Tim said, 'Tony and I will view the images in detail; we might find the answer Sergeant Drew's query relating to the black plastic bag.'

Eric asked. 'What about Kelly Glover and her aunt?'

'An unclear situation; please question Mrs Glover on what we've discussed.' He threw Eric a forthright smile and then said, 'ask Mrs Harold if you may examine the roof again and then check the dwelling's history.' He rose from his chair.

Tim Wilding thanked everybody. 'I'll phone you after my team and I have looked at the material in detail.'

Eric thanked him, stood and then escorted the two forensic scientists out of the room.

15

Eric Bolton was discussing Tim Wilding and Tony Simpson's observations and comments with his colleagues when Glyn Salmon and Norma Taylor escorted Kelly Glover and Josie Harold into the incident room.

Once he'd introduced them to the team, Eric part-described the discussion with the forensic team and then told the two women: 'They had to leave, reviewing new evidence; they might need to speak with you in the near future.'

Glyn Salmon handed Eric a type-written sheet of paper. 'The phone numbers plus service providers you requested.'

'Thank you.' He whispered to Glyn Salmon and Norma Taylor: 'This meeting might take some time; I'll update you later.'

The two officers left.

Jimmy Elson smiled at Kelly Glover and asked her: 'How many doors into the garage?'

Kathy, dressed in a black polo shirt, beige V-neck sweater, wine-coloured jeans, brown trainers and a leather bag resting on her lap, said, 'Two; the main door, and the side one at the foot of the steps.'

Jimmy nodded and then said, 'An iron ladder, fixed to the side of the garage, leads to the roof. Why?'

Kathy said, 'A three-foot high timber windbreak built around the roof is ideal for sunbathing.'

Jimmy asked her: 'Mrs Glover, is there access to the roof from inside the garage?'

Kelly shook her head. 'No, sir.'

Jimmy looked at Eric.

Eric turned his blue fabric swivel office chair to look directly at Josie and then threw her a rhetorical question 'You own the property, Mrs Harold?'

Josie, dressed in a black shirt, grey trouser-suit and black leather shoes, shuffled in her chair, agitation trawling through her voice, tugging at the strap of her leather shoulder bag with one hand as she answered: 'Yes, Chief Inspector,' and then described how she came to buy it.

'Were you shown the plans of the flat, Mrs Harold?'

'My solicitor scrutinised them; they meant nothing to me. I wanted a holiday place in north Wales; this was spot-on for my purpose. I have a copy of the plans in the flat.'

'When was the house built, Mrs Harold?'

'Second half of the nineteenth century.'

A smile crossed Eric face as he said, 'A house built several yards from the foreshore of a large bay, perfect beaches for mooring boats,' he paused , then considered: 'stage of the moon's cycle and tides permitting in the quiet of the night -'

A feisty Josie interjected: 'I don't follow you, Chief Inspector.'

'Ideal landing stage for smuggling; any history of a concealed entrance on the shore near to the house? It would have been constructed before cars existent in this part of the world. My thought only.'

'I'm not aware of smuggling or human trafficking in the past, Chief Inspector.'

Eric didn't comment; threw Josie an impish grin, realised that she had followed his line of questioning with an acute perceptive mind. He decided to end the interview 'Thank you, Mrs Harold, that'll be all for now.'

Eric looked at the wall clock, then told the women. 'I won't keep you here much longer; would you like a coffee break?'

Both appreciated the offer.

'WPC Norma Taylor will take you to the ladies' room and then she'll make the coffee; everyone back in fifteen minutes.'

Everyone returned to the room.

Eric looked at Kelly and, in a discreet soft voice, asked her: 'Have you thought of anything that might help us?'

'When I'm in Criccieth, especially when I'm alone, I read until about eleven-thirty at night, then check the flat and look out over the bay. I often see lights moving on the distant beaches.'

'Moving lights? Explain.'

'Maybe people wandering along the beach, Inspector, carry lanterns or torches. I've seen them during my previous visits, but I've have noticed more in the early dark nights. I mentioned the sightings to Ray. He felt I read too much make-believe rubbish, and undermining realistic thoughts.'

Eric looked at her, said nothing.

'Ray and I walked one night along the beaches at low water, we saw lights moving below the head of the rocky protuberance that separates Criccieth beach from another vast sandy area;' a loud sight and Kelly said, ' seconds later, they disappeared. There are several caves on each side of the headland. Ray said that some of the lights were probably spotlights attached to the fishermen's caps while seine netting. Other lights, he reckoned, were from lightweight lanterns as fishermen moved with the incoming tide to behind the peninsula.'

Eric asked her: 'Did you believe Ray's possible explanations?'

'I regarded them as being a distant possibility,' a sigh, then: 'though since I've been here, alone, this week, I saw similar scenes on Wednesday night: lights moving, zigzagging along the beach before they disappeared behind the peninsula. During the high tides the expanse of sand beyond that point is not accessible by foot from Criccieth's south beach,' a short pause again and then she stated: 'why did these lights appear at a certain stage of the tide every night? I thought that tide times were not always favourable for fishing -'

Iwan Drew jumped in: 'That is correct; I live near the castle and see fishermen's lights on the adjacent beach, mainly at weekends, when tide times are favourable.' Iwan thought for a few seconds and then said, 'they carry halogen lamps. On colds nights, however, fires are built from flotsam and other wooden debris. Timber of all shapes and sizes is deposited on the tidemark, more from gales and big tides. The men stay for several hours,' a smirk, then: 'I also enjoy fishing, join them occasionally.' He asked her: 'Do these lights disturb you?'

Kelly's answer was a convincing: 'No, Sergeant; they captivate me. It's Halloween time, the last night of the old Celtic calendar year, a pagan holiday and a night of celebration for spirited witches. This corner of the Principality celebrates such rituals

Iwan gave a nervous cough, nodded once and said, 'True.'

Kelly, raising her eyebrows, asked Iwan: 'Are you interested in poetry?'

Iwan, surprised by the question, looked at her, shook his head and said, 'Please explain.'

'Have you heard of Robert Graves, the World War One poet?' His combat ended in 1916 by a bullet piercing his lung.'

A bemused Iwan stared at her.

Kelly responded to Iwan's silence: 'This man spent many holidays in the family's property near Harlech castle. He wrote poetry about the area. I'm reading one of his poems for the umpteenth time; it's called *Welsh Incident,* written in 1929. The beginning reminds me of the lights I see on the foreshore.' She opened her bag, brought out a sheet of paper and handed it to Iwan. 'One of several photocopies of the poem, Sergeant, the text is in bold lettering, easier to read. Your colleagues might be interested.' A smile and then she said, 'Please read it while I quote.'

Iwan read whilst Kelly recited:

"But that was nothing to what things came out
From the sea-caves of Criccieth yonder."
"What were they? Mermaids? Dragons? Ghosts?"
"Nothing at all of any things like that."
"What were they, then?" Unquote.'

Kelly smiled and looked at Iwan.

An expressionless Iwan didn't comment.

Kelly told him: 'It's a long poem, Sergeant; please keep it.'

Iwan thanked her and then turned to Eric Bolton. 'Sir.'

Eric, tapping the middle finger of his right hand slowly and gently on the desktop, eyed Kelly for a few seconds and then he asked her: 'When did you last see lights on the beach. Mrs Glover?'

A sigh, clenched her teeth while considering the question, and then, neurones synchronising, a nervous, high tone tweaked her voice as she answered: 'Saturday night just after midnight; the wind was still howling, the rain had eased, a few stars were visible and .I saw, albeit veiled, lights moving on the far beach.'

Eric said, 'They could have been produced by early Halloween revellers.' He wrote in his desk pad and then asked Kelly: 'Did you mention this to your aunt?'

'No Chief Inspector.' She bit her lower lip, shook her head once, then looked at Eric and, in a firm voice, insisted: 'The lights I saw were not produce by fireworks or burning torches.'

Eric turned to Josie. 'Are you able to see the beaches from your bedroom window?'

'Yes, but Saturday night's weather was foul up until midnight, Inspector. I couldn't sleep, so I made a mug of coffee in my room and then stood at the window;' a pause, then: 'although the terrible weather had abated, I didn't see any lights.'

Eric reflected on Kelly and Josie's answers for several moments and then told them: 'You may leave; WPC Norma Taylor will drive you back to Criccieth. We'll speak with you again on Wednesday.'

Both women didn't speak and followed Norma Taylor out of the room.

Eric told Iwan: 'Continue a low-key surveillance,' then to everyone else: 'a rest day tomorrow, meet back here on Wednesday morning at nine to discuss the evidence.'

16

On Wednesday morning, the first day of November, Eric Bolton, presiding over the planned plenary discussion in Madogton police station, admitted: 'The info we have is repetitive-,' a wry smile, then: 'like a radio and television newscaster, wanting to tear their hair out at the unyielding prospect of repetition, despite using different words, the same news in an attempt to enthuse their respective listeners and viewers.' He sighed. 'Boring. Has anyone any news since Monday and, any problems with last night's Halloween parties?'

'Quiet on the beaches,' Iwan said; 'it was a dry, bitterly cold frosty night; fireworks' displays were absent. Criccieth has unpredictable weather in November,' a grin, 'it seldom fulfils the official forecast. Exasperating.'

A shake of heads was the answer from the other colleagues to Eric's question.

Eric Bolton, pointing at the evidence board, declared: 'No significant additions to the scribble since the first days. I apologise for the lack of info and the scrawl. PC Alan Reed who, in addition to his policing and station duties, updates the board every day, is on a week's holiday, golfing on the Lancashire links.' He smiled then, tapping his fingers on the desktop, said, 'It's *status quo.*' The despondent Eric then asked: 'How do newscasters control their emotions and avoid expletives when facing a similar scenario?' He grimaced then, looking at Helen Manning and Norma Taylor, said, 'Having anticipated this evidential void, I checked my notes; I'm uneasy about the insipid answer Kelly Glover gave Sergeant Drew when he asked her on Monday if the lights she'd seen on the beach disturbed her.'

Helen Manning asked. 'What's our m.o., sir?'

'I want you and WPC Norma to visit the two women this morning; not too early, update them. Ask the usual:

any correspondence, etcetera,' a sneer, then: 'mobile calls are unlikely in this signal void, and check if they need shopping. Report back by one.'

Helen and Norma left.

Eric told Iwan: 'Continue to monitor the property.'

Iwan said, 'Two constables, Martin Ford and Sion Parry, who live in the locality, have been briefed. They'll report to me on any unusual activity in the area, and be part of a team if required,' and then he left.

Eric Bolton pointed at the evidence board again, then he looked at Jimmy Elson, then at Glyn Salmon and asked: 'What are we missing?' He grimaced a tad, then: 'What haven't we considered?'

Glyn Salmon pointed to Kelly Glover's name and, his intense north Wales accent dominating his voice, said, 'Knowing only part of this woman's history, do we accept that the man in the garage was her husband?'

Eric shook his head. 'Not yet, hence my impatience regarding news from forensics and,' running a forefinger across his brow, added: 'it won't be the first time an ID is incorrect.'

Glyn Salmon left his chair, walked to the evidence board and, directing the tip of his pencil onto Josie Harold's name, said in a resonant voice: 'As to this woman? I have a gut feeling that she embraces the internecine tumult.'

Eric and Jimmy remained silent.

Glyn Salmon, after a subtle pause of two seconds, asked: 'What info have we on Josie Harold? Little. We know she's in her mid-forties, is attractive and a wealthy widow. Has she a partner as per today's definition of that vague noun? Not to my knowledge. Kelly Glover hasn't

71

mentioned such. Josie lives alone, is she sexually active or a loner?' A thin smile, then: 'She, of course, could have a penchant for both. Does she remain indoors when here? Positive information: Kelly Glover is her only relative; they obviously get on well, but,' he hesitated for a few seconds before continuing: 'what of Josie Harold's friendship, if any, with Kelly's husband? I believe we should consider if a love triangle is a motive for the events.' He returned to his chair, shrugged his shoulders and looked at his colleagues.

Eric said, 'Your thesis is not only interesting but a possible representation of the situation, Glyn,' he added: 'the three people have criteria for your submission: friendships, and a linked romantic component.'

Contemplative silence followed, then Eric rose from his chair, walked to the evidence board and pointed to Kelly Glover's name. 'Teaches English literature, reads poetry, married for twelve months, spends time in north Wales; maybe often but we don't know that.' He pointed at Ray Glover's name. 'A consultant anaesthetist who spends a great deal of his professional time away from the marital home. He has a private practice,' he paused for a second and then said, 'a friend is looking into that. I'm expecting a call from him this morning.' He then pointed at Josie Harold's name. 'Assuming there is a love triangle, is she the third person? Are the two women, unwittingly, competing for Ray Glover's love, or is it the reverse? Does he split his attention between them?' He shook his head, structured a wry smile and said, 'We keep an open mind on that possibility -' the phone rang.

Eric lifted it. 'Chief Inspector Bolton -'

'Howard Baker; news as promised.'

Eric told him: 'I've been discussing the case with my colleagues, DS Jimmy Elson and DC Glyn Salmon; they are aware that I've asked for your help regarding Ray Glover's life. Is it okay with you if they listen in?'

'Not a problem, Eric; you and I are friends I'm a retired investigative newspaper reporter, but I will not reveal my contacts to you.'

'Noted, Howard. Thanks.' He gestured to Jimmy and Glyn to lift the extension phones and then told Howard: 'OK, shoot.'

'The Glover marriage has undergone an uneasy twelve months: the husband spends many hours in the hospital and his wife, Kelly, is alone most nights; being in a local drama group is her only social activity.'

'What info have you gleaned on Ray Glover's private work?'

'Unusual for an anaesthetist to have such; he rents a ground floor consulting suite, which he shares with a surgeon and a physician, in a large detached Victorian house in north Manchester.'

'So what's his line?'

'Hypnotherapy.'

'What? Hypnotherapy?'

'Correct, Eric.' Howard continued speaking in a firm voice: 'He practises hypnosis, comforting patients who are polysymptomatic and lacking in confidence when, in fact, they have no discernible illness. He encourages self-esteem in people who lack self-control, call it a form of brain washing.' He stopped speaking for a few seconds, and then said, 'He has a busy practice; details of his profession are on line.'

Eric commented: 'A thought-provoking formidable skill; I need that info.'

'Indeed,' Howard concurred. 'He has the power, a startling authority to influence emotions in a receptive person: greed, love, jealousy and then control and manipulate them to perform his desired deeds. Is his wife prescient? Is she being stage-managed, hence her lack of confidence? Is Ray insecure in his work, maybe has dubious recreational activities and, perhaps, plays a perilous game inculcating his wife's impressionable mind with dangerous psychological rubbish,' a short pause, then: 'a possible perilous scenarios. Have you paper and pencil?'

'Yes.'

Howard gave him Ray Glover's private practice address and phone number.

Eric thanked him and then, in a meaningful tone, commented: 'Frightening power,' a long sigh, then: 'my colleague and I will discuss your info.'

Howard confirmed: 'I'll look into Josie Harold's history, be in touch before the weekend,' and ended the call.

Eric and his colleagues returned the phones into their cradles.

17

Eric leaned back in his chair, balancing it on the hind legs and, while thinking, gazing at the plain white ceiling for a few moments before returning it to its correct stance. He looked at each team member and then asked: 'In view of Howard Baker's news, should we interview Kelly again -'

Jimmy Elson interjected: 'I suggest we wait for forensics news then question her about that plus Harold Baker's info and the photos of the black plastic bag containing her clothes.' He stopped speaking for a few seconds then, tapping a foot on the floor, carried on in an upfront voice: 'ask her to comment on the photograph of the black bag when the body was in the garage with the one when the body had disappeared.'

Eric, rubbing the nape of his neck with paper tissues, asked Glyn Salmon. 'Your views please?'

'I agree with Jimmy,' was the astute Detective Constable's instinctive response. He continued: 'we are dealing with a cunning woman; I suggest we adopt a patient strategy, divulge nothing to her yet,' he paused to consider further, shrugged his shoulders.

Eric leapt in: 'Continue, Glyn.'

'House to house inquiries revealed nil, no one heard or witnessed anything on that Thursday's horrible night,' a sigh, then: 'Police constables Martin Ford and Sion Parry, who live in the area, have also questioned local inhabitants without success.'

Eric chipped in: 'Unfortunate, but nobody of sound mind would have been be out in that weather. Carry on.'

'While we wait for forensics news I thought we try and view the tragedy from Kelly Glover's aspect: there is, apparently, turmoil in the marital camp, a husband and wife bondage seems minimal, she's capable of being self-sufficient lecturing; her husband spends hours away from home. Question to her should include: does she know of his private practice? How well does he know Josie Harold? Nevertheless, before we raise these questions, we must determine if the body inside the garage was Ray Glover.' Glyn paused, then pointing at the evidence board, asked: 'Do we believe that there is marital unrest?' He chuckled as he confessed: 'that was my original thought, but then a cynical query: did the couple devise a clever ploy to divert us from their private agenda with an explicit end. Is Josie Harold privy to this?'

Several silent moments followed while Eric and Jimmy considered Glyn's words, then Eric looked at his colleagues and said, 'Even if forensics produce crucial news, we play dumb and allow the women to leave the flat, but we watch them.' He looked at the wall clock, checked his wristwatch and said, 'we wait for -' he lifted the ringing phone: 'Chief Inspector Bolton.'

A frustrated-sounding Tim Wilding said, 'Chief -'

'Sorry, can't help you in that personal department, but -'

'Frisky, Chief? I'm frosty.'

Eric chuckled. 'I'm listening, I thought you were Lucy Grange from forensics HQ.'

Both laughed.

Tim Wilding said, 'Mouth swabs from the two women confirm their ID; the profiles are on the UK database, compulsory for a college lecturer or a secretary in a High Street bank.'

'Go on.'

Tony Simpson and I viewed the photos taken in the garage again, came to an opinion but, before finalising our observations, we asked our colleague, Edward Brown, I stress he hadn't seen the police or Tony's photos previously, for his opinion.'

'And?'

'He agreed with us: considering the atrocious weather, the setup was inappropriate; he asked if the scenario was structured. I found that question interesting, especially when he, also, was adamant that the black plastic laundry bag in the initial photos was more bulky than the one snapped in the empty garage.'

'Interesting,' Eric said. He then described the discussion with his colleagues and stated: 'we'll line up the black bag photos for Kelly to view.'

Tim concurred and then said, 'We checked the samples taken from the garage floor and, considering its location, we found no marine elements or microbes. Dust samples weren't helpful; remarkable negativity.'

'Thank you,' Eric said, 'we'll continue digging; you'll be updated,' and ended the call.

Eric placed the phone back in its cradle and was about to discuss Tim's news with his colleagues when a knock on the door stopped him. 'Come in.'

WPC Helen Manning entered the room. 'You wanted a report on my visit to Criccieth, sir.'

Eric, splaying the fingers of both hands, asked her: 'Where's Norma Taylor?'

Helen described the meeting with Kelly and Josie. 'Nothing new to report, sir, but Kelly, who remains disturbed, wants to return home. We explained the position to Kelly, told her that I had to consult you and that I'd return with your answer. Norma is still with her.'

'Please sit, Helen,' Eric said, gesturing to a chair in front of the desk, 'we'll discuss her request over a coffee.' He filled the kettle, switched on the power, made four coffees and handed everybody a mug.

Eric drank some of his and then looked at Jimmy. 'Your view on Kelly Glover's request.'

Jimmy exhaled, scratched his left temple and, after a sip of his coffee, said, 'In view of the scarcity of evidence, we discuss the photographs with her and then, irrespective of her reply, allow her to return to Manchester, ask the local force to watch her, interview her colleagues and family again.'

Eric turned to Glyn Salmon. 'Your opinion?'

'Jimmy's m.o. seems credible; a part-answer to the mystery might be in Manchester.'

Eric smiled at Helen and said, 'A female perspective please.'

Helen thought for a few seconds and then, confidence skating through her voice, said, 'A complex state of affairs; I sense a scary disharmony in the marriage, an unnatural background. Do the couple spend many days apart? The husband, Ray Glover, is preoccupied with his profession and his private practice while Kelly, a fulltime lecturer, spends her free time with local dramatics. Then the aunt, Josie Harold, an attractive wealthy widow in her mid-forties, no immediate family and, as far as we know, is without a partner and has been without a close male companion since being widowed.' Helen stopped speaking then, a moment later, said, 'An ominous situation. I sense there's a love triangle; someone, I don't know who, is tethered and that is a possible motive for what's occurred?'

Eric, surprised by Helen's splendid insight, asked her: 'How did you arrive at your theory?'

'It's a model for a crime, sir,' a pause, then a firm: 'if there was or is one in this mystery.'

'Elucidate please,' the attentive Eric said.

Helen asserted: 'We have no evidence to suggest there's such a triangle, but I do have a question: are we looking at a ploy, maybe someone is bluffing, planning with friends to commit a crime later-a team effort?'

Eric considered Helen's words and then said, 'I want to speak with Kelly Glover and Josie Harold again.' He looked at Helen and told her: 'Return to Criccieth, inform Norma of our talk, then bring Kelly and her aunt here.'

Helen left.

18

Eric Bolton and his colleagues were in the incident room discussing future options for their investigation when Jimmy Elson suggested: 'We broach the subject of Kelly's return to Manchester after we've asked her about the photos of the black bag and,' a sigh and then, in a firm, probing voice, said, 'if it *was* her husband on the garage floor.'

Glyn Salmon piped up: 'Helen Manning described a possible scenario but,' in a raised voice, asked: 'was the man on the garage floor actually dead; or a clever illusion?' He pointed at Ray Glover's name on the evidence board. 'An anaesthetist who practices hypnotherapy could self-hypnotise, simulate death or, he'd hypnotised another person who was privy to an intricate plan and,' a pause -

Eric encouraged him: 'Go on.'

'Is Kelly Glover mendacious?'

'Interesting concepts,' Eric confessed, 'I aim to determine what Dr Ray Glover's private practice entails. My friend will look into that and obtain Ray Glover's private practice portfolio.'

Glyn Salmon asked: 'Do we ask Kelly if she is aware of her husband's private work?'

'Not yet,' Eric said, 'I'll ask Josie Harold that we want to look inside the garage again. If she is unwilling, I'll acquire a warrant.' He then said, 'I don't want Josie or Kelly confined to the flat any longer than is necessary, otherwise we might have the human rights brigade hammering on our door. We examine and consider the evidence, allow Kelly to return to Manchester, but stipulate that she could be called back at short notice.' He checked the wall clock. 'I move that we have a snack lunch while we wait for the women to arrive.' He handed Glyn a twenty-pound note. 'Meat rolls and a selection of cakes from the nearby supermarket; I'll eat my lunch here while I try to analyse the evidence.'

His two colleagues left.

Lunch completed, the CID officers were back in the incident room discussing Eric's collated evidence when a single knock on the door interrupted their confab.

'Come in,' Eric shouted.

Helen Manning and Norma Taylor escorted Kelly and Josie inside.

'Interview room two please, 'Eric said to the WPCs, 'we'll join you soon, ask Sergeant Drew to be present.'

'Will do, Chief,' Norma said, and the four women left.

The two WPCs had arranged chairs at the desk for the three CID officers.

Kelly, her ruffled short black hair bordering red-eyes, highlighted an expressionless pale face, masking its previous healthy-looking features, the result of frequent walks along the beach. Her clothing consisted of a heavyweight white parka, red shirt and a light grey trouser-suit. Black ankle boots completed the attire.

Combed long blonde hair, edging Josie's part-furrowed pallid face, exaggerated her sullen eyes. She, also, had considered the weather: clothes were shower-proof, fleece-lined black anorak and a light grey woollen polo shirt underneath a medium weight navy trouser suit. Shoes were lace-up black brogues.

Eric invited the two women to remove their coats. 'Please hang them on the back of the chairs,' and then he addressed them: 'I apologise for the short notice, but we have reasons for your attendance.'

He turned to Josie. 'I'll be questioning your niece for a while; I ask you to be patient, we'll talk afterwards.'

An expressionless Josie remained silent.

Eric thanked her and then summarised the discussions between his colleagues and members of the forensics team. He waited for Kelly's response.

There was none.

He looked at her, then said, 'Mrs Glover, some of the photos taken inside the garage are puzzling us,' he paused, handed Jimmy Elson a memory stick and said, 'DS Elson is in charge of the computer.'

Jimmy inserted the memory stick into the computer, and then Eric told Kelly: 'Please concentrate on two particular photos, then I'll ask for your opinion on them.'

A tight-lipped smile was Kelly's silent answer.

'Okay,' Eric said.

Jimmy, pressing the view button, said, 'The photos, separate and superimposed, will be on the screen in a few seconds.'

A confused Kelly eyeballed the screen, furrowed her brow, but remained silent.

Eric told her: 'Before you see the images I must explain that Dr Tony Simpson, the official forensics photographer, and Dr Tim Wilding, head of the department, have viewed and compared the photos taken by Tony Simpson with those taken by PC Roger Young. Before commenting on them they acquired their colleague, Edward Browns, opinion.' Eric then stressed: 'Dr Brown, not having seen the photos before agreed with his colleagues' observations.' He nodded to Jimmy Elson.

Jimmy scrolled to the particular photos and said, 'I'll explain.' He pointed with his pencil at the images of the black bag. 'This one was taken when the body was inside the garage, and the other,' he pointed to it, 'was taken when the garage was empty. The third image shows the two superimposed.'

A trembling Kelly, on tenterhooks, whispered: 'I don't understand.'

Jimmy spoke in a soft voice: 'Please try and focus on the first two photos of the black plastic bin bag, then concentrate on the superimposed image.'

She leaned forwards for a better view.

Seconds later Eric asked her. 'Do you notice anything of note?'

A shake of the head. 'No.'

Josie Harold coughed, then asked: 'May I comment, Chief Inspector?'

A startled Eric looked at her and, in a cautious voice, decreed: 'Of course, Mrs Harold.'

A confident-sounding Josie declared: 'The bag in the second photo, compared with the one in the original; looks smaller; this is confirmed in the overlain shot.'

'That is our, and the forensics team's, conclusion,' Eric said. He looked at Kelly. 'Please concentrate again, Mrs Glover.'

'Now that you've highlighted the difference, yes, they do differ in size.'

Eric looked at Josie. 'Anything you wish to add, Mrs Harold?'

'No, Chief Inspect.' she stopped speaking, stared at the photos again and then said, 'but -'

'Yes, Mrs Harold?'

'The knots securing the bags are different.'

Eric asked Jimmy Elson: 'Please enlarge the images, concentrate on the knots.'

Seconds later they appeared on the screen.

Eric rose from his chair, walked to the screen and, pointing at the knots, said, 'A distinct difference in the way they're tied.' He turned and looked at Josie Harold.

A wry grin, then a sarcastic: 'Correct, Chief Inspector.'

Eric asked Kelly: 'Are you able to account for the bags' different sizes and the securing knots?'

She shook her head and muttered: 'No, Chief Inspector.'

Eric, having considered the physical and mental turmoil Kelly was experiencing, decided to close the session. 'OK,

Sergeant Elson, thank you, please shut down the computer.'

Eric stood, looked at the two women and said, 'You may leave,' and then to Kelly: 'I believe you've requested a return to Manchester?'

'Please,' a few seconds-long pause, 'but I won't return to college until this mystery is solved, and I wish to apologise the North Wales College for my absence on Friday. I haven't been able to contact them.'

Eric said, 'We'll inform that department and your wish to return to Manchester is granted but, you may be called back here at short notice.'

He then turned to the two WPCs. 'Please drive Mrs Glover and Mrs Harold back to Criccieth,' and then he advised Josie Harold: 'If you think of anything please contact us.'

Josie smiled, remained silent.

Eric addressed the two WPCs as they were about to escort Kelly and Josie out of the room: 'Please have lunch when you return; I guarantee you won't be disturbed.'

19

Back in the incident room, Eric Bolton leaned back in his chair and asked Jimmy Elson: 'What do you make of those two?'

Jimmy spoke in a thoughtful tone: 'Kelly Glover seemed perplexed with the situation; her description of the lights on the beach was intriguing. Did they disturb her?'

Eric asked Iwan Drew. 'Do you see lights on the local beaches often?'

Iwan, while shaking his head, said, 'Fishermen on the shore; I've lived here for many years and haven't witnessed what Kelly Glover described.'

A frustrated Eric asked: 'What the hell has and, seemingly, is continuing? The few facts we have are vague; the more I think about the paucity of evidence, my gut feeling is that the married couple are partaking in a ploy. I'll contact Manchester Police, update them and ask them to monitor Kelly's movements.' He wrote a memo in his desk pad, then looked at the ceiling for a few seconds and then asked Glyn Salmon: 'What's your take on Josie Harold?'

A smiling Glyn needed no time to think about his answer: 'I recap: an attractive mature woman, experienced in many ways, wealthy and, as far as we know, has no definite male friend.' He tapped a pencil on his note pad and said, 'Chief, your description of her was spot-on; she tried to annoy you. She could be a handful; I wouldn't risk my marriage on her-'

'I, also disregard such, Glyn,' was a smiling Eric's retort, and then he asked Iwan Drew: 'Do you wish to add anything to DC Salmon's analysis?'

Iwan grinned and said, 'She left a curious, playful imprint, Chief.' He carried on in a steadfast tone: 'A street-wise person, oozing assurance and self-sufficiency; and has a forthright attitude, is not afraid to question anyone.' A short pause, then: 'Maybe a hint of acrimony in her voice; it's possible she's experienced vitriol in her life?' He stopped speaking and waited.

No comment was forthcoming so Iwan carried on: 'another question: what, if she has any, are her views on Ray Glover? She hasn't mentioned him by name,' then: 'to answer your match-making quip with DC Salmon, sir; I couldn't handle her but,' a sideways nod of his head at Jimmy and then suggested: 'she could be a challenging prospect for bachelor DS Elson.' He laughed.

A smiling, silent, Eric raised his eyebrows and looked at Jimmy.

Jimmy, recognising Eric's reaction to Iwan's words, threw a wry smile and shook his head.

Eric carried on: 'I agree that Josie Harold is a clever woman, maybe devious; she needs careful consideration. I agree with you, Iwan, as to her obtuse attitude towards Ray Glover. We'll allow her a few days to settle in her flat before we question her-' the phone rang; Eric picked it up. 'Chief Bolton.'

'It's WPC Manning, sir, we're on our way back from Criccieth; just to let you know that Kelly Glover is returning to Manchester tomorrow morning; she'll keep us informed of any developments. Josie Harold said that she'll probably stay until Kelly returns.'

'Thanks, 'Eric said. 'Sergeant Drew is here; I'll inform him and, unless there are dramatic events, our next meeting is aimed for nine on Friday morning; enjoy your lunch.'

Eric conveyed Helen Manning's info to his colleagues and, as he was about to ask if anybody had any queries, the fax machine groaned into action.

He ambled over to the machine, collected the sheets; had a brief look at their contents, then returned to his chair and, tapping the type-written communication, declared:

'More information from my friend, Howard Baker; he has news on Ray Glover's private medical practice. He's sent me brochures describing the man's medical expertise in hypnotherapy.' He opened up the copying machine and five minutes later handed everyone a print of the faxed package.

'Please read it all,' Eric said, 'it won't take long. Howard, a retired investigative journalist, has a knack of obtaining news. He's also, researched hypnotherapy, especially self-hypnosis; that info is on the last page. We'll discuss the fax later.'

He placed the bundle on the desk and said, 'I was asking if anybody had any queries.' He tapped a pencil on the desk and admitted: 'Several unanswered questions remain.' He looked at his colleagues.

Jimmy Elson asked; 'Now that Kelly Glover's returning to Manchester, what news regarding surveillance of her movements there?'

'The Manchester Police have her relevant particulars.' He picked up Howard Baker's faxed report and said, 'I'll ask Howard to confirm details of Ray Glover's private practice,' then added: 'I'll explain the problem regarding the lack of evidence to our Manchester colleagues and that we'll be in our HQ, retuning here on Friday. Now that Kelly Glover is home, I'll ask Howard Baker to check on her.'

Jimmy, Glyn and Iwan approved.

'Any further queries?'

Iwan Drew asked: 'Any particular tasks for the local force?'

Eric shook his head and then asked him: 'Tide times and patterns during the next two days p3ease.'

Iwan told him, then advised: 'they are at their minimum at the weekend, then they increase on Monday, but not to any great height. Largest tides accompanied the full moon last week. We'll visit the caves again; neap tides don't extend into them, consequently vehicles can enter and exit at any time during a four-day window.'

Eric, glancing at his note pad, said, 'Good. Josie Harold will be alone in her flat, ask one of your WPCs to use their car, expense courtesy of the police expenses budget. Visit the area morning and afternoon while the other WPC, mobile signal permitting, contacts Josie and speaks with her,' he smiled, 'a compassionate call.'

'OK, sir,' Iwan confirmed, and then advised Eric: 'I'll contact you in HQ if any new developments arise.'

Eric nodded. 'We'll leave now, meet on Friday morning at nine. Afterwards, we interview Josie Harold and then we have a look inside the garage again.'

20

A few minutes before nine on Friday morning, the three CID officers, together with Iwan Drew and his team, gathered in the incident room.

'Seems Criccieth's been quiet,' Eric Bolton remarked, 'nobody with any news; no incidents?'

Iwan said, 'Quiet, Chief; there weren't that many people about, weather was windy, cold and wet. Financial circumstances and term time were understanding factors for the absence of any festivities in the town.'

Eric then asked Iwan: 'Any noteworthy activity on the beaches?'

'Despite the small tide and a biting breeze, only two retired men, exercising their dogs were seen on the expansive Black Rock beach south of the peninsula. I spoke with both men; they came to the beach most days, but gave it a miss during the severe stormy weather. Neither man had seen anyone else or vehicles in the vicinity recently.'

Eric wrote in his desk pad and then asked Iwan again: 'What news of the caves?'

'We've investigated them numerous times during this year, reason being that homeless numbers have increased in several areas of north Wales. Quarry caves above a seaside resort on the north Wales coast have been sealed off, preventing them being used as shelters for these people. The worry is that they'll seek refuge in towns such as Criccieth and the immediate coast. Kelly Glover mentioned she'd seen lights on the foreshore on several occasions; I thought that it might be homeless people using the caves .We examined them thoroughly; several had generous space for such people to settle for the night and also, a car could be parked there and not be visible from the caves' entrances. Nothing suspicious was found in any; the firm sandy floors were devoid of footprints and tyre marks.' Iwan shrugged both shoulders and added: 'Neap tides would not reach the caves' entrances. Sorry, not helpful, sir.'

'Not necessarily, Sergeant,' Eric said, 'we'll analyse everything eventually.' He turned in his swivel chair and directed his gaze at the WPCs. 'What's your news on Josie Harold?'

Norma Taylor spoke: 'I visited her twice, she's been shopping, bought wine and gin, was home by one on both occasions, bought instant meals, mostly curry. When I called on her again at five last night she was watching television, seemed relaxed.'

Eric then turned and said, 'WPC Manning?'

'I phoned Josie Harold at eight last night, managed a chat despite the poor signal. She seemed fine, had nothing to add, and was grateful for the police's assistance and presence.'

Eric scribbled notes and asked: 'Any queries?' He smiled and then quipped: 'Haven't we all?'

Glyn Salmon said, 'Not a query as such, sir but, in view of the weird situation inside the garage, I suggest we speak with Josie Harold this morning.'

Eric threw Jimmy Elson a questioning look.

Jimmy approved of Glyn's proposal.

Eric then turned to Iwan. 'Sergeant Drew?'

'Yes, sir?'

'Where is PC Roger Young?'

Iwan, his north Wales's accent rolling along each syllable, explained: 'He's on a mission, sir, plain clothes, it concerns this inquiry. He phoned me earlier, said he should be back early this afternoon. I'll ask him to report to you.'

Eric, opting not to pry into Iwan's schemes at this stage, said, 'Good, in the meantime I request permission, once more, for your WPCs' help.'

Iwan looked at Norma and Helen.

They smiled.

Iwan then asked Eric: 'When do you want to question Josie Harold, sir?'

'Eleven o' clock,' then to the two WPCs: 'please collect her.'

'Consider it arranged,' Iwan said. He beckoned to the two WPCs to follow him, then told Eric: 'Sir, I wish to speak with you and your colleagues as soon as I've organised your request; it's important, relevant. Fifteen minutes?'

'Of course,' the bemused Eric said.

Iwan and his female colleagues left the room.

Eric Bolton gazed at his two colleagues and then, his Merseyside accent vibrating in a robust voice, demanded: 'We must double our efforts.'

A tetchy Jimmy Elson reacted instantly: 'We are without help, sir, nobody has any concrete news, and we have no leads.' His Cheshire accent heightened as he carried on: 'many avenues with dead-ends.'

Glyn Salmon agreed with his colleague. 'I've not known such poverty of evidence during my time in the CID, boundary walls without gates everywhere.' He shook his head and asked: 'Where do we go from here -' a loud rasp on the door interrupted him.

Eric shouted: 'Come in.'

Iwan Drew, an A4 pocket folder in one hand, entered, shut the door and looked at Eric Bolton.

Eric reacted instantly: 'Are you ill, Sergeant?'

Iwan didn't reply; handed Eric the folder.

'Thank you,' Eric said, and then commented: 'you're frowning, sporting a troubled look, Sergeant.' He waved at a chair. 'Please sit and explain.'

A perspiring Iwan lowered his muscular, frame into the chair, ran fingers through his short brown hair and, staring at Eric, said, 'The situation arose Saturday, the weekend before Halloween.'

An alarmed Eric stared at Iwan. 'Six days ago?'

Iwan's local accent was hardly evident as he continued in a low voice: 'I received a phone call that evening regarding the disappearance of Ray Glover and was asked to attend a flat in Criccieth. The continuing inclement weather hindered the Halloween revelry so, consequently, police activity was negligible,' he sighed, then coughed to clear his dry throat. 'Sorry.'

Jimmy Elson asked. 'Water, Sergeant?'

Iwan accepted and then emptied the glass. 'Thank you.'

'Please continue,' Eric said.

'The flat belongs to WPC Manning; I had no idea as to why I was asked there,' he stopped speaking for a few seconds and then said, 'Helen was nervous, shaking and, after a gin and tonic, she told me that she'd been asked to visit a cottage in a village near Criccieth.' Iwan stopped speaking again then, pointing to the folder he'd given Eric said, 'I ask you to read its contents and print copies for your colleagues.'

Silence filled the room.

Eric gave out a long sigh and then furrowed his short black hair with the fingers of one hand while evaluating the text. He underlined sections of the typescript, then went to the printer, made numerous copies, stapled them, handed each colleague a copy and returned to his chair.

He placed the remaining copies in a drawer, locked it, raised his head slowly, looked at Iwan and asked him: 'Has anyone else seen this document, Sergeant?'

'Only WPC Manning, sir.'

A stern-looking Eric stared at Iwan and, in a demanding voice, asked: 'Why has it taken this long for you to inform me?'

A clammy Iwan stressed: 'Miss Manning was stunned, unsure as to how she should tell you, hence her call to me. She was distressed.' Iwan then emphasised: 'I repeat, none of the station's other personnel are privy to it; WPC Manning is sworn to secrecy.'

Eric raised his hand in response and said, 'Not informing the inquiry of relevant significant information.....' he stared at Iwan for several seconds and then emphasised: 'is a serious matter,' he paused for a few seconds and then said, 'I'll speak with WPC Manning.'

Iwan remained silent.

Eric doodled on his desk pad for several seconds and then told Iwan and the colleagues present: 'Only the Manchester Police will be informed of this news. Howard Baker, plus this station's personnel not involved in the inquiry, will not be privy to the information.' He stressed: 'Secrecy is paramount, divulgence might hinder the investigation,' and then, in a strengthening voice, commanded: 'the inquiry continues as if we are without this knowledge. Do you all understand?'

Everyone did.

Eric checked the wall clock, then turned his gaze on Iwan and told him: 'My colleagues will read your text.' He sighed, looked at the text again and said, 'I'll question Josie Harold at eleven.' He then insisted: 'Sergeant, you and WPC Manning will report here at two o'clock this afternoon' then he advised Alan Reed. 'I hope to provide new info for your evidence board later.'

21

Eric Bolton leaned back in his chair, sighed, inhaled and exhaled loudly, then told Jimmy and Glyn: 'Read Iwan's story while I phone Manchester Police. I'll call Howard Baker later, I've more work for him.'

The Manchester Police answered on the third ring.

Eric gave his rank, explained the reason for the call. A click, then: 'Chief Inspector Paul Henson.'

Eric updated him. 'Kathy Glover is returning to Manchester today; I'm interested in her movements while there. Her aunt is staying in north Wales, returning to Manchester next week.'

The Manchester Police would cooperate.

Eric thanked him, then added: 'We'll keep you informed, I believe we should share our info with you.' Eric then summarised Iwan Drew's dossier, emphasised that it be regarded as secret, that wide knowledge of the contents might hamper the inquiry. 'I'll fax it to you after this call.'

Eric replaced the phone in its cradle and then dialled Howard Baker's number, updated him, but declined to inform him of Iwan's news. 'I need gen on Kelly's movements in Manchester,' he gave him the address again, 'plus her friends and colleagues, and any slant on her husband and Josie Harold's social activities.'

Howard had contacted more friends. 'This woman will be trailed every hour of every day she's back home,' then: 'did you receive my latest news on Ray Glover's private work?'

'Thank you, yes, Howard; I've discussed it with my colleagues; his expertise might be connected with his disappearance.'

'I'll look further into his medical practice; might discover something new, I hope so.'

A grateful Eric said, 'I do appreciate your help -'

Howard interjected: 'An uncanny situation, Eric; I hope to have constructive news for you during the next days.' Howard sighed, then carried on speaking: 'I'm at a loss as to how to plan further,' and ended the call.

Eric replaced the phone in its cradle, rose and left for a toilet break.

On his return Eric spent a few moments writing in his desk pad, looked at his colleagues and asked them: 'Anyone with suggestions as to our next moves? Howard Baker's groundwork continues; he hinted that he'll require further instructions afterwards.'

A contemplating Glyn Salmon proposed: 'When we quiz Josie Harold; I suggest we inform her of our phone calls and our plans, emphasise there might be evidence we've missed inside the garage; make her think.' He raised his voice: 'Disregard her melodrama, I believe she's not the disturbed woman she's portraying -'

Jimmy Elson jumped in: 'An act? What of Kelly Glover?'

Glyn Salmon flicked him a sideways nod. 'An option is the answer to your first question,' then, speaking in a soft, measured voice, reasoned: 'as to your second: Kelly is well educated, agrees that her subject revolves around other people's literary material. She may be living in a professional cloistered environment, but she mixes with a variety of male and female students,' a pause to consider, then: 'she marries a doctor who has a bizarre work ethos. Question: Does she know his hospital and private practice timetables? Is the marriage one of convenience? Is there infidelity involving either partner? Have they planned or are they in the process of planning a secure future and abridge their working life?' A knock on the door stopped Glyn's deliberation.

'Come in,' Eric announced.

Helen Manning and Norma Taylor escorted Josie Harold into the room.

Eric stood, welcomed Josie Harold and, after he introduced her to Glyn Salmon and Jimmy Elson, invited her to sit opposite him.

Eric turned to the two WPCs. 'Please stay,' he said while beckoning with a wave of his hand to chairs.

Josie Harold, wearing a white shirt under a stylish light grey trouser-suit, a black shoulder bag hanging down her left side, appeared refreshed: the facial ruts had vanished, lustre had returned to her hair. She sat.

Eric asked Josie: 'Coffee?'

A curt 'No thank you, Chief Inspector, had one half an hour ago.' She stared at Eric and, in a distinct voice, asked him: 'Why summon me here this morning?'

Eric waved a hand at Glyn Salmon.

Glyn answered her question: 'Routine, Mrs Harold; we are progressing with the investigation, need to update our information, trying to form a picture of what's happened. We thought that being Kelly Glover's relative, you might be able to help us -'

Josie interrupted him: 'Stop waffling, ask me what you want to know; Mr Salmon.' She sat upright, stared at Glyn and, in a formidable tone, said, 'I'll tell my age, my connection with Kelly and where I was born. You have my address in Manchester, I'm a widow, financially secure, physically and mentally fir, and I don't shag men.'

Astonished by Josie's outburst, Glyn had a drink of water, collected his thoughts and then told her of the phone calls the police had made. 'There might be evidence inside the garage we've missed.' He raised his voice as he asked the obvious question: 'Has the situation affected, troubled you in any way? Melodrama I can do without, Mrs Harold.' He stared at her and said, 'I ask myself: do I believe you are an anguished woman -'

Jimmy Elson jumped in: 'A pretence, Mrs Harold?'

An expressionless Josie didn't respond.

Glyn asked Josie: 'How long have you known Ray Glover?'

Josie answered in a dull voice: 'About three years, met him when he and Kelly were dating.'

'Do you know him well? Has he stayed with you, alone, in your flat in Criccieth?'

Josie challenged Glyn: 'Meaning what, Mr Salmon; are you suggesting we were lovers?'

'Just routine questions,' Glyn paused and then asked her: 'did you know that Ray Glover was friendly with Amy Coleman?'

Josie, startled by the question and displaying uneasy body language, shook her head and answered quickly: 'No.'

Eric, noticing her unease, said, 'It's lunchtime; that's all for now, Mrs Harold. Thank you for your help. I'll arrange transport for you to return to Criccieth.'

22

After snack lunches bought from the local supermarket, Eric buzzed Alan Reed on the internal phone and asked him to brief him and the team.

The twenty four-year old, six-foot tall and athletic conscientious bachelor, had short black hair crowning hazel eyes and highlighting a golf links' begot bronzed face. An only child, his parents lived in Conwy and he dwelt alone in a two-bedroom first floor flat in a small village near Criccieth. A non-smoker, he was teetotal and his professional priority was ascending the police ladder in this area. His main duties were operating the station's front desk and patrolling the locality. He checked, and if necessary, updated the evidence board daily. Unable to make sense of the info on the board, Alan, his north Wales lilt gliding over his soft voice, admitted: 'The events are without obvious connections. I try to create a chain from the events -' a loud knock on the door interrupted the discourse.

Iwan Drew and Helen Manning entered the room.

Eric Bolton told Alan: 'Thank you; we'll meet again later.'

Alan left.

Eric reiterated Iwan's news, explained that he, and his colleagues, had read Iwan's text and, staring at her, said, 'Explain please, WPC Manning.'.

Helen Manning did.

Eric explained the seriousness of withholding info from the inquiry.

She apologised, then explained: 'Amy Coleman is affording Ray Glover refuge; he's a friends, she's the widow of one of his fellow medical students who died in a climbing accident; Ray has remained in contact with her since. She travels to Greater Manchester frequently, visits her husband's parents and, I believe she meets up with Ray Glover.'

Eric remained silent, nodded to her to continue.

Helen handed Eric a piece of paper. 'Amy Coleman's address, phone numbers and her email address.'

Eric thanked her, then asked: 'Is Ray Glover still staying with her?'

'Yes, sir.'

'Both to be here just before three this afternoon for interviews and statements; you and Sergeant Drew collect.'

Helen nodded.

Eric, looking at Jimmy Elson and Glyn Salmon, told them in a forthright voice: 'If necessary, charge Ray Glover with deceiving the police and wasting forensics time We'll question him and Amy Coleman in separate interview rooms, record their fingerprints and I'll ask forensics to swab their mouths for DNA profiles.' He lifted the phone, dialled forensics and told Tim Wilding.

Tim said that Dr Edward Brown was working south of Caernarfon, a body had been found in one of the rivers. He'd ask him to call into Madogton station on his way back to the department- 'around four o'clock.'

Eric thanked him and then informed his colleagues.

Iwan Drew said, 'I'm assuming that an explanation for Ray Glover's disappearance may be forthcoming, so why continue the inquiry in secret mode?'

'I have a hunch, Sergeant; please accompany WPC Manning to Mrs Coleman's abode; inform DS Elson and DC Salmon of the time you'll visit her, they'll join you. -' the phone rang.

Eric lifted it. 'Chief Inspector Bolton.'

He listened, remained silent, writing in his desk pad during the five-minute-long one–sided call. He thanked the caller and replaced the receiver.

Eric inspected his notes, then he looked at everybody and said, 'We'll have a break; be here at two o'clock. PC Roger Young will have returned before we interview Ray Glover and Amy Coleman. We should have an interesting and, hopefully, a constructive afternoon.'

23

During the break, Eric Bolton phoned Howard Baker, updated him and then said, 'A request, Howard: I need information on Kathy Glover's movements and more background on her husband, especially his social life. 'You know the game.'

'Give me a couple of days,' Howard said, and ended the call.

A minute before two o'clock, PC Roger Young, dressed in a white open-neck shirt, single-breasted light grey suit, and his lengthy black hair covering the cream fleece-lined parka's collar, knocked once on the door and walked into the incident room.

Chief Inspector Eric Bolton was alone.

They greeted one another.'

Eric told Roger Young: 'Remove your parka,' then, pointing to the door, told him: 'hang it on the peg and sit opposite me.'

Roger Young did as told.

Eric looked at Roger, threw him a thin smile, and said, in a soft voice, said, 'Sergeant Drew told me you've been working for him,' he stopped speaking, raised his eyebrows and said, 'well?'

'Sergeant Drew told me to report to you when I returned.'

'Returned from where, Roger?'

'Manchester, sir, is vibrant; a city on an upward curve.' Roger smiled and then said, 'I visited Ray Glover's private consulting rooms. The receptionist told me he was away, explained that he consults on two evening most weeks and, occasionally, on a Saturday morning. I was handed a brochure describing his expertise: hypnotherapy and self-hypnosis.' He handed Eric an A4 envelope and, in his deep-rooted north Wales accent, said, 'Interesting two days, however, no progress, negative news, frustrating.' '

Eric grinned. 'I know,' was his quiet, but influential, reply.

'You know?' was the bewildered Roger's remark.

Eric Bolton didn't expand, asked the Police Constable: 'Where else did you visit?'

Roger Young looked at Eric again, didn't comment, and then described his movements: 'I visited the college where Kathy Glover works; no classes arranged for her at the moment; sickness was mentioned as the reason for her absence from college, hence no new students are being admitted to this course.'

'Understandable', Eric said, adding: 'a friend, a retired investigative journalist informed me about Ray Glover's practice.' He tapped a pencil on the A4 envelope and said, 'I'll read your full report later.' He smiled and, encouragement in his voice, added: 'You might think your trip was unnecessary, but it's a beneficial exercise for your learning curve,' a grin, then: 'I've been told that your aiming for a rapid climb up the police ladder.'

Roger nodded.

'Patience,' Eric advised, 'always consider the basic ABC of a police inquiry,' he stopped deference speaking and looked at Roger.'

The young PC, not understanding Eric's words, apologised, explained: 'I don't follow you, sir.'

'Listen to what I say, Roger; you'll probably hear these words again when in training school.'

'Sir?'

'During a major police inquiry the letter A stands for assume nothing, B for believe nobody, and C reminds you to check all the evidence with care.'

Roger remained silent, jotted down a few words in his note pad and said, 'Thank you, sir.'

Eric grinned and then, a reticent tone to his voice, said that he and colleagues had held a constructive meeting that morning. 'It's startling news; only those present at the meeting are privy to the info.' He stopped speaking, frowned and, in a measured tone, implied: 'Please report on your activities to my colleagues here at three o'clock. Afterwards, you might witness incredulity. If you do, I order you to keep it a secret.'

A bemused tight-lipped Roger gazed at the ceiling.

Eric responded with a second-long smirk, then said, 'Get some lunch.'

24

Eric Bolton and PC Alan Reed were in the incident room.

Alan Reed, busy setting up a new and larger evidence board, told Eric: 'I've collected photos of all associated with the mystery, thought their presence on the board might help the deliberations.'

Eric Bolton thanked him. 'I agree, Alan; please stay.' He glanced at his desk pad, then raised his head slowly, looked at him and said, 'News of PC Roger Young: he returned earlier and reported to me about the days he was away from the station. I told him that we obtained interesting news during the morning's meeting but didn't divulge the contents. I insisted the outcome was privy only to the people present at the meeting. PC Roger Young will be here at three; he'll describe his clandestine work before we interview Ray Glover and Amy Coleman.'

A firm single knock on the door interrupted him, then 'Come in.'

DS Jimmy Elson and DC Glyn Salmon, followed by Iwan Drew and Helen Manning, entered.

Iwan Drew informed Eric that he'd updated a PC and a WPC and advised them to escort Ray and Amy to separate interview rooms, emphasising that their interviewers wouldn't concur, were privileged info.

Eric thanked him, then invited Iwan, Helen Manning and the two CID officers to sit and was about to update them on bus conversation with Roger Young when a loud knock on the door interrupted him. 'Come in.'

PC Roger Young entered.

Eric greeted him, waved to a chair and said, 'Our colleagues await your report, please sit next to me.'

'I'll be brief,' Roger said, smiling at his small audience as he sat. He described his time in Manchester: 'I didn't see Ray Glover, no mention of him in the local press, police have no idea where he is, or whether he's alive or dead. His car hasn't been located and he has not contacted his family or his hospital colleagues. I checked his private consulting rooms; no one there knew of his whereabouts and no appointments to see him were available at the moment. I also, inquired about Josie Arnold, nothing untoward to report. Chief Bolton has my full written report.''

Eric thanked him and then added: 'that's fine, the local police had similar results: Ray Glover's car had not been seen and he hasn't contacted Josie Arnold.'

Roger Young looked at his colleagues, shrugged his shoulders, and didn't speak. '

'The no-go situation continues, Roger,' Eric confessed. 'Thank you.'

Roger Young left the room.

Eric leaned back in his chair, looked at his assembled colleagues and said, 'News of your afternoon's work please.'

Jimmy Elson described the trip.

Eric Bolton looked at everybody, waited.

DC Glyn Salmon proclaimed: 'I've warned Ray Glover that depending on his story he might be charged with deceiving the police and wasting their time, ditto regarding the forensics team but emphasised he wasn't under caution.'

Eric nodded, then: 'What about Amy Coleman?'

Glyn said, 'No evidence yet as to whether she was involved in an unlawful act.'

Eric wrote a note in his pad, then tapping his pencil on the desk, said, 'We'll take their fingerprints before we begin questioning them.' He thought for several seconds and then said, 'Jimmy Elson and,' looking at Iwan Drew, 'a WPC, I suggest Norma Taylor, to question Amy Coleman in interview room one.'

Iwan agreed

Eric then told Jimmy: 'I'll wait thirty minutes after you begin questioning Mrs Coleman, then Iwan Drew and I will begin quizzing Ray Glover in room two.' He swivelled his chair, looked at Glyn Salmon and specified: 'You are not without work, Glyn; please remain in the incident room; I'll contact you once the questionings have been completed.'

Glyn smiled as he left, glad he was excluded from a possible confrontational session.

Eric scribbled in his note pad, considered what he'd written, and then told Iwan. 'I suggest PC Alan Reed takes charge of the front desk pro tem; I might have to make phone calls.' He smiled at Alan and then told him: 'We'll need you to taxi us to various locations eventually.'

'Will do,' a tense Alan said, and then sighed as he left the room, pleased that he wouldn't be involved in either interview.

Eric looked at his colleagues. 'Any questions?'

There was none.

Eric tossed Helen Manning an understanding smile and told her: 'You are involved with Amy Coleman plus Ray Glover's stories. Therefore, please stay away from the hub, have a coffee, remain in the station's operational room, you'll be updated subsequently.'

Helen rose from her chair and, before she left the room, looked sideways at Eric, pitching him a shrewd, short gratifying smile.

Eric Bolton reacted with a slim grin and then declared: 'Preliminaries over.'

Silence for several seconds followed then, a contemplating Eric blew a silent whistle, opened the desk drawer, took out a large brown envelope and handed it to Jimmy Elson: 'It's time to quiz Amy Coleman, the envelope contains enlarged photos of the body in the garage, and added: 'I've made copies for us, to be used when I interrogate Ray Glover.'

Eric then addressed Iwan: 'Inform the officers in the two interview rooms of the respective timetables and, before you return here to discuss our strategy, ask one of your station officers to collect a selection of sandwiches from the local supermarket, sufficient to feed us, the station's staff and those being interviewed.'

Iwan Drew buzzed Roger Young, thanked him for his report, told him of Eric's request and then said, 'I have another assignment for you; I'll brief you after you've returned with the food.'

25

The five-nine tall, slim and attractive sixty-kilogram Amy Coleman, a navy leather shoulder bag hanging against her slim waist, looked smart in her red shirt, light grey trouser-suit, quality low-heeled laced black shoes and white fleece-lined long anorak. Her fingerprints were recorded in the police station's operational room and then Norma Taylor and Jimmy Elson took her to interview room one.

Norma invited Amy to remove her anorak. 'Hang it on a peg on the back of the door,' then waving a hand at a chair, told her: 'please sit opposite DS Elson.'

Active hazel eyes highlighted Amy's healthy colour she'd obtained from walking in the Derbyshire and the local Welsh hills plus the briny onshore breezes on the north Wales beaches. She wore no makeup. Below collar-length red hair framed her oval face's attractive features, and hazel eyes and pristine white teeth completed an eye-catching figure.

Preliminaries over, Jimmy Elson pointed to the back of the room. 'The water vending machine, please ask if you need a drink.' He pitched Amy Coleman a short grin and then, in a soft voice, asked her: 'Do you know the reason for your presence?'

Hands clenched, a nervy and perspiring Amy gave Jimmy a short hollow smile and then, a slight north-east Wales accent flicking through her anxious-strewn voice, said, 'I'm aware of your problems regarding the whereabouts of Dr Ray Glover during recent days.'

'We require answers, Mrs Coleman,' an assertive Jimmy Elson said. He turned and gazed at Norma Taylor, but didn't speak, a tacit signal for her to question Amy.

Norma Taylor was about to speak when Amy Coleman asked: 'Do I need a solicitor?'

Jimmy Elson looked at her for a few seconds and, realising her evident unease, said, 'The questioning, Mrs

Coleman, is routine, part of our ongoing inquires,' a pause then, in a soft voice, added: 'if you want your solicitor to be present, please contact him or her. I remind you that you haven't been charged with any offence and you're not being questioned under caution.' He pointed to a tape recorder, switched it on and advised her: 'This interview is reordered for future reference.' He specified the time and date.

Amy unfurled her white-knuckle fingers, looked at the floor for a moment, and then she raised her head slowly and, despite looking tense, said in a self-assured voice: 'I'll listen to your questions before I decide.'

Jimmy looked at Norma Taylor, raised his eyebrows and smiled at her.

Norma checked her notes, looked at Amy and, in a firm voice, asked her to confirm her name and address.

Fundamentals over, Norma looked at her notes again and, in a compelling voice, said to Amy: 'Please describe what's happened to you from last Thursday evening.' '

In a quiet, nervous soft voice, Amy recounted the events: 'Thursday night was wicked, severe wind, pitch black and incessant rain. Light from the only street lamp was meagre, battling to breach the downpour -'

'Please,' Jimmy Elson interjected and, pointing at the tape recorder, advised her: 'Please raise your voice, Mrs Coleman.'

Norma Taylor lifted a jug of water, poured some into a plastic mug and handed it to Amy.

Amy's responded with a twitchy smile, then followed it with a hasty: 'Thank you.' She drank some and then, her darting eyes full of trepidation, encountered Jimmy Elson's stare. She shivered, realised she hadn't answered his question and had more water. Brow and hands covered with perspiration, she grabbed a wad of paper tissues, wiped away the greasy films and then, anxiety engulfing her soft slow nervy voice, said, 'The time was a few minutes after eight, I watch a mystery thriller on television every Thursday night, and then the phone rang. Ray Glover was on the line, sounding distressed: voice hoarse, spoke quickly, said he was driving from Manchester, the journey was hazardous in the horrendous weather and that he wanted to see me -'

Jimmy jumped in again: 'Did the call startle you?'

Amy wiped her hands as she thought, and then answered: 'Yes, Detective Elson; although we often had a chat,' slight hesitation followed, then: 'after the death of my husband, Mark, in a climbing accident, Ray, who was a contemporary and friend in medical school has kept in touch with me since.'

Jimmy asked: 'Any sexual relationship?'

A blushing Amy shook her head, remained silent.

'You rent a flat in a village near Criccieth, Mrs Coleman?'

Another drink of water, a further wipe of her forehand with a fresh set of tissues and then Amy said, 'Yes; it belongs to WPC Manning; I've been her tenant for nearly two years.'

Silence descended on the proceedings for several moments, and then Jimmy asked: 'What time did Ray Glover arrive, Mrs Coleman?'

'Just before nine, after Ray's call I couldn't relax to watch the television, so I made a mug of coffee, switched off the set, listened to the radio and waited. The news was about to begin when the doorbell rang.'

Jimmy Elson jotted down her words in a large notepad, then filled a mug with water, looked at Amy, had a few sips of the drink and then asked her: 'Describe his demeanour.'

'Agitated, looked tired, pale, and was carrying a large holdall. He said his wife was staying in her aunt's flat in Criccieth and that they had planned to celebrate their first wedding anniversary in a local restaurant at the weekend,' a pause, then: 'yes, Sergeant Elson, he stayed the night in my flat.'

'What was his reason for wanting to stay with you.......... and not with his wife?'

'He was anxious about Kelly; she'd been depressed recently. He decided not to disturb her, would call on her in the morning.' A quick shrug of one shoulder and then she said, 'He didn't elaborate and I didn't question him.'

'You visit your late husband's family in Greater Manchester?'

'Yes, every six to eight weeks, not a regular pattern.'

'Do you meet up with Dr Glover when there?'

'Not every time.'

Jimmy Elson changed tack: 'What time did he leave your flat on Friday morning?'

Amy gulped, then said, 'Around nine-thirty.'

'What clothes was he wearing?'

'Skimpy; summer weight, no anorak or cap, well, nothing ideal for the wet, stormy weather.'

'Did he use his car?'

A quiet: 'No, we swapped car places; his Mercedes is in the garage; my Mini is now parked on the driveway.'

'You drove him that morning to where?'

Amy clenched her hands. 'Yes, sir.'

'I repeat, to where?'

'The garage adjoining Kelly's abode. He ran to the side of the building, sheltering from the weather, and I returned home.'

'How long was Dr Glover away?'

'He phoned me, just after one, from a payphone; asked me to collect him near the shelter at the end of the south beach. He was drenched, shivering. We were back in my flat before two, he has not been outside until today.'

Jimmy stared at her. 'Did you ask him where he'd been?'

Amy shook her head. 'No, sir.'

'Did he mention what he did during those hours?'

'Hardly spoke, he was wet, perished, clothes clinging to his body. A hot shower was his priority when he returned to my flat.'

'What did Ray Glover do with the clothes he'd been wearing?'

'They were machine-washed and tumble-dried. I gave him some of my late husband's clothes, especially large, heavy woollen sweaters,' she raised her eyebrows and added: 'I wear them occasionally, over other clothes, when I walk along the beach during the autumn and winter months.'

'Then?'

'He had vegetable soup and a bread roll, then he went into his bedroom, stayed there until early evening.'

A silent Jimmy Elson studied her body language.

Amy glared at him and, vehemence in her voice, told him: 'Nothing happened, Sergeant; we had a curry, then we watched television. Ray was in his bed before ten.'

'Have you contacted Kelly while Dr Glover's been staying with you?'

'He told me not to, said he needed time to think, didn't divulge the problem, and I didn't ask.'

'Did he say if he'd contacted his wife during the week before he travelled to north Wales?'

Amy shook her head. 'No. Since arriving here he's stayed in the flat, has not used my phone and, although he has charged up his mobile twice, I'm not aware he has called anyone.'

Jimmy Elson thanked her, then looked at Norma and said, 'Over to you, WPC Taylor.'

'How old are you, Mrs Coleman?'

'Forty-two next month.'

'Any family?'

'I'm an only child, have a distant cousin in London. I have no children.'

Norma changed tack. 'Are you aware of the police's interest in Dr Ray Glover?'

She shook her head. 'No, didn't realise they were.'

Norma, silent, stared at Amy for several seconds,

Amy repeated her answer.

Norma spoke in a slow deliberate soft tone: 'On Saturday, Detective Sergeant James Elson and his colleagues from the North Wales CID, met the press and the media in Madogton Police Station.' She described the events that led to this particular meeting and then she looked at Amy. 'You're reaction. Mrs Coleman.'

There was none.

Norma continued speaking in a monotone: 'Bizarre events, the police are not certain of the man's identity and, despite extensive searches of the foreshores and surrounding areas during the past week. Nothing, including Ray Glover's car, was found.... we now know where Ray Glover's car is. The Greater Manchester Police are helping us but they are without information from Ray Glover's colleagues and family in Manchester.' She glanced at her watch, then looked at Jimmy Elson and waited.

Jimmy checked the wall clock and said, 'We've been here for over thirty minutes. Before we take a break, Mrs Coleman, I want you to look at some photographs.'

Amy agreed.

Jimmy opened the envelope given to him by Eric Bolton, selected three photographs and placed them on the desk. Pointing at them with a pencil, he said in a quiet voice: 'Not a pleasant sight, Mrs Coleman.' He placed the pencil on one. 'This is the first photo taken of the body, please note it is a man; he's wearing summer-weather clothes and flimsy shoes. In spite of the atrocious weather, he was without other clothes.' He waited for a reaction.

Amy flinched, didn't speak.

Jimmy carried on: 'The man is face downwards on the garage's concrete floor;' he paused and then, in a slow measured voice, said, 'when Mrs Glover saw the body, she told us it was her husband, her identification was based on the wristwatch he was wearing.' He passed her a photograph of the watch. 'Please look at the watch; does it belong to Ray Glover?'

A silent Amy winced.

Jimmy Elson then pointed to the other two photographs. 'Look at the man's clothes again and the garage floor; please note the man's hair and clothes are dry

112

and,' a seminal pause, 'there are no wet footprints on the garage floor.'

Amy said, 'I dropped him outside the garage, he hurried to the garage wall for shelter from the weather. So, if that is Ray, I'm not surprised that he and his clothes were dry.'

Jimmy asked: 'Do you recognise the watch and,' another pause, then: 'did you wash the clothes he was wearing?'

Amy leaned back in her chair, looked at Jimmy and, in a firm voice, said, 'No to the first questions, Sergeant. As to the clothes he was wearing, I threw them into the washing machine. I repeat: he had a shower and then he put on my late husband's clothes. Why do I hang on to them? Sentiment, Sergeant.'

Jimmy collected the prints, placed them in the envelope and said, 'I suggest we adjourn for thirty minutes. During that time our colleagues will question Dr Glover. A member of the forensics team, Dr Edward Brown, will be here later and, with your permission, will take a swab of the inside of your mouth to obtain your DNA profile. Chief Inspector Bolton might speak with you later.'

A trembling, edgy Amy Coleman answered with a hasty: 'I understand.'

Jimmy Elson stood and told her: 'WPC Taylor will see to your requests and provide food and drink.' He then left the room.

Iwan Drew returned to the incident room, placed two sandwiches on the desk: one containing prawn, the other filled with chicken and mayonnaise. Smiling, he declared: 'Food, soft drinks, plus fresh milk are available for everyone, sir.'

Eric Bolton thanked him and then said, 'Jimmy Elson and Norma Taylor have questioned Amy Coleman for over thirty minutes.'

Iwan declared: 'It's time we spoke with Dr Glover.'

26

The tall, broad Ray Glover, wearing a cream shirt under a weighty beige crew-neck woollen sweater, brown cords, white socks, black shoes, and carrying a small black backpack, had his fingerprints documented before he was escorted, by a designated police constable, to interview room two.

Ray Glover, while waiting to be interviewed, had reflected on his student days in medical college, how he came to meet Kelly, an attractive student of English and History - it was at the fresher's dance. Possessing a strong personality and a determined academic, Kelly strived for good results, then afterwards her aim was advanced qualifications to boost her ambition: a teacher of English Literature in a higher education establishment.

Considering the college days, he reckoned his philosophy had a similar edge with Kelly's, desiring higher qualifications, developing an expertise in anaesthetics. Their ambitious traits, aiming for personal success, affected a married life, met infrequently, slept in separate beds. Ray recalled those unnatural times: were they playing a dangerous flirtatious game against one another? Yes, was his considered inference: each was receiving physical and psychological slaps from one another by their respective actions? Were their separate academic minds on a collision course? He stopped drinking, placed the mug on the desk, sighed and widened his lips into a wry grin.

Several seconds passed as he considered further: was their marriage an act following a student romp? Both, sporting immature personalities at that period in their lives, happened to be in a particular college environment and, without having experienced life in the real world, became engrossed in a new surreal life. Their diverse personalities, both striving for recognition by their peers in their respective professions was destined for a stressful married relationship at times. Such was their ambition, their lives lacked passion, no social integration. Ray felt he was socially active, while Kelly, who was well-off financially, confined her recreational hours to the written word and her wealthy widowed aunt. Without a leaning towards any particular political party, Kelly was distressed following the outcome of June's UK general election. Uncertainty as to her future in academia continued to pervade her active mind, and this continuing mental turmoil compounded her insecurity most days. A black cloud hovering often above her troubled emotions, shaped her daily life most weeks. A loud knock on the door interrupted his reverie.

Eric Bolton and Iwan Drew entered.

Eric thanked the constable who had monitored Ray Glover, and then whispered to him: 'Have a coffee and produce a record of your observations of Ray Glover's actions.'

The PC left.

Eric Bolton and Iwan sat at the desk and introduced themselves once more to Rat Glover.

Eric opened one of the desk's drawers, took out a tape recorder and asked Ray Glover if he wanted a legal adviser.

Ray Glover asked: 'Do I need one, Chief Inspector?'

Eric advised him: 'The interview will be recorded; time now is sixteen o six on Friday the third November.'

Ray Glover stared at Eric and asked: 'Am I being charged, Chief Inspector? Am I being interviewed under caution? If yes is the answer to one or both questions, I do request legal advice.'

Eric answered him in a soft controlled voice: 'DC Glyn Salmon told you that you may be charged with wasting police time, ditto regarding the forensics team and their expert resources. You were, also, informed of your legal rights. You're not being questioned under caution.'

Ray Glover nodded, and waited a few seconds before he asked: 'Why fingerprint me and swab the inside of my mouth to determine my DNA profile?' Disapproving of these actions, he shook his head a few times and then said, 'That personal info is available on my registered file in the hospital's Anaesthetic Department. Phone my secretary, she'll e-mail or fax you the data.'

'You agree to such, Dr Glover?'

'Of course.'

'We might, if necessary, contact the department later, Dr Glover,' Eric confirmed and then explained the police's interviewing procedure to him.'

Ray Glover accepted the prescribed details and glanced at his wristwatch.

Eric said, 'May I see the watch?'

Ray Glover showed him his left arm.

'Were you wearing it on Friday morning, the twenty-seventh of October?'

'It's the only one I possess.'

Eric changed tack: 'Please describe your professional expertise.'

'Anaesthesia, both local and general applications. My specialty is anaesthesia relating to brain and other neurological problems mainly, but I'm regarded as being proficient in its general utilisation.'

'I believe you were working in the hospital on Thursday, the twenty-sixth of October?'

'Yes, sir.'

The patient Eric spoke in a controlled quiet voice as he delivered Ray Glover a rhetorical question: 'The surgical session finished earlier than expected and,' in a challenging tone asked him: 'you left the hospital around six that evening?'

'Yes.'

Another rhetorical question from Eric: 'It was an arduous drive from Manchester to north Wales in that horrendous weather, Dr Glover?'

'Yes, sir.'

'You drove to Criccieth?'

'No,' a hesitant Ray said, 'I called in a service station, phoned Amy Coleman around eight and asked if I could stay in her flat that night. She lives a few miles from the town'

'Any sexual interest?'

A firm: 'No.'

'I believe you see Mrs Coleman when she visits her husband's family in Greater Manchester.'

'We've known one another since my college days; her husband was a fellow student.

'I ask again, Dr Glover, have you had a sexual relationship with her?'

Ray shook his head. 'No romance.'

Silence fell over the proceedings for a few moments and then Eric asked: 'What time did you arrive at Mrs Coleman's flat, Dr Glover?'

'Just before nine.'

'Why didn't you contact your wife?'

Ray Glover clenched his teeth for a few seconds, then stroked the back of his neck with one hand and then, in a quiet, nervy voice, explained:: 'Kelly has been depressed and anxious during the past few months, takes prescribed medication for the problem,' a long sigh then he added: 'because of the atrocious weather I had no idea as to the time I would arrive at the flat. So, not wishing to frighten her, I decided to contact her in the morning,' a shorty nervous smile, then: 'so I phoned Amy Coleman.'

'No culpability, Dr Glover?'

A thinking Ray Glover shook his head then, affirmation in his strong voice, said, 'Yes.' A sudden closing of his eyes, a sniffle then, after a short dry cough and. staring at the desk top, explained: 'Kelly. Yes, Kelly,' he hesitated for a few seconds, then: 'this part of Wales influenced her mind, especially when it involved myth and poetry; she developed a passionate relationship with the history of this particular part of north Wales, the axilla between the country's trunk and the arm that is the Lleyn Peninsula.'

Iwan Drew then addressed Ray Glover: 'We are aware of your wife's profession and her interest in a drama school in Manchester.' He then described his meeting with Kelly in the flat and said, 'She quoted the first five lines of the poem while I read them.' He eyed Ray Glover.

Silence.

Determination trickled through Iwan's controlled voice as he asked Ray Glover: 'Do you believe that Criccieth's local history, and this particular poem by Robert Graves, dominate her behaviour when she is here?'

A thoughtful Ray shook his head a few times and, tapping the fingers of both hands on the desktop for several seconds, answered in a soft clear-cut voice: 'Yes. The castles, but mainly Robert Graves's poem. Why? Because it was beyond her comprehension,' a loud sigh, then: 'it became a dominant psychological challenge- a riddle depicting caricatures of the local people or maybe, prisoners, zombies, from the castles all those centuries ago?'

A few-seconds of silence followed then, Eric Bolton, having observed Ray Glover's anxiety and agitated body language, declared: 'A fifteen-minute break.'

Approving sighs followed the announcement.

Eric handed Ray a small sheet of blank paper and a pencil. 'Please write down your Manchester home telephone number, your wife's email address and her mobile phone number.'

Ray Glover obliged and was then escorted out of the interview room.

Minutes later the phone rang: Dr Edward Brown had arrived.

Eric thanked the desk officer and then told him: 'Ask him to call here after he's seen Mrs Coleman.'

27

Fifteen minutes later everyone was back in interview room two.

Eric Bolton, pointing to a jug of water and a small stack of plastic mugs, said, 'Please help yourselves to a drink.' He then took several photos from his case file, placed them, face downwards, on the desktop and looked at Ray Glover, didn't speak.

Ray Glover remained silent.

Eric played with the photos for several seconds and then addressed Ray Glover: 'Where is your car?'

'It's in Mrs Coleman's garage until I decide to leave. The garage is unlocked; there's ample room in the drive for me to reverse out and pass Mrs Coleman's car, now parked on the drive.'

'That problem solved; the Manchester Police will be updated,' and then Eric asked: 'What happened to the wet clothes you were wearing when you returned to Amy Coleman's abode?'

A tense Ray Glover said, 'Mrs Coleman washed them in the machine while I had a shower' and then, tapping his chest and trousers, said, 'she gave me these clothes that belonged to her late husband. The black slip-on leather shoes are mine.' A cynical grin, then he said, 'The garb is neither elegant nor fashionable, but comfortable and warm, Chief Inspector.'

An expressionless Eric noted the answer, then fingered the photos and, a subtle tone to his voice, said, 'I shall show you several photos that were taken inside the garage, Dr Glover.' He turned over the first photo. 'Is this person you, face downwards on the floor?' Eric stopped speaking, hoping for a response.

None was forthcoming.

Eric turned over another photo, pointed to the image's left arm. 'Your wife identified you from the wristwatch.'

Ray Glover didn't react.

Eric raised his voice, turned over another photo. 'This has been enlarged to demonstrate the clothes you were wearing, plus a view of the garage floor.' Tapping his fingers on the desktop, he added: 'a question: despite the foul weather, why were your clothes, your hair, shoes and the garage floor dry?' A short pause to consider the situation, then Eric said, 'You would be soaked if you had been in that hostile weather for just a few minutes,' then Eric, eyebrows raised, stared at Ray Glover and declared: 'The setting inside that garage is implausible.' He stopped speaking again and waited.

Ray Glover remained silent.

The tolerant Eric Bolton had a drink of water, checked his notes and then, in a demanding tone, challenged Ray: 'Explain how, on a stormy, wet night, a male person, wearing enters a garage wearing dry clothes and sporty shoes. He is subsequently assumed to be dead, but then that person disappears into nature's harsh elements. Alive and soaked, he seeks refuge from a female friend.' He passed another two down-turned photos across the desk to Ray Glover, then upturned one with a pencil and said, 'You are on the garage floor; please look at, and note the size, of the black plastic bag next to the tumble dryer.'

Ray Glover nodded, then, in a defiant voice, said, 'I don't follow you, Chief Inspector.'

Eric turned over the second photo and said, 'You are no longer in the garage, but please note again the black plastic bag next to the tumble dryer. Compare it with the one in the previous shot,' a pause while Ray scanned the two photos, then Eric asked: 'A parallel question: what do you see, Dr Glover?'

A hesitant Ray Glover, shook his head and said, 'An empty garage and a black plastic bag.'

'Compare the bags' sizes, Dr Glover.'

Ray Glover clenching his hands, said, 'The one in the empty garage seems less bulky.'

'Correct,' Eric said, then he asked: 'are you able to account for the disparity?'

'No, sir.'

'Did you remove towels from the bag, hence the difference in the sizes?'

A perspiring Ray Glover looked at Eric and, in a moulded voice, answered: 'I arrived at Amy Coleman's flat around nine on Thursday evening, spent the night there. The next morning she drove me to the flat's garage. I have a spare key to the side door and unlocked it,' a pause, 'and then I entered…..you know the rest.'

His patience splintering, Eric claimed: 'We do not, Dr Glover. How did you feign death, an act that has wasted police and forensics teams' schedules? You may be charged regarding these.' He looked at his notes, scribbled a few more, then raised his head and told Ray Glover: 'Mrs Josie Harold has shown us the plans of the garage; there is no tunnel from it to the beach.' A wry smile, then: 'That negative finding is surprising because smuggling was a possibility along this coast during the nineteenth century.'

'A complex story, Chief Inspector. Is that finding significant?'

'It could have been a way out from the garage.' Eric said.

Ray Glover said, 'Kelly's family had no connections with north Wales, but her wealthy widowed aunt, Josie Harold bought the   first-floor flat in the   large house situated near Criccieth castle. From the rear of the property, a twenty-yard long private, part concrete and part sandy, walkway provides access to the nearby high water mark., ideal to enter the beach and then a walk along the foreshore.'

'I'm listening,' Eric said.

'Kelly became engrossed in the local history dating back to the 13th century, the castles in that area and Robert Graves's family had a home near Harlech castle. My wife read his poetry and became interested in poems he'd written appertaining to this part of north-west Wales. It engulfed her thinking. Enamoured by the history of the area and the poetry of the acclaimed poet, Kelly, who has an interest in the late 19th and early 20the century poets, became fascinated with stories of the area. Why such a near-obsession with this prose?' Ray shook his head and then, in a thoughtful tone, carried on speaking: 'Kelly often recites one particular poem that involves this part of north Wales; how he spent weeks on holiday in the area, especially in the vicinity of Harlech. His father, Alfred Percival Graves, also a poet, known for his Celtic compositions, had built a large house within walking distance of the castle. The vast open countryside and the nearby mountains appealed to Robert Graves. He loved the area.'

Eric asked: 'Which one poem appealed to your wife, Dr Glover?'

'It's titled *Welsh Incident,* fifty-one lines long, unclear dialogue between two unidentified people,' a shrug of his shoulders, 'or perhaps someone is reminiscing, having a conversation with himself. I'm interested because of Kelly's obsession.'

'Obsession?'

'On several nights Kelly proclaimed she saw lights moving on the beach, or maybe the beaches; I'm not sure which. Following late night trips there I couldn't confirm what she claimed. When we returned to the flat I sked her why was she convinced of such visions. She felt that the poem described what happened in Criccieth and Harlech castles: the way prisoners were treated and killed. Kelly was convinced their ghosts marched along the beaches into the caves, never to be seen again, sensed the castles' histories were being analysed by Robert Graves's poem. There's a book of English verse in the flat in Criccieth; a red bookmark indicates the particular poem.'

'That was noted by the police when they were with Kelly in the flat. Sergeant Iwan Drew has a copy of this poem. Your wife quoted the first five lines to him.'

Ray sighed and then said, 'It's a profound beginning, but I'm clueless as to what it conveys,' a sigh again, then: 'Kelly, I repeat, regarded it as a possible fable relating to the area's history.'

Eric asked: 'Are you able to recite any section of the poem that might relates to our inquiry, Dr Glover?'

'Kelly's thoughts on the poetry strikes an emotional, maybe historical chord; the poem describes nameless persons, human facades simulating surreal procedures in north-west Wales. The castles ruins, also, influenced her philosophy, regarded them as emitting creepy atmospheres, and reflecting insecurity that, to her, was ever-present in the present century and in particular this decade. Uncontrolled past and present human behaviour burdened her.'

'What was your wife's response when you chatted about this?'

Ray Glover shut his eyes, thought for a few seconds and then said, 'I asked her to describe what she'd seen;' a shrug of a shoulder and then: 'she quoted parts of the poem. I got the impression that she had divided the composition into definite, graphic segments.' He opened his backpack, took out a book and, a tint of sour humour trickling through his voice, said, 'I carry this when I'm in north Wales in case Kelly wants to read the poem when we walk along the beaches.' He opened it at a particular page and handed the book to Eric.

'The *Welsh Incident* ', Eric said.

'Photocopy the pages in bold type, Chief Inspector, hand the copies to you team, they might discern some of the enigmatic profiles.'

Minutes later, Eric, having printed several copies, returned the book to Ray Glover. 'Thank you.'

Ray Glover elucidated: 'Kelly's obsession with seeing lights moving on the foreshore relate to Criccieth and Harlech Castles' histories.' He quoted the first section's lines, then said, 'I'm unable to analyse the poet's thoughts, but have questions appertaining to the words: was he meditating aloud, trying to elucidate visions, real or imaginary, that he believed he'd witnessed on the sands?' He stopped speaking and looked at Eric.

Eric was impassive.

Ray gave out a deep sigh, and then continued: 'Was he speaking with somebody? He is asked about these visions in the poem, but by whom? The reader isn't told the identity of the questioner in the stanza.' He looked at Eric, then at Iwan and said, 'both of you please read the first five lines of the second part of the poem while I quote.'

Eric put on his reading glasses. 'OK.'

Ray recited: *"All sorts of queer things,*
Things never seen or heard or written about,
Very strange, un-Welsh, utterly peculiar
Things. Oh, solid enough they seemed to touch,
Had anyone dared it."?' Ray stopped speaking, then a moment later, said, 'that last line suggests that no-one challenged or defined the events.'

Iwan, in a soft reflective voice, asked Ray Glover: 'Does anyone know what the poet was describing?' A shrug then further questions: 'Why focus on this poem? Is your wife impressionable?'

Ray shook his head. 'No, yet I have no idea of what the poet is expressing; I can't imagine what sort of life forms are seen leaving the caves,' he sighed, thought for a brief moment and then, in a sombre voice added: 'I told her that I had three queries concerning the poetry: First; why were these things inside the caves; second: how did they live there and third: who are they? She answered with a quotation: *"Marvellous creation,"'* Ray Glover tendered a cynical smile as he said, 'It's in the poem's second part, the tenth line. Is the poet describing migrants, ghosts, zombies- part of folklore?' Another sigh then: 'Is he seeing zombies of the castles' thirteenth century prisoners; or, is he describing members of an alien civilisation, controlled freaks, obeying a powerful force or forces?' A wry smile and then he continued; 'Is he fantasising, has he a flamboyant and pictorial mind that produces atypical creepy images?'

A perplexed Iwan asked: 'You have no explanation-' a rap on the door interrupted him.

Dr Edward Brown entered.

Eric introduced him and then explained to Ray Glover the reason for the forensic scientist's presence.

The swab for DNA profiling was taken from inside Ray's mouth and then Edward Brown left.

Eric looked at the wall clock and said, 'We adjourn for a comfort break, all back in ten minutes.'

28

Once everyone was back in the interview room, Eric nodded to Iwan.

Iwan, targeting Ray Glover with a thin smile, said, 'Returning to my question, Dr Glover, are you unable to explain your wife's fascination with this poet?'

Ray Glover scratched one temple for a few seconds, smiled at his small audience, and said, 'I hope I'm not repeating history. I'm sure you are all aware of such.' He waited for a response.

No one commented.

Ray Glover, a resolute tone tinting his strong voice, continued: 'My wife's is interested in Harlech and Criccieth castles' histories; the latter built by a Welsh Prince in 1239, it became a prison for a Welsh Prince, then in 1283 the edifice was captured by Edward 1st army, and then it housed Scottish prisoners until 1295 until the English garrison was conquered by a Welsh Prince who attacked it with sea power. It remained, however, a prison up until 1403, when Owain Glyndwr seized and set it alight. Relics of that fire are still visible in the ruins.'

Iwan asked: 'Why is your wife so interested in these castles?'

Ray Glover gave out a deep sigh and then said, 'Kelly believes they are what Robert Graves describes in his poem: the castles' prisoners, after years of incarceration, are now ghosts enjoying freedom in their deaths. Who knows? This poem influences her thinking. Is she deluded? Maybe. Harlech castle has a different history from Criccieth's. Edward's troops reached Harlech in 1283 and work started immediately to build a structure to cow the Welsh. Which it did. Edward survived a fierce siege, one of many, by a Welsh Prince in 1294.'

Eric, intrigued by Ray Glover's imaginable interpretation of Kelly's thoughts, asked him: 'What other parts of the poem influenced your wife's thinking?'

'The last section of the poem's second part, sir; I believe to be a dialogue,' a pause, then: 'I'm unable to ascertain as to whether the poet is taking part in the conversation. I'll quote again: **"Marvellous creation,**
All various shapes and sizes, and no sizes,
All new, each perfectly unlike his neighbour,
'Though all came moving slowly out together.'
'Describe just one of them.'
'I am unable.'
What were their colours?'
'Mostly nameless colours,
Colours you'd like to see; but one was puce
Or perhaps more like crimson, but not purplish
Some had no colour."'
Silence followed.

Ray Glover fractured it: 'Kelly believes that the persons on the beaches are zombies, walking dead released from captivity, allowed to roam the sands, have caves as refuge and, somehow, they exist inside them.' He raised his voice as he stressed: 'I'm not aware however, that people, and there are many, who have visited these caves and not witnessed such. It's another Welsh myth.'

Eric sighed from disbelief, then said to Ray: 'You mimic the state of death, and your wife is obsessed by this poem.' He tapped a pencil on the desk top as he added: 'We'll speak with Mrs Glover when she returns from Manchester.' He ran a finger along the inside of his collar and addressed Ray Glover and Iwan Drew: 'This info is to be kept secret, no other persons, certainly not the press or the media, are privy to it. We play dumb, and,' with a wave of his hand at Ray Glover, announced: 'your disappearance remains a mystery. I've decided not to charge you with any offences at this stage of the inquiry therefore, you remain in north Wales until we say you're free to return to Manchester. Do you understand?'

'Yes, sir.'

'Good, I'll update the Manchester Police, ask them to inform the hospital's authorities that you are unable to attend there indefinitely, personal reasons.'

'I understand.'

Eric then turned to Iwan and said, 'Contact the station's duty police officer; he's to attend here during your short absence, and also, tell WPC Manning to be present. Afterwards, ask DS Jimmy Elson and WPC Norma Taylor to bring Mrs Coleman here.'

Ray Glover stared at the floor while Eric Bolton and the attending police constable were unfolded canvas chairs in the room.

Iwan returned with WPC Manning, DS Jimmy Elson, WPC Norma Taylor and Amy Coleman and the police constable left the room.

Eric invited Jimmy Elson and WPC Norma Taylor to sit on each side of him, then requested everyone else to sit opposite. In a firm voice, he declared. 'Each of you has been associated directly or indirectly with the bizarre events that took place in Mrs Josie Harold's flat on the last Thursday and Friday in October.' He describe the events again and the people involved, then looked at Amy Coleman and at Ray Glover. He addressed both. 'Weather was wicked that Thursday night. Ray Glover, having driven in those conditions from Manchester, seeked refuge for the night in Mrs Coleman's flat, decided not to meet up with his wife, Kelly, who was staying in her aunt's flat in nearby Criccieth.'. He tapped the interview sheet. 'The reasons for such actions are here.'

Eric turned to Jimmy Elson, whispered in his ear, then looked at his audience and declared: 'We have statements from Mrs Coleman and from Dr Ray Glover regarding the Thursday night. First, I invite DS Elson to read Mrs Coleman's accounts of what happened.'

Amy Coleman's statement was read and then Jimmy Elson said, 'Chief Bolton and Sergeant Iwan Drew have quizzed Dr Glover regarding that period.'

Eric thanked him and then stated: 'We have a record of events from the main characters in this mystery. Mrs Coleman drove Dr Glover to the garage in Criccieth on Friday morning, then she collected him in the afternoon from the beach and they returned to her flat.' He paused for several seconds, then looked at WPC Manning and Sergeant Drew, took out two documents from his case file and said, 'I also, have statements from Sergeant Drew and WPC Manning appertaining to the events described.' He opened one document and said, 'This is a statement from Sergeant Drew; I'll summarise the contents.'

Five minutes later, synopsis completed, Eric Bolton said, 'WPC Manning was obviously worried, anxious as to what had occurred, wanted to speak with someone about it and contacted Sergeant Drew.' Eric sensing Iwan's tense body language, asked him: 'Anything you wish to add at this stage, Sergeant?'

'No, sir.'

'We now know that Sergeant Drew attended WPC Manning's flat so, I'll open the second document and summarise her statement.'

Eric read it, then closed the document and said, 'I've spoken with Sergeant Drew and WPC Manning about these events. I now ask Miss Manning: do you wish to add anything to what I've just disclosed?'

Helen Manning shook her head and whispered: 'No, sir.'

Eric carried on speaking in a slow monotone: 'Sergeant Drew and WPC Manning volunteered the information, albeit days after the incident in the garage. I've asked both as to why the delay. Miss Manning was stunned, distressed, unsure as to how she should tell the CID, hence her call to Sergeant Drew. None of the station's other personnel are aware of these events; WPC Manning has sworn to secrecy.'

Eric raised his hand and stated: 'Withholding significant information in a police inquiry is to be considered a lapse of professional responsibility. However, having considered, at length, the unusual circumstances, the officers' attitudes and, withholding the information wasn't deliberate, it did not affect the inquiry I deem the matter closed.'

Iwan and Helen, both fighting back tears, gave out long sighs.

Eric sipped water, then gazed at Amy Coleman and said to her: 'You helped Dr Glover, allowed him to stay in your flat, realised he was distressed but, at no time did you know what his problem was,' a pause, then: 'he may still have one. I see no reason for you to be cautioned.' Eric threw her a thin brief smile and then said, 'You were not aware of what occurred in that garage on the Friday morning.' He stopped speaking.

Amy Coleman offered no response.

Eric checked the wall clock: 'It's nearly five o'clock; everybody will be offered food and a hot drink before I call it a day.' He turned to Ray Glover and Amy Coleman and told them: 'I want to speak with you later,' then he looked directly at Ray Glover and told him: 'In the meantime, you stay with Mrs Coleman until your wife returns. You're only allowed incoming calls on the landline; if you have any mobile phones or laptops, please surrender them to the police. Emails answered and sent only with police supervision.' He emphasised: 'You do not contact your wife until I advise you.' A quick glance at Amy Coleman and then he asked: 'Do you both understand?'

'Yes, sir,' was their simultaneous replies.

Eric replaced the cap on his ball-point and then, placing the pen slowly on his file, told Ray Glover: 'Once you've finished eating your snacks WPCs Norma Taylor and Helen Manning will take you and Mrs Coleman back to her flat. Then, Dr Glover, the WPCs will check your clothes Mrs Coleman washed; photograph them and compare them with those you were wearing when you were inside the garage.'

Ray Glover didn't react.

Eric then told him: 'An unmarked police car will call for you tomorrow morning to attend here at ten o'clock.'

Ray Glover nodded, remained silent.

Eric then announced: 'I want everyone, plus DC Salmon, to be in the incident room at ten tomorrow morning.' He picked up the internal phone, dialled the incident room's number, briefed Glyn Salmon and then asked: 'Any significant phone calls, Glyn?'

A jaded Glyn said, 'None, Chief.'

29

Nature had mellowed overnight: a crimson sun heralded Saturday's dawn with a few high fluffy benign-looking cumulus clouds hovering in a quiet sky. However, the legacy from the elements' recent ferocity was evident: roadsides' hedgerows were grey and the grass banks devoid of colourful wild flowers as Eric Bolton sped to Madogton police station.

He arrived before nine, then his team and the local officers joined him in the incident room.

WPC Norma Taylor placed a file on the desktop and told Eric: 'Shots I took of Ray Glover's washed clothes; Helen has phoned the restaurant.'

Helen explained: 'The manager confirmed the couple's Saturday evening booking; I clarified the situation, there will be no penalty payment.' She smiled and sat in a chair.

The team, drinking coffee, was checking and discussing the evidence when, a few minutes before ten, PC Alan Reed escorted Ray Glover into the room.

Eric nodded, thanked Alan Reed, who then left.

Eric gestured with a wave of a hand. 'Dr Glover, we'll continue the interview in interview room two.'

Everybody entered the stark, dimly-lit grey-walled, interview room, the weak winter sun struggling to shine through the small single window at the top quarter of the west wall.

Eric thanked both women, took out several photos from his case file, placed them next to Norma's file, waited until everybody was seated and then he advised Ray Glover: 'Detective Sergeant Glyn Salmon has joined us this morning, you've met everyone else.' Eric tapped the tape recorder and, switching it on, said, 'This session is being recorded; do you understand?'

'Yes, sir.'

Eric, pointing to the photos, told Ray Glover: 'My team and the local police officers have seen these,' and then he added: 'I want you to look at them; bring your chair up to the front of the desk.'

Eric showed him photos of the person on the garage floor.

Ray Glover looked at them for several seconds and then said, 'That is me on the floor, the watch is mine,' and then he described the clothes he was wearing. 'Yes, they were flimsy, Chief Bolton, the pockets were empty, hence no ID.'

Eric showed him Norma's photos. 'These were taken in Mrs Coleman's flat, clothes she had washed for you.'

Ray, shaping his lips into a second-long thin wry grin, continued: 'They are the clothes I was wearing in the garage; I planned such so that I could move swiftly in the atrocious weather.' A derisive smile, a shake of his head and then: 'Not the ideal clothing, I know. I was perished and, within minutes of leaving the garage, I was soaked.' He stared at Eric and, a sarcastic tone flanking his voice, said, 'Do you think that those were the only clothes I brought from Manchester? Mrs Coleman's has a large holdall containing suitable clothes for this time of the year.'

A silent Eric looked at Ray Glover.'

Ray Glover described how he hurried to the farthest point of the south beach, found a payphone and, reversing the charges, phoned Amy to collect him.

Eric declared: 'We can check that call, Dr Glover,' and then: 'you were drenched when you returned to Mrs Coleman's flat.'

Ray locked his eyes on Eric's stare and, in a soft, yet confident-sounding voice, said, 'I've already stated that Amy washed them and confirm they are the ones in the photo.'

Eric nodded; considered this man: a self-assured presence and was anxious not to pressurise Ray Glover. He glanced through his case notes once more and then lifted his head. He studied Ray Glover's body language for a few moments and thought: this man emits supreme self-confidence. Eric judged the present situation: despite the adverse circumstances, Ray Glover's remained unflustered, displaying composite ease and aplomb, the latter maybe artificial but, he exuded charisma. A plausible act? Maybe: Ray can manufacture his demeanour, his subtle body actions and his words before answering a question. Eric considered the dialogue for several seconds and then realised he was dealing with a perceptive professional who possessed programmed edicts. He decided to change tack: 'How well do you know Mrs Josie Harold?'

'Several years before I married Kelly, we became friendly and, following the marriage, I was accepted as a member of the family,' a pause, then, looking directly at Eric, he said, 'there was no financial or sexual frenemy on my part.'

Eric ceased this line of questioning and, after a few seconds silence, looked at Glyn Salmon.

Glyn asked Ray Glover about his private practice: 'Doctor, anaesthetist?'

'A qualified doctor in anaesthetics, psychoanalyst and hypnotherapist, all relate to a medical practitioner.' A wry smile followed and them a droll addition: 'is an archaeologist an alleged grave robber? Semantics is interesting.'

Glyn threw him a wry smile and then looked at Eric.

Eric looked at Jimmy Elson. 'Any questions for Dr Glover?'

'None at present, Chief.'

Eric thumped his case file, glared at Ray Glover and demanded: 'Tell us what happened in the garage that Friday morning.' An impatient Eric continued: 'We have interviewed your wife, your friend Mrs Coleman, and now we await your account of what happened.' A long pause, a substantial sigh and, exasperation creeping into his voice, said, 'If my colleagues and I are dissatisfied with your explanation of the events and consequences, I will charge you with wasting police and forensics time.' He made a note, and then said, 'please observe that the tape recorder is still running; as from now your answers to my questions and, to those from members of my team, will be recorded and may be used as evidence.' Eric gave him a copy of the official legal advisory document and told him: 'You are entitled to have a legal adviser.'

Ray Glover eyed the floor for several seconds, then lifted his head slowly and said, 'I'll describe the situation, Chief: it's an intricate story that could take a considerable time to describe; contains many factors and varied factions requiring analysis.'

Eric responded with vigour: 'This inquiry has involved police, forensic expertise and paramedics' proficiency.' A firm 'we need answers.' He then looked at the wall clock. 'In view of the time and what you've said, Dr Glover, I suggest we have a break for lunch; we reconvene at one o'clock,' and switched off the tape recorder.

Eric, looking at the two WPCs, said, 'Your expertise is required, ladies; please chose a selection of snacks from the supermarket. He glanced at his notes and then said, 'It could be a long session this afternoon.'

Helen Manning and Norma Taylor left.

Eric picked up the internal phone, contacted Alan Reed and explained the situation to him. 'We continue at one o'clock.'

Seconds later, PC Alan Reed entered and escorted Ray Glover out.

Alone in the room, Eric picked up the phone, dialled home and, in a soft contrite monotone, explained the situation.

30

Eric, as he resumed the meeting in the afternoon, switched on the tape recorder, summarised the morning's proceedings and then said, 'Dr Glover will explain the reasons for his behaviour and, especially, how he feigned his demise on Friday morning, the twenty-seventh of October.' He nodded to Ray Glover and said to him; 'Water and a plastic drinking mug is on the table.'

'Thank you.'

Eric told him: 'Please describe your actions that Friday morning.'

Ray Glover stood and, speaking in a strong, confident voice, described how he and Kelly met: a college romance, then they became established in their chosen professions, appointments were Manchester-based, so they decided to marry. A sullen tone entered his voice as he added: 'Professional demands on us were such that some days we only met at breakfast and late at night,' a pause, 'yes, this led to difficulties, affected our marriage. Yet, I was willing to curb my work to accommodate Kelly's desire to progress in academia and her hobby of poetry reading classes and amateur dramatics.' He stopped speaking.

A drink of water later, he continued in a monotone: 'She declined my offer, refused to discuss it, was obsessed with poetry and also, she became interested in the sixteenth century Spanish painter, Diego Velasquez. She regarded him as a genius, an obsessive painter who became the chief artist in the court of King Phillip the Fourth of Spain.'

Silence prevailed.

Ray Glover continued: 'Velasquez's story fascinated her,' a pause, then a question: 'what attracted her to this man? I felt she was drifting away from reality, I strived to speak with her, assess her thinking. The painter's literary and artistic circles enthralled her, notably during the five years when he was an apprentice in Seville. He married his teacher's daughter and afterwards produced notable works.' Ray stopped speaking, sipped water and then carried on: 'Velasquez eventually became the senior artist in the King's court and painted a portrait of Phillip in less than one day. Soon afterwards he was admitted to the royal service. At that time, his paintings were regarded as being risqué by the Catholic Church but, because of this appointment, he escaped the censorship of the Inquisition. Velasquez had many fans and, especially one, who brought himself a lifetime of misery. I was afraid that this was Kelly's problem.' He explained: 'I'm interested in psychoanalysis, so I questioned her as to why was she infatuated by the Spanish painter, a specific type of poetry, and -'

Eric raised his hand. 'Please stop there, Dr Glover; you say you're interested in psychanalysis. I understand you have a private medical practice -'

Ray Glover interjected: 'It comprises psychoanalysis and hypnotherapy, the latter concerns treatment of an illness such as an addiction, an obsession plus emotional or psychogenic state by hypnosis. It is imperative that the patient reveals his or her problem to the psychoanalyst. I believe Kelly had developed an obsessive category, a dangerous deviance, possibly suffering from illusions, so I believed she required help.'

Eric asked: 'You suggested treatment?'

'Psychoanalysis to begin with, sir.' Ray inhaled deeply, then he spoke in a deliberate slow, firm voice: 'Sigmund Freud believed that a person's mind was dictated to by the local weather that shifted from tempestuous to clement without reason. He was of the opinion that each of us has an unconscious life, sections of which are hidden from our own view and initiate unwitting remarks and behaviour. He felt there should be a free association between patient and analyst, an intimate therapeutic conversation, meaning mutual trust is fundamental for success.'

Slow moving black dark clouds eliminated the afternoon's feeble sun from the room and the temperature dropped. 'That's the end of the day's light,' Eric commented.

Ray Glover stared at each police officer for several seconds, then told Eric Bolton: 'I'll enlighten you and your colleagues: to carry out hypnosis you require a participant, even a group of people that are interested in a particular subject matter can be receptive.'

A tense silence filled the room for several moments, some officers shivering in the room's cooler conditions.

Ray's voice developed a purposeful tone as he spoke in a measured, unhurried manner: 'I felt Kelly was developing a manic state, yes,' he stared at each officer for a few seconds and emphasised: 'yes,' then a louder: 'manic.'

Ray drank more water, leaned back in his seat for a moments, clasped the back of his neck with one hand and then rose. His hands shaking, a slight tremble rippled through his hesitant voice as he said, 'I decided on an extreme form of treatment, devised a ploy to frighten her, an illusion that might terrify her, annul her fantasises and return her to realism. No one else knew of my plan.'

Eric, sensing Ray Glover's distress, glanced at the wall clock, raised both hands and said, 'You seem uneasy, Dr Glover; what you were about to describe is, from looking at your body language, intense and personal,' a short tight-lip smile, then: 'I suggest we adjourn the proceedings at this stage.'

Ray slumped onto the seat.

Eric asked his colleagues. 'Are we all agreed?'

Silence, and an affirmative nod from each person was his answer.

Etic told Ray Glover: 'I shall arrange transport for your return here on Monday morning, at eleven o'clock, to complete your version of what happened.'

A tired-looking Ray uttered a grateful: 'Thank you, sir.'

Eric turned to Iwan Drew and the two WPCs: 'Please inform Mrs Coleman of our decision, then arrange transport for Dr Glover today, and for his return on Monday morning.' He looked at Jimmy Elson and Glyn Salmon and said, 'We'll return to the relative luxury of the incident room.'

Back in the incident room, Eric rose from his chair and said, 'I'll make coffee.' He ambled to the kettle, made mugs of strong coffee, placed them on the desk and said, 'We need to discuss what we've seen and heard this afternoon; try and fathom out Kelly Glover's past and present life. Ray Glover describes her as being detached from reality.' He lifted the internal phone and hit three digits.

A minute later PC Alan Reed entered.

Eric briefed him, then handed him an A4 writing pad and told him: 'Record our conversation.' He made him a mug of coffee then, pointing to the evidence board, told him: 'Update it by Monday morning.'

'Yes, sir; all such info is also stored in my laptop.'

31

Coffees consumed, Eric Bolton looked at the wall clock and announced: 'It's four-fifteen; time we consider today's proceedings,' he smirked and added: 'I aim to be home by six.' A shrug of his shoulders, then: 'Recovering lost marital stripes.' He smiled and said, 'Please describe your thoughts on the day's stories.'

Glyn Salmon, notes in hand, said, 'Questions, which I believe we must reflect upon, are first: is Kelly's mental state as her husband describes? Two: is the particular poem and her apparent infatuation with the Spanish painter- Diego Velazquez's life, sufficient for her to compare her life with these two men? Three: if yes is the answer to the last question, is her comparison a compelling influence on her where she is at the point of possible mania? But,' he paused and considered again: 'she may be in an abyss, her mind in an indeterminate state without direction, dominated by metaphoric tunnel vision. Has she submitted her life to this poem when she is in this part of north Wales? Is it a magical restructuring of her mind, or is it the result of a cunning application of hypnotherapy? Will there be a conclusion? I liken her mind to a computer after an electrical malfunction; it requires re-programing.'

Jimmy Elson, respecting Glyn's words, reacted in a considered voice: 'Yes is the answer to all your queries, Glyn. If we believe Ray Glover, the reaction his wife displays when she hears his story on Monday afternoon could be crucial.'

'What *did* Kelly Glover actually see on the beaches?' a thoughtful Eric asked, then, after considering his question, stated: 'she could not describe any of the persons.' He took out a copy of the poem from his case file. 'You've all read this,' and then he asked: 'where did these animated figures originate? Why did they remain inside the caves? No one has seen them there. Has poetic imagination influenced her thoughts -'

Glyn Salmon interjected: 'If the husband has subjected his wife to hypnotherapy, he controls her, uses the poem as a catalyst for a devious psychological exercise?' He gave out a long, deep sigh and then continued: 'Does she becomes hallucinated, maybe deluded? Vulnerable to suggestions and develop an indefinable protracted obsession devised by her husband? Has he manipulated her emotions, stemmed her thoughts into manoeuvred, controlled compulsive convictions or, are we witnessing a well-crafted confidence trick? Yes is my conclusion to my last suggestion so, what is the motive for such? Let's remind ourselves of the main ingredients for committing a crime: love, money, emotional upsets, jealousy and redemption.'

Several seconds of silence followed while his colleagues reflected on his potent analysis of the mystery.

Eric turned to Alan Reed and broke the quiet ambience: 'Getting all this down?'

A smiling Alan tapped a pencil on his writing pad and said, 'I have my own short hand system to record proceedings, sir.'

Eric took out an A4 sheet of paper from his case file, handed it to Alan and said, 'This is the poem involved in our discussion....it's an important factor in the inquiry.'

Alan thanked him.

Jimmy Elson asked Eric: 'Do we believe Amy Coleman and Ray Glover's accounts?'

A contemplative Eric said, 'We'll allow them a *yes* for now; re-assess their words on Monday. I'll update Manchester Police and ask then to inform Kelly Glover to return to her aunt's flat in Criccieth by lunch time on Monday.' He eyed his colleagues and declared: 'Kelly Glover is not to be told of recent events. We'll hear from Ray Glover again on Monday morning. Kelly is to be brought into the room after lunch, then everyone, including Ray Glover, return. The reaction of the married couple when they meet will be interesting.'

Jimmy Elson and Glyn Salmon thought it was a shrewd ploy.

'Emotions will run high,' Jimmy said, 'the initial responses between them might prove to be crucial in our quest to untangle the mess and,' looking at Alan Reed, said, 'link up the evidence, try and construct a definite chain of events.'

Alan Reed smiled, but didn't speak.

Eric then told Alan: 'The interviews are privy only to those taking part: actions seen and words heard are not to be divulged to anyone else.' He closed his case file and then affirmed: 'We four meet again, here, at nine on Monday morning; check the evidence board again, refresh our minds, while we wait for news from Howard Baker; his news could determine our future m.o.,' and placed the case file in his document case.

The eager Alan Reed said, 'The info on the evidence board will be in chronological configuration.'

Eric grinned at Alan, then stood, lifted his document case, stretched his lower back muscles and declared: 'That's all for today, thank you, see you all on Monday morning.'

After they'd left, Eric phoned Manchester Police, then left, hurried to his car, slid a *Lighthouse Family* CD into the console's slot and was home before six.

32

Black-clouds had countered the arrival of Monday's dawn when Eric Bolton arrived in Madogton police station at eight-fifteen.

'Good morning, sir,' Iwan Drew said, 'the unpredictable weather is par for this time of year,' and then, noticing Eric's attire: white shirt, red patterned tie and a charcoal suit under the lightweight white anorak, asked in a dutiful tone: 'Important action this morning, sir?'

Eric flicked a hand to Iwan, 'Follow me into the incident room; how was Bonfire night?'

Spoilt by the weather and, being a Sunday, only one small fire was lit on the north beach near the castle. Police and the emergency services had a peaceful time.'

Eric, his mind focused on the day's schedule, uttered a weak: 'Good.'

Alan Reed was in the incident room, updating the evidence board, when Eric and Iwan entered.

Alan greeted the two men and then said, 'I decided to come in early to update the board; no news since yesterday, sir,' then to each: 'a mug of coffee?' '

Both men welcomed Alan's words.

Eric placed his document case on the desk, removed his anorak, hung it on the peg on the back of the door, then he turned to Iwan and threw him a rhetorical question: 'You witnessed Ray Glover's words and body language when we interviewed him?'

'Of course, sir.'

Eric acknowledged with a wave of his hand, then recapped Saturday's meeting. Afterwards, he explained the present strategy and, grinning, said, 'Like many plans, it might get derailed.'

Iwan nodded once.

Alan Reed announced: 'Coffee coming up now.'

Eric opened up the computer, checked for any new e-mails, not one. He drank his coffee and then told Iwan: 'My colleagues and PC Alan Reed are the only people privy to the meeting and interviews. All will be revealed to you later.' Eric then said, 'That will be all for now, Sergeant.'

As Iwan was about to leave, Jimmy Elson and Glyn Salmon entered. They exchanged pleasantries and Iwan left.

Eric walked to the evidence board, scrutinised it then, pointing at the names of Amy Coleman, Josie Harold and Ray Glover, asked: 'Who's controlling these strange events? My hunch is that Ray Glover has power over his wife and maybe, Josie Harold and Amy Coleman. None of these two has criticised him or accused him of unprofessional behaviour.'

Jimmy Elson scratched his chin a few times and then asked Eric: 'Where does Josie fit in this unfathomable jigsaw? Did she not know of the disharmony within the Glover's marriage? No vibes, but I have a gut feeling that she was unhappy as to what happened a week ago.'

'Yes,' Glyn Salmon said, 'I have that impression.'

Eric asked: 'Is Amy Coleman an innocent observer? We need more info on her -'

Glyn butted in: 'WPC Manning seems to know her. Shall I ask her .to try and suss out if Amy has an active part in this?'

'That could be helpful,' Eric conceded. 'Okay, pull up a chair for her, Glyn, and then bring her in.'

Five minutes later Glyn Salmon escorted a nervous-looking Helen Manning into the room.

Eric waved to the chair. 'Please sit.' He smiled at her. 'Nothing serious, Miss Manning, relax.'

Eric outlined their earlier discussion and then said, 'We thought you might be able to give us some background on Mrs Coleman's life since her husband's death.'

Helen spoke in a soft voice: 'You're all aware of the association between us; Amy Coleman has rented a flat that I own in a village near Criccieth, for about two years. Although she has no connection with the locality, she wanted to begin a new life after her husband's death.'

'Are you good friends?'

'I saw her only occasionally, Chief, she's a private person, travels to Manchester occasionally to visit her husband's family. I didn't know of her link with Ray Glover. When I saw her recently she was distressed, crying, described their friendship. I asked how she came to know him. She explained the college days and admitted to a long-standing friendship, emphasising they're not and never have been lovers.'

Eric jotted down a few notes, then told her of today's plans: 'I want you to visit Josie Harold, use an unmarked car, be there by noon and explain that we want to speak with Kelly again, routine police work. Wait until Kelly arrives from Manchester, allow her to have some food and drink, and then bring her to the station by two o'clock. Be sure no one sees you entering the building.'

Helen wrote in her notepads and then said, 'It's all been noted, Chief.'

'OK, inform Alan Reed when you arrive with her, he'll buzz me, then we go from there. I'll see you this afternoon.'

Eric waited for Helen to leave and then turned to his colleagues and PC Alan Reed. 'We'll study Josie Harold's evidence now, try and decide if she's involved in the obscure story.' He checked the time: 'Nine-thirty-five;

Howard should be phoning soon.' He looked at Glyn Salmon and stressed: 'I know you have an opinion on Josie Harold, Glyn.'

'Restating, sir.' Glyn smiled as he carried on speaking: 'An attractive mature woman, experienced in many ways, wealthy and, as far as we know, has no definite male friend.' He turned to a page in his note pad, tapped a pencil on it and said, 'My opinion of her? She could be a handful and, I repeat, a challenge for many men but, I wouldn't jeopardise my marriage frolicking with her. She's left an impression for us to mull over, Chief.' He grinned, then carried on speaking in a steadfast tone: 'Sergeant Drew was of the same opinion, he felt she's street wise, self-sufficient with a forthright attitude: a clever, rich and attractive widow that plays her part well.' Another smirk, then: 'I wonder whether or not Ray Glover is a match for her?'

Eric nodded. 'She's intriguing,' a smile, 'maybe tricky -' the phone rang.

Eric lifted it.

A solemn tone muffled Howard Baker's usually positive attitude: 'I believe Kelly Glover has been at home for the past three days; no sign of her leaving the house, and no sign of the husband or his car. Neither the college nor the hospital, respectively, have heard from either.' A slight cough. 'Sorry, Chief. I also checked on Ray Glover's private practice. There has been no contact with him, and his appointment book is empty.'

Eric asked: 'Any news on Josie Harold's life?'

Howard Baker's voice remained a dull monotone as he continued: 'Zilch, she's not a socialite I then checked with Ray Glover's family, no news from him or Kelly. Weird, sorry. Is there problem concerning the two families, an atmosphere between them?'

Eric said, 'Not to our knowle4dge, Howard.' He decided to update him: 'We still lack a pattern to the happenings. Thanks, phone me if you hear anything of note.' He ended the call, replaced the receiver in its cradle, looked at the wall clock, then at Alan Reed and said, 'It's time to collect Ray Glover we'll be in interview room two.' He gave Alan the address. 'Take an unmarked car.'

'Yes, sir,' and Alan left.

Eric told Jimmy and Glyn of Howard Baker's negative news and asked: 'Any suggestions?'

Neither man could oblige.

'Okay,' Eric said, 'we'll have a coffee'. He made the drinks, then picked up the internal phone, dialled three digits and told Helen Manning. 'Leave for Criccieth now.'

Eric sipped his coffee, looked at his two colleagues and, opening up the computer, said, 'While we wait for Ray Glover I'll furnish the computer with our evidence; see if it can realise potential reasons for this chaotic setup.'

Fifteen minutes later, the computer, despite being fed with several permutations of the participants and the obtuse evidence, failed to provide an answer.

Eric shrugged his shoulders. 'The experienced copper's brain remains a superior computing machine when it comes to solving crime,' and shut it down. He then rose from his chair and said, 'It's time we transferred to the interview room.'

33

The time was a few minutes before eleven; torrential rain, driven by a strong winds, had returned to the area when Alan Reed escorted Ray Glover into the interview room. Alan then left.

'Welcome, Dr Glover,' Eric said, stood, and then he introduce Jimmy Elson and Glyn Salmon. Eric invited him to sit in a chair, and then Eric, pointing to a jug and plastic mug on the table, said, 'Water is available.'

Eric sat back in his chair, glanced through his case file and then declared: 'I'll remind you of the statement you made on Saturday afternoon.'

Ray Glover, wearing an open-neck navy shirt under a thick woollen light grey crew-neck sweater, light blue jeans and sturdy brown lace-up leather ankle boots, nodded once.

Eric, after summarising the statement, said, 'An important point, Dr Glover; you say that your wife is in a -'

'A manic state, Chief Inspector.' Ray stared at Eric, then at Jimmy Elson and Glyn Salmon and, in a firm voice, repeated; 'Kelly's mind was and remains in a potentially pre-manic state, yes,' and then declared: 'manic; gentlemen. Remember that word. He then stressed: *'manic.'*

Jimmy Elson asked: 'Why are you certain of this, Dr Glover?'

'Her increasing agitation, her obsessive behaviour, relating her life to this poem, then quoting passages repeatedly. The poem made no sense to me,' a pause, then: 'was she experiencing a message, a transference from local mythology? Possibly.'

'Such as?' Jimmy asked.

Ray Glover said, 'Do you all have a copy of the poem?'

The three CID officers produced one from their case files.

Ray Glover said, 'Please note my previous quotation; it ends with: **"Some had no colour."'**

Glyn pointed to the passage. 'That, and the previous quotes are meaningless to me. I'm unable to understand the theme or, is there a message within that, one that I'm missing?'

Ray Glover said, 'Look at what follows, please read what I quote, then consider the prose again.'

The three officers nodded.

Ray Glover spoke in a distinct voice: This particular section follows the last: **"Tell me had they legs?'**

'Not a leg nor foot among them that I saw.'

'But did these things come out in any order?'

What o'clock was it? What was the day of the week?

Who else was present? How was the weather?'

'I was coming to that. It was half-past three

On Easter Tuesday last. The sun was shining."

Ray Glover drank more water and then, in a contemplative voice, asked: 'Gentlemen, do the words make any sense to you?'

Eric exhaled, checked the prose Ray had quoted, and then said, 'No is my answer to your question,' and then, determination flowing within his firm voice, asked: 'are you implying that your wife is psychologically conditioned by this?'

'Yes, Chief Inspector.'

A frowning Eric looked directly at Ray Glover and said, 'You are asking my team to believe this?'

'A significant factor,' was Ray Glover's compact reply, 'the poem's characters cast long shadows over my wife's mind.'

Ray drank more water then, for a few seconds, clasped the back of one shoulder with his hand and then, in an authoritative voice, said, 'I decided on an extreme form of treatment, devised a ploy to frighten her. I told you on Saturday that I created an illusion to this effect. My objective was to annul her fantasises in the hope she'd return to realism.'

Eric looked at his two colleagues. 'Any questions for Dr Glover?'

Glyn Salmon answered: 'Not at this stage.'

Jimmy Elson shook his head and said, 'Later.'

Eric, staring at Ray Glover, said to him: 'You are about to see two photos of the inside of the garage.' He handed him the first shot. 'There's a body, yours, on the floor,' Eric declared, then handed Ray Glover the second. 'You have disappeared. Please explain how you were in the garage on Friday morning at that particular time and then clarify the two photos.'

'Kelly has a ritual when it comes to washing clothes, early morning every Tuesday and Friday; because of the vile weather in Criccieth, I guessed, correctly, she would dry it in the tumble dryer. I calculated that she'd take the washing into the garage at around ten. I have a key to the flat and two for the garage's doors.' More water, then: 'Amy Coleman gave me a lift to Criccieth on Friday morning. I ran from the car to the lee of the garage from the weather. I entered the garage through the side door, placed the keys behind the tumble dryer and then,' he looked at Eric Bolton and said, 'to answer your third question, Chief, I lay on the floor and underwent self-hypnosis.'

'Please enlighten us,' Eric said.

Ray spoke slowly: 'It's a self-induced trance, makes use of self-suggestion to create a superior resilience -'

Eric interjected: 'In simple English please, Dr Glover.'

'It can counter pain, anxiety, a depressive illness and skin conditions. Asthma and emotional states can be managed by it.'

'And in your case?' Jimmy Elson asked.

'Four steps are commonly used for self-hypnosis; the first is motivation, without this an individual will experience difficulty practising it. Second, the person must be relaxed as to what is happening, distraction is avoided, so the empty garage was a suitable scenario. Third, the person must concentrate completely as energy is created when the mind focuses on a single act or image. The fourth: direction; this is an option used when a person wants to work towards a specific goal. In my case, feign death. I was able to stop my main organs such as the heart and lung functioning for several moments, hence feigning death. At the beginning of the twentieth century a French hypnotherapist described the method to accomplish such a phenomenon as *conscious autosuggestion*, To recover from this particular state of self-hypnosis you require a stimulus to awaken you, I decided the shutting of the garage's side door would be the desired one for me. It worked. I got up, undid the knot on the plastic bag, fished out a couple of towels to counter the wet weather, then tied up the bag, picked up the keys and left the garage, locking it after me. I ran in the horrid weather to Criccieth's south beach, threw the soaking towels into public bins, and then stayed in the beach shelter while I waited for Amy Coleman to collect me.'

A tense silence followed Ray Glover's mystifying story.

Jimmy broke it: 'Dr Glover, you hoped that this dramatic action would frighten your wife, re-set her mind, return it to reality. As yet we have no idea as to whether you were successful.'

A thinking Ray, shaking his head slowly from side to side, commented: 'Not until I meet her again; I'll be able to assess her mental state from her reactions, her voice, her general attitude and body language.' He stopped speaking, considered his words for a few seconds and then said, 'The definitive test will be when I show her the poem.'

Glyn Salmon turned to Eric Bolton. 'Chief, you asked earlier if I had any questions for Dr Glover. I have listened to his accounts of how he came to meet Josie Harold and Amy Coleman. My question concerns his expertise in hypnotherapy. Dr Glover, did either woman receive advice, counselling, or treatment from you relating to their husbands' deaths?'

An irate Ray Glover asked: 'What is the purpose of your question, Mr Salmon?'

'You treated your wife,' a wry smile and then: 'is this ethical, Dr Glover, had you not thought of considering consulting an independent practitioner?'

'I was aware of her problems, her phobias and her obsessions. I've lived with them for a considerable time. No other person would have succeeded in obtaining this information.'

Glyn Salmon then remarked: 'You came to know both Josie Harold and Amy Coleman well. Were they grieving, mentally distressed, by their personal tragedies?'

Ray Glover shook his head. 'No.'

'Thank you.'

Eric Bolton, glancing at the wall clock, said, 'We'll break for lunch, meet back here at one-forty-five.' He buzzed Alan Reed. 'Please escort Dr Glover to the incident room. Return at one-forty five.'

Eric waited until Ray Glover had left the room, then phoned and updated Iwan Drew and then he told his colleagues. 'Meet back here at one-fifteen, we'll discuss Ray Glover's account before his wife arrives.'

34

Late on Monday morning, Helen Manning checked Chief Bolton's directive regarding her visit to Criccieth, then hurried through the rain to an unmarked police car and arrived at Josie Harold's flat a few minutes before noon.

She climbed the iron stairway slowly and heard a carpet cleaner's distinct whining-sound as she approached the door. She rang the bell a few times, then knocked the door until silence prevailed.

Josie Harold, dressed in a sky blue shirt, navy jeans and a beige sweat shirt was surprised when she saw her visitor. She managed a short twist of her lip. 'Good morning Miss Manning,' she paused, then, a soft Manchester accent skimming through her voice, apologised: 'I'm sorry, do please come in; you have news for me?'

'Indeed, Mrs Harold.'

'Coffee, Miss Manning?'

'Thank you, but no, I had one less than an hour ago.'

'Come into the lounge,' Josie said, 'it's warmer in there, I've just turned the heating on.' Josie gestured to the sofa. 'I'll take your anorak and hang it on the back of the kitchen door.'

Helen gave it to her, then sat on the sofa.

Josie returned, chose an armchair and then, looking directly at Helen, said, 'Well?

Helen specified the reason for her visit. 'Following recent happenings, Chief Bolton and his colleagues wish to speak with Kelly again. I've been asked to call on you to advise you that Kelly Glover has been asked to return from Manchester, to be here at lunchtime,' she glanced at her watch, 'that could be any time now. After refreshments she is to accompany me to Madogton police station, we need to be there by two-o'clock.'

Josie asked: 'Are you able to tell me the reason for her recall?'

'Sorry, Mrs Harold; I'm under orders from Chief Inspector Bolton not to divulge the reason.'

Josie stared at Helen. 'Does she know that Ray is alive?'

'She hasn't been told; we keep it like that until she attends the police station.' She looked directly at Josie. 'Understood?'

Josie nodded. 'As you wish Miss Manning -' the doorbell rang twice.'

Josie hurried to the door.

Kelly had arrived. They hugged one another and then Josie carried Kelly's holdall and anorak into a bedroom and then they entered the lounge, Kelly holding her handbag tightly against her chest.

Helen rose from the sofa and greeted Kelly. The young woman looked tired, had lost weight, face was pale and drawn, and the dark clothes: navy shirt, navy jeans and a dark grey sweater, exaggerated her thin features. She slumped on an armchair and removed her white trainers.

Kelly, surprised at seeing Helen Manning, placed her handbag on the floor then, lifting her legs onto the arm of the chair, sighed and then said, 'Driving affects my feet, although it was a good journey, just two and a half hours, They still ache, especially the right foot, I drive an automatic.'

'Coffee, Kelly?' Josie asked, then to Helen: 'are you ready for one now?'

Both women nodded.

'I'll make some tomato and salad sandwiches; I'll be five minutes,' Josie said and left the room.

A nervous Kelly looked at Helen and, a slight tremor in her voice, asked: 'Why are you here, Miss Manning?'

'Chief Inspector Bolton told me to meet you; he wants to speak with you again.' She checked her wristwatch. 'He wants you to be in the station at two o'clock.'

'Why does he want to question me again?'

'New developments; I'm not privy to the details, but he thinks you might be able to enlighten him on some recent developments.' Helen threw Kelly a short smile. 'So here I am.'

Josie entered, carrying a tray with three mugs of coffee, milk, sugar and a plate of sandwiches. She placed the tray on the large coffee table. 'Please help yourselves.'

Fifteen minutes later the plate and coffee mugs were was empty.'

Josie rose and addressed Helen. 'Does Kelly need a change of clothes?'

Helen shook her head.

Josie lifted the tray and ambled into the kitchen.

Helen smiled and said to Kelly: 'Do you wish to freshen up, comb your hair before we leave?'

Kelly left for the bathroom.

Josie returned, sat in the armchair and said. 'Do you want me to come with Kelly?'

'The Chief didn't say such; those present will be myself and Kelly but, if you wish, you can come to give her support, but you will not be allowed attend the proceedings.'

'She doesn't look well, 'Josie commented, 'she's lost weight, lacks sparkle and her hair is lacklustre, not her usual standards.'

'She's a worried woman,' was Helen's comment, 'has had an emotional shock, does not know what's happened, and has no idea as to what's occurred since that Friday morning.'

'She was anxious and tense prior to the incident, 'Josie remarked. 'I hope the problem will be solved soon. She needs to get well again before she returns to her teaching post.' She stopped speaking when Kelly, carrying her anorak on her left arm, entered the room.

'Freshened up?' Helen asked, noticed Kelly's bloodshot eyes; she'd been crying.

'I'm feeling better after the meal and then splashing my face with cold water.'

Helen rose from the sofa, checked the time and said, 'We should be going now.'

'Do you have everything, Kelly?' Josie asked while she collected her own bag and put on her fleece–lined white anorak.

An unsettled Kelly nodded, put on her anorak, picked up her handbag and both women followed Helen out of the flat.

35

Eric Bolton and his two colleagues were in the incident room at one-fifteen.

Eric summarised the morning's proceedings then, tapping a pencil on his case notes, asked: 'so what do we make of Ray Glover's performance?'

Jimmy Elson, sitting on Eric's left, said, 'Ray Glover has a professional agenda concerning his patients, but also, I'm certain he has devised a separate one involving his wife,' a pause, then: 'and possibly Josie and Amy.'

'Big question,' was a thinking Eric's response and, a sense of turmoil in his hesitant voice, asked: 'how do we ascertain such possibilities?'

Glyn Salmon, sitting on Eric's right, piped up: 'We ask Ray Glover specific questions on his relationship with the women; is he more than a friend to Kelly's aunt and Amy Coleman?'

Eric said, 'Glyn, spell out the method you believe we should adopt to establish our suspicions.'

'We attack his expertise. Yes, he is a consultant anaesthetist but, compared with his medical and surgical colleagues, his contact with patients, albeit important, is minimal.'

Jimmy Elson asked: 'How do we approach the delicate subject of his clinical work and his private practice?'

Glyn Salmon's voice strengthened as he elucidated: 'We use the police's formula for profiling a person. He has a razor-sharp analysing mind, so we make him feel ill at ease by asking personal questions to produce vulnerability to suggestions, aware that he's been stung by a wasp and its toxin is still causing pain,' he stopped speaking, looked at Eric, then at Jimmy and asked: 'your views please, gentlemen?'

Eric, doodling on a piece of paper while thinking of Glyn's scheme, nodded once and then said, 'Play him at his game, I use the word *game* carefully because I, like you, Glyn , believe he has and, is still playing a deceptive enjoyment with the three woman.' He turned to Jimmy Elson and said, 'Your opinion of Glyn's strategy?'

A positive grin from Jimmy as he agreed with the plan, then said, 'I concur. Ray Glover is playing a game, is manipulative, clever and details a careful plan; a shrewd operator.'

'So we go with Glyn's m.o.,' Eric said. 'We build a picture of him and then, when he's uneasy, vulnerable and influenced by our style of probing, we play our trump card.' He checked the time. 'It's one-forty.' He buzzed Alan Reed. 'Okay, Alan, we will be in interview room two in five minutes, I'll contact you when we're ready for Ray Glover.'

Alan Reed escorted Ray Glover into interview room two at one-fifty and then returned to the station's operational room.

'Please sit,' Eric said to Ray Glover and confirmed: 'we'll continue this morning's proceedings.' He then asked: 'Do you wish to say anything before we commence, Dr Glover?'

'No, sir.'

Eric switched on the tape recorder, confirmed those present and then, in a soft persuasive voice, said, 'Dr Ray Glover, we are aware of your professional qualifications and specialities. Being interested in your private practice of hypnotherapy, my first question is: 'Are you actually living in the real world?'

Ray Glover stared at Eric. 'What?'

'I'll repeat the question -'

'I heard it, Chief Inspector.'

'Please answer.'

Ray Glover wriggled in his seat, clasped the muscles at the back of his neck with one hand and then said, 'I don't understand your question, Chief Inspector.'

'Having listened, on several occasions, to your evidence regarding your wife's demeanour, you describe your concern about her mental health. Our concern is whether you are describing your own behaviour at times -'

'A preposterous suggestion.'

Eric continued speaking in the soft voice: 'Your private practice involves dealing with people who are suffering from a mental, psychological state. Is it possible there is transference between your clients and you?'

'None, Chief Inspector, I'm able to detach myself from such a phenomenon.'

Eric turned to Glyn Salmon.

Glyn said to Ray Glover. 'We sometimes find a transference between villains and their families, many become part of a criminal system; a similar happening can occur in the medical profession.'

Ray Glover remained silent.

'You've had no extramarital relationship with either Josie Harold or Amy Coleman?'

'A ridiculous rhetorical question, Sergeant. I've already explained how I became friendly with both women.'

Glyn tapped his pencil on the desktop for a few seconds and then said, 'Dr Glover, I'm aware that contact with patients in your work as an anaesthetist is minimal compared with your hospital colleagues, but contact with people in you private work involves intense concentration and thought. Are you capable of lateral concepts when interviewing them?'

A perspiring Ray Glover, wriggling in his seat, and blinking rapidly, said, 'Of course; I need to look at all aspects of their problems.'

'Dr Glover, do you have lateral designs when analysing your wife's problem, or do you focus on her possible tunnel vision?'

'My concern with Kelly has a similar formula to the one I use professionally,' was Ray's tetchy answer. 'I seek to analyse and consider the best approach, each person's has a different response, reaction, to a problem. For example, if ten patients suffer from an anxiety state, there are usually ten different reasons for the dilemma. Therefore, you try and adapt to each situation.'

Glyn continued in a strong, unrelenting tone: 'We believe from evidence we've gathered during our inquiries that there is turmoil within your marriage -' the ringing phone interrupted Glyn's questioning.

Eric looked at the wall clock as he picked it up; it was two-fifteen. He listened to the caller and said, 'Thank you. Alan; I'll contact you soon.' He replaced the receiver and nodded to Glyn to continue.

Glyn, realising the nature of the phone call, said. That is all my questioning, for now, Chief.'

Eric turned to Jimmy Elson. 'Any questions for Dr Glover at this stage?'

Eric, staring at a stressed Ray Glover, asked him: 'Do you have any questions for us, or wish to clarify any of your answers before we continue?'

Ray Glover drank more water, thought for several moments and then said, 'You might think that my actions on that Friday morning were extreme, but I maintain that I believe they were important. I repeat, it was an attempt to rid my wife's mind of her hallucinatory, impending manic state.' He had more water and then said, 'To answer Detective Constable Salmon's statement regarding my marriage, our professional careers took us along distinct ways, affected our domestic and social life,' he nodded and then added: 'no third party was involved.'

Eric thanked him, then lifted the internal phone and contacted Alan Reed.

36

Five minutes later, Alan Reed, followed by WPC Helen Manning and an agitated, pale and tired-looking Kelly Glover, entered interview room two.

Kelly's knees gave way when she saw her husband.

Helen Manning caught her, helped her to a chair and sat next to her.

Kelly, head bowed, began to cry.

Eric handed Helen a box of paper tissues and, empathy in his soft voice, said, 'It is a distressing situation, Mrs Glover. Your reaction from the mental and physical shock was expected; take your time.'

Helen Manning handed Kelly and Ray Glover each a mug of water.

Eric, eyeing a startled Ray Glover, asked him: 'Do you wish to speak with your wife, enlighten her on what's happened since that Friday morning?'

Ray Glover coughed once, had a drink of water and then said, 'Not here, Chief Inspector; I'll tell her later,' then he asked: 'may I return with her to Mrs Harold's flat?'

'We'll consider that request at the end of this meeting and discuss it with Mrs Harold.' He looked at Helen. 'Does Mrs Harold know the situation, what's happening?'

Helen explained her chat with Josie and said, 'She is waiting in the operational room, a supportive role for Mrs Glover.'

Eric nodded and then he addressed Kelly. 'Are you feeling better; able to answer questions?'

A perspiring and fidgety Kelly, wiping perspiration from her brow and tears from her red eyes with a shaky hand full of tissues, gulped and then, in a wavering, quiet and hesitant trembling voice, said, 'Yes, Inspector.' She raised her head, sat upright and looked across the room at her husband, but said nothing. Her head shaking and, vocal strain evident in her voice, told Eric: My husband has a great deal to answer for, Inspector and, with your team's support, I demand a full explanation from him.'

Eric said, 'Detective Sergeant Elson will ask you a few questions now.'

Kelly nodded.

Jimmy threw her a smile and said, 'We are aware of your professional qualifications and your present position in a college in Manchester. There was a seminar in the North Wales Teacher Training College during the last week in October and you travelled to Criccieth on the Wednesday to stay in Mrs Harold's residence. Your husband was due to join you on the following day.' He looked at Kelly and then threw her a rhetorical question: 'Celebrating your first wedding anniversary on the Saturday?'

'I arranged the evening,' Kelly said in a moist voice.

Jimmy, intertwining his fingers asked: 'Has anything upset you during recent weeks?'

'I'm sorry, sir, I don't understand.'

'Anxious, depressed, circumstantial problems?'

Kelly shook her head.

'I believe you've seen lights moving along the beaches,' Jimmy said, then paused, looked at Kelly but didn't discern any reaction. He continued: 'I must tell you that we've interviewed your husband and he is of the opinion that a poem by Robert Graves titled *Welsh Incident*, and the Spanish painter. Diego Velasquez, have a profound influence on you.'

Kelly, managing a short nervous smile, answered: 'Been interested in both men, more especially the poetry of Robert Graves concerning this part of Wales. I can explain the circumstances,' she looked at her husband, then addressed Jimmy Elson: 'I suggest you ask my husband as to how I came to be obsessed by the poet.' She grinned. 'Oh, yes, Sergeant, I've travelled along a tumultuous emotional path. I have now recovered from my husband's influence on my judgement.' Her speech gathered momentum: 'He is cunning; has a manipulative mind -'

'I am not that,' an angry Ray retorted, 'that is a lie.' He looked at Eric Bolton. 'You have my statement regarding my professional aspect on my wife's behaviour. I've shown no anger towards her; sympathy, yes. I've tried to help her.' He waved his hands and said, 'What she implies is untrue.'

Eric raised his hand. 'Please, Dr Glover,' then to Kelly: 'a short pause while I discuss, what are, a married couple's personal difficulties and accusations that I and my colleagues have witnessed this afternoon.'

A tense silence governed the uneasy ambience while Eric conferred with Jimmy and Glyn.

Helen Manning comforted Kelly.

Ray Glover stared at the floor. No eye contact between man and wife.

Eric wrote in his pad and then, directing his gaze at Kelly, then at Ray, said, 'My colleagues and I are of the opinion that your personal difficulties need to be discussed in private, an interview room in a police station is not the ideal place for such.' He turned to Glyn Salmon. 'Please explain our thoughts.'

Glyn, speaking in a firm decisive voice, said, 'What I'm about to say involves only Dr Glover and his wife, Kelly. Dr Glover will not be charged with any malfeasance at this stage of our inquiry; we have considered the domestic picture and are of the opinion that the couple should discuss their problems in the flat in Criccieth.' He glanced at the couple and waited for a response.

Kelly and Ray looked at one another for several seconds and remained silent as they both nodded at Glyn Salmon.

'Good, we are pleased with your decision,' Glyn said, 'we do, however, need to ask Mrs Harold regarding this.' He looked at Helen. 'Please ask her to join us.'

Helen hurried out of the room and returned less than two minutes with Josie Harold.

Josie was invited to sit next to Kelly.

Glyn Salmon summarised the events then asked her about accommodating the married couple while they considered their difficulties.

Josie Harold agreed. 'Although the flat has only two bedrooms, the sizeable sofa in the main lounge is actually a three-seater sofa bed with storage.'

Eric thanked her, then said, 'Transport will be arranged for you and Dr and Mrs Glover to return to Criccieth.'

Ray Glover said, 'I need to collect my holdall from Mrs Coleman's flat.'

'That will be arranged, Dr Glover,' Eric said, then: 'A car will collect both of you at ten-thirty this Friday morning, to be here for further questioning at eleven o'clock. In the meantime WPCs Manning and Taylor will visit the flat in Criccieth each day until then.'

Glyn looked at Ray and Kelly, then turned to Eric. 'Over to you, sir.'

Eric looked at Ray and Kelly Glover. 'My colleagues and I have no notion of what's causing your domestic turmoil.' He sighed and then said, 'We will allow you, Dr Glover, to bring your car to Criccieth. Park it outside the flat's garage door.'

Ray nodded.

Eric, in and understanding voice, said. 'In view of your obvious distress, Mrs Glover, we could arrange for a local doctor to visit you.'

A sniffling, tearful Kelly, dragging a wad of tissues across her wet face, declared: 'No, thank you, sir. I am upset but not in a state of panic; I require no medical advice. I'll recover, my welfare depends on what my husband tells me. I need to be compos mentis to assess his words.'

Eric appreciated her candour and then told Helen. 'Please phone Amy Coleman, inform her of what's occurred and that a police car, with Ray Glover on board, will be at her flat in about half an hour.'

'Yes, sir.'

Eric continued: 'Tell Mrs Coleman I wish to see her in the station at ten tomorrow morning. Routine questions.' He looked at Josie Harold and said, 'Be here at midday tomorrow.'

Helen left the room and, on her return five minutes later, confirmed: 'Amy Coleman has received the message.'

Eric thanked her then added: 'Please inform Norma Taylor of our plans; discuss the hours you both wish to attend the flat in Criccieth, come to a shift-work agreement.'

Eric picked up the internal phone, divulged the gist of the proceedings to Iwan Drew, and then told him he'd like his permission for Helen Manning and Norma Taylor to chaperone Kelly in the flat and then he told Alan Reed of the situation. 'Use a large unmarked police car, your passengers will be waiting outside the station in five minutes.'

37

Eric Bolton, wearing a white shirt with a blue necktie under a grey woollen V-neck sweater, thick navy trouser, a navy blazer, durable black lace-up leather shoes and a winter-weight lined white anorak, arrived in Madogton police station at eight-thirty on a cold, frosty Tuesday morning.

He checked with the front desk officer: No mail or phone calls.

He then called into Iwan Drew's office on his way to the incident room.

PC Roger Young was with Iwan.

Eric, greeting Roger with a handshake, remarked: 'I haven't seen you in the station recently.'

'Out of town duties, sir.'

A perceptive Eric looked at him, then scanned Iwan's expression and decided that the two had an agenda, probably connected to the inquiry. Iwan would notify him eventually, so he decided not to pursue his question and, in its place, .informed Iwan of the morning's interviews with Amy Coleman and Josie Harold. 'You'll be updated, Iwan.'

Iwan smiled, then: 'DS Jimmy Elson and DC Glyn Salmon are in the incident room.'

'Is it warm in there?'

Iwan smiled. 'Yes, sir.'

'It's an icy morning,' Eric said, 'frost sparkling on the roads' grassy banks as I drove to the station; typical British weather,' a smirk, then: 'winter, officially, begins in December,' a, simper, then: 'the weather boffins should be told that it's arrived early this year.'

A smiling Iwan agreed.

Eric said, 'Time we met our colleagues in the incident room.'

'Good morning, gentlemen,' Eric announced, then advocated: 'Coffee for everyone before we start?'

'Mugs prepared for completion,' Glyn Salmon said, 'milk and sugar are available,' then, grinning as he rose from the chair to switch on the kettle, added: 'we were waiting for you, Chief.'

Eric took off his anorak, hung it on the peg in the back of the door, then sat in his chair and opened his case file.

The three men discussed the previous day's events in between sipping their caffeine drinks, and then Eric, tapping his index finger on the file, asked a broad-spectrum question: 'How do you think yesterday's domestic tension pans out? Did we learn anything new, was our questioning intense enough? Conflict between a fraught woman and her confident husband seems difficult for both.'

Jimmy Elson reminded everyone: 'The marriage has experienced difficulties, but there is no evidence that Kelly was, or is, mentally disturbed. Her reaction to weird and frightening circumstances was, in my experience of questioning people, natural.'

'I agree,' Glyn said, then a fiery addition: 'I also, believe they need forty-eight hours to discuss their problems; we question them further on Thursday morning.'

Eric ambled up to the evidence board and, using a black marker pen as a pointer, asked: 'What do we have? A specialist medic who deals in psychology and the treatment of distressed clients.' He pointed to Kelly's name, then to Josie Harold and Amy Coleman names. 'Three women whom he knows well.' He waited for a response.

There was none, both wanting their boss to continue.

Eric, after pondering what he'd said for several moments, looked at his colleagues and, in a reflective voice, declared: 'Helen Manning did broach the possibility that there might exist a love triangle within this group. Well, any opinions on that prospect?'

The astute Jimmy Elson answered immediately: 'I don't believe you require our assessments, Chief; you've summoned the two widows to attend here this morning.' A wry grin, then: 'I'm sure you'll ask them about your perspectives on the mystery.'

A grinning Glyn said, 'You *have* considered the mystery's obtuse framework.'

Eric agreed, adding: 'Since Helen Manning announced her feminine vibes.'

Glyn, pointing at the evidence board with his pencil, asked: 'Do the events point to possible infidelity by Ray Glover?'

Eric drew black arrows between the three women, then lines connecting them with Ray Glover's name and then he said, 'There are pros and cons to this possible association;' he drew a hand along his forehead and as he carried on: 'what's on this board does not, necessarily, parallel what has happened in real life.' He returned to his chair and told his colleagues: 'That is why you and I are reviewing these Josie and Amy's testimonies today.' Eric checked the time. 'We'll have the coffee break now; meet in interview room two at nine-forty-five.'

38

Amy Coleman drove into Madogton police station's car park a few minutes before ten on Tuesday morning.

She was wearing a black woollen polo-neck sweater under a thick-neck long-sleeved fleece sweater, and a beige thigh-length heavyweight fleece-lined anorak. A woollen beanie hat, thick cotton-lined gloves, stone-coloured cord trousers and lace-up brown leather walking shoes completed her outfit.

Shivering and looking perished, she hurried across the car park into the warmth of the station and reported to the duty officer.

They exchanged pleasantries; Iwan Drew had told the officer of Amy's visit and had written it in the appointments' book.

The duty officer hit three digits on the internal phone, told Eric Bolton and then, after replacing the receiver, told Amy: 'I'll inform WPC Taylor that you're here.'

At ten o'clock Norma Taylor escorted Amy Coleman into interview room two.

Eric greeted Amy and, after introducing her to his two CID colleagues, guided her to a chair, then asked: 'Coffee?'

'Thank you, but no.'

Eric said to her: 'We've requested your presence this morning, Mrs Coleman, to see if you can throw any light on the inquiry.'

Amy's reply was silence and a thin smile.

Eric advised her 'You are not being questioned under caution, but the proceedings will be taped,' and then, opening his hands, said, 'pleas prompt me of parts I might have missed in our previous chats.'

A daunted Amy, fidgeting with her wristwatch, nodded she'd understood, but didn't speak. She stared at Eric Bolton.

Eric remained silent for a few seconds and then told her: 'Not easy, but try and relax, Mrs Coleman; our questions shouldn't take long.'

A churning stomach, a hint of nausea, maybe over breathing controlled her thinking as she tried, desperately, to reason her presence. Why more questions concerning her?

Eric turned to Jimmy Elson.

Jimmy threw Amy a cursory smile and then said to her: 'We've looked at the statement you made regarding that Thursday night, the twenty-sixth of October.' He paused for a second, then in a forthright tone, said, 'You gave Dr Glover refuge without knowing the reason for his request. Did you not know that his wife was staying in her aunt's flat in Criccieth at the time? I believe you know Kelly well from the time your husband and Mrs Glover's husband were students.'

A shaking Amy, a handkerchief now in one hand, garbled: 'I rarely had contact with her, had no idea she was in the neighbourhood that week.'

Jimmy wrote in his pad and then asked her: 'Did Dr Glover's phone call on that horrendous night startle you?'

A feeble 'Yes, sir.'

'Did you wonder as to why he was calling you when you knew he had access to a flat in Criccieth?'

'No, sir.'

'Really?'

'Yes, sir,' was a quiet answer and wiping away tears with the handkerchief.

'Please explain.'

'It's a convoluted picture, Sergeant,' a fraught Amy said, 'we've known one another for many years, you know this from my previous statement. Ray Glover helped me after my husband's tragic death.' She stopped speaking, gulped, retched a few times and then Norma Taylor handed her a mug of water.

'Sorry, sir.

'Take your time, Mrs Coleman, you're testimony could be important.'

Amy blushed as she continued: 'I've been asked if there was any sexual relationship with Dr Glover. He helped me through the months following my husband's death. He's an adept counsellor, relaxed me,' she shrugged, 'a close friendship.' She drank more water. 'He visited me when he was in Criccieth.' She exhaled, then continued: 'After several months of therapy, treatment by hypnosis, a mutual agreement, was considered to help me to counter my grief.'

More water and then, in a quivering whisper, Amy said, 'A relationship did develop soon afterwards -'

Eric jumped in: 'Please speak in a sound voice, Mrs Coleman.'

She coughed, cleared her throat and said, 'We formed an allegiance, Chief Inspector.'

'I'm listening, Mrs Coleman.'

A susceptible Amy, wriggling in her seat, said, 'About six months after my husband's death I became depressed,' a pause, a sigh, then: 'defenceless, welcomed sympathy.'

'Vulnerable?'

'For many months I felt lost, Chief Inspector, had frequent panic bouts, was afraid of being alone, lost confidence, wanted support and then Ray phoned me, a courtesy call, and from then interactions developed.'

Glyn Salmon piped up. 'Explain what you mean by "interactions", Mrs Glover.'

'We met when circumstances were convenient, our friendship blossomed, and yes, I haven't been honest with you, we had a sexual relationship, but,' she hesitated, remained silent for several moments, contemplating, then: 'it's difficult to explain, Mr Salmon, he spoke with me most days when he was in north Wales and we met occasionally. Kelly had no idea of our clandestine activities. He devised a formula to relax me, then hypnotise me, and we'd have sex, usually in my flat.' She had another drink of water, then said, 'The sex was devoid of any carnal sensitivity; I couldn't remember what occurred. When he released me from my hypnotic state I was naked, yet warmth circulated between my thighs.' She cried.

Norma Taylor comforted her for several seconds and then, a patient Eric said, 'What you've described has been a difficult delicate route for you, but,' targeting Amy's eyes, he asserted: 'I need to ask you a few more questions, then you may leave. Are you able to continue?'

Despondency coloured her voice: 'Yes, sir.'

'Take your time.'

Appreciating Eric's understanding of the situation gave Amy a degree of confidence; she spoke in a clear tone: 'Dr Glover brought me to a specific cave in north Wales, a secluded environ, no contact with the outside world. He supplied food and drink. The varying ghostly intense echoes within the cave were signals for him to approach me. I obeyed Ray's directives and we had sex there,' a pause, then a firm: 'on reflection, Chief Inspector, despite my susceptibility to his demands at these times, I'm ashamed of my actions.'

'You were not in control of your activities?'

'Correct.'

'Despite the weather, the roar of the sea, the noisy gulls, that could be distractions, he still dominated you?'

Amy's reply was an anguished: 'Yes.'

'How did he launch this power?'

'By speaking one word, my maiden name of Price. I became mentally, physically and emotionally vulnerable.'

Eric massaged the sides of his face with the palm of one hand, then looked at her and, in a soft voice, said, 'Two further questions, Mrs Coleman.'

The tense Amy nodded.

'I assume Dr Glover was staying with his wife in the flat in Criccieth when you visited this cave,' a pause, then: 'have you any idea as to how he organised the trysts?'

'During small tides the upper reaches of the beaches weren't covered by water, easy access to the cave.' Amy squeezed the fingers of both hands and, looking at Eric, then at Jimmy and at Glyn, said, 'He called for me and, to answer your question; he controlled the tryst,' a wry sneer, then a symbolic assertion: 'it's possible that he also, disciplined his wife.'

'Does he still dominate you?'

Amy shook her head. 'No, he realised that, after many sexual encounters, he became remorseful and ended his trance-stimulating expertise,' a pause, then she added: 'the dalliances ended last March, the start of the tourist season in the area. He no longer had the privacy of the previous months when the beaches were quiet, no one entered that particular cave, but we saw dishevelled people entering and leaving others. They seemed high, probably on drugs, perhaps alcohol, or a combination of both, inhabiting their idiosyncratic world and they didn't see us, didn't even check inside the cave despite Ray's parked car nearby.'

Eric looked at her then, sympathetic to her distress, said, 'That will be all, Mrs Coleman, I'll arrange for someone to take you home; another officer will drive your car to your flat. Keys for your car please.'

A tearful Amy obliged and then, speaking in a watery voice, struggled to thank everyone.

Norma escorted her out of the room, then arranged the transport and returned to interview room two for further instructions.

Eric wrote in his pad, then checked the time and said, 'We have over an hour before Josie Harold arrives.' He sighed. 'We'll have a comfort break and afterwards we'll discuss Amy's story.' He shut his note pad, then remarked: 'If Josie's story is also enlightening, we can be more ruthless with Ray Glover.'

39

Josie Harold, clad in a beige woollen shirt under navy crew-neck sweater, plus grey trousers and black lace-up leather shoes, drove her white BMW into Madogton police station's car park at five minutes before noon. She got out, put on her heavy, three-quarter-length camel coat, zap-locked the car and hurried into the building.

WPC Norma Taylor, standing at reception, greeted her and took her into interview room two.

The three CID officers stood.

Eric said, 'Please remove your coat, Mrs Harold.'

Josie acknowledged with a smile and then handed it to Norma Taylor who hung it on a peg on the door.

Eric, waving with his arm to a chair, invited Josie to sit and then, after everyone had settled, told her: 'Thank you; I'm seeking your help in our ongoing inquiry into the baffling events of the past weeks.'

A curt riposte: 'I'm listening, Chief Inspector.'

Eric looked at Josie: she appeared composed, expressionless, and thought: was she mentally tuned in for a challenging meeting? Pointing his pencil at the tape recorder, he said, 'Although, you are not under caution, Mrs Harold, I will tape our conversation to write the proceedings, ad verbatim, in my case file.'

Josie stared at Eric, didn't speak.

Eric, a dour tone to his voice, said, 'The events are obscure, Mrs Harold. We haven't found a pattern to what's happened, hence the reason for your presence today; maybe clarify some aspects of this conundrum.' He looked at her.

Josie remained impassive.

Eric said to her: 'Detective Sergeant Elson will ask you some questions.'

Jimmy thanked Josie for her presence, then summarised the events from the crucial Friday morning and then said to her: 'You came to Criccieth on the following Monday, and stayed because your plans to check the flat and lock it up for the winter have been delayed.'

A fretful Josie said, 'You know the sequence of the events, Sergeant; I've given you statements, have supported my niece and now, with Ray also there, a tense atmosphere pervades through the flat.'

Jimmy nodded once at her and then spoke in a soft voice: 'It's a difficult, involved setup.' He flicked through several pages of his file and, tenting his fingers, asked Josie: 'How long have you known Ray Glover?'

'Numerous years; from the time he and Kelly were college students.' A groan, then: a vexed: 'I've already told you this.'

The professional Jimmy waited for several seconds, then asked her: 'Did Ray Glover, in his professional capacity as a hypnotherapist, help you with any psychological problems that you might have had following your husband's death?'

Josie reacted with a firm: 'No,' and then, raising her voice, added: 'I felt grieved on occasions but, that was understandable.' She stopped speaking, shook her shoulders once and then stared at the floor.

Norma handed her a mug of water.

Josie took a few sips and then handed the mug back to Norma.

Jimmy said, 'That is all I wish to know, Mrs Harold. Thank you. DC Salmon has questions for you.'

Glyn, having watched Josie's reactions to Jimmy Elson's last question, felt that Josie's iron lady image might be, following that personal question, softening. A rational approach, similar to Jimmy's tactic, was his plan. He smiled at Josie and, in a slow monotone, advised her:

'Take time to consider your answers to my questions, Mrs Harold; you're evidence is important.'

Josie shrugged her shoulders again.

Glyn Salmon, sensing her tentative vibes, spoke in a measured, clear voice: 'DS Elson asked you if Dr Glover might have helped you during times of personal unease, possibly depressive bouts,' a pause, then: 'felt he was somebody with whom you could discuss personal problems?'

Josie exhaled, sighed and, after a few seconds considering the question, said, 'A sexual relationship did develop......Ray provided solace.' She stopped speaking for a few seconds, and then asked aloud: 'Was I overcome by the man's proficient approach to my dilemma?' She wriggled in her seat. 'Yes; totally.'

Glyn, staring at her; sensed she wanted to talk about her experiences with Dr Glover. He remained silent, waited.

While gazing at the wooden floor, Josie confessed: 'He helped me, albeit years after my husband's death. He counselled, relaxed, me,' she shrugged, 'a close friendship developed.' She drank water, then continued; 'he visited me at my home in Manchester and, following several consultations in his private rooms, hypnosis was deemed as possible therapy.'

Norma handed Josie another mug of water.

Josie had a few sips, then handed Norma the mug, looked at Glyn Salmon and, her voice a wobbly whisper, told him: 'We became sexually active; our friendship grew and, yes,' she hesitated, remained silent for several moments, then: 'it's difficult to explain because I became dependent on him. Kelly had no idea of our furtive meetings in his private consulting room.' A long sight, then: 'When he released me from the hypnotic state I was naked, yet warmth swept through my body. Ironic, but when I came out of the trance, soft background music was evident, always Nina Simone singing *I put a spell on you.*'

'When was the last time you had such an assignation with Dr Glover?'

'About a month ago.'

'Did you succumb to his hypnotic persuasion then?'

'Certainly; a thirty-minute-long talk relaxed me, then he'd whisper my maiden name, Noble, and I was under his spell.' Josie gulped. 'Sorry.'

'Thank you, Mrs Harold.' Glyn looked at his boss.

Eric said, 'Kelly and Ray Glover are in your in your property, and you've described the atmosphere there as being tense.'

'They sleep in separate bedrooms; I sleep on the sofa; I'm last to bed and first to get up in the morning.'

Eric said, 'I appreciate it's been a difficult, delicate route for you, but,' focusing on Josie's eyes, he asserted: 'I need to ask you a few more questions, then you may leave. Are you able to continue?'

Josie nodded, cleared her throat and said, 'Now that I'm here, I might as well continue; this is not a place I relish visiting.'

'Does Ray Glover still dominate you?'

'No, realising that I was a cheap thrill, I threatened him; told him that Kelly would be notified of our actions.'

'And?'

A forthright Josie said, 'That is no problem now, Chief Inspector; he no longer can seize my mind and body.' She sighed, eyed Eric and continued: 'I'm glad that I've explained his actions. He is a female predator; goodness knows how many women he's controlled,' she stopped speaking, stared at the wall behind Eric and, a determined tone in her voice, added: 'what I'm about to say may seem odd, Chief Inspector but, reflecting over recent happenings, I'm not convinced that Kelly is psychologically disturbed.' She switched her gaze from the wall to Eric and declared: 'Please consider my point of view.'

Eric, impressed by Josie's remarks, wrote a few notes, then thanked her. 'That will be all, Mrs Harold; please don't divulge our conversation to anyone. Do you feel capable of driving back to the flat?'

She nodded. 'Yes, I'll be all right, sir. I'll unwind during the short journey.'

Norma fetched Josie's coat and they left the room.

Eric stopped the tape, then lifted the internal phone and asked Alan Reed to join him in the interview room.

A minute later, Eric handed Alan the tape. 'All the info on the meeting with Josie Harold. Once you've heard the discussion please return it, I need to type the essentials for my case file.'

Alan thanked him, then: 'I'll update the evidence board this evening,' and left.

Eric turned to his colleagues. 'Well?'

A baffled Jimmy Elson voiced his frustration 'Two explicit vivid stories, both critical of Ray Glover's behaviour.' He ran fingers through his hair and admitted: 'Kelly Glover's story should be interesting, then we consider the man's behaviour, especially his blasé attitude towards the police and forensics.'

Eric agreed and then he glanced at Glyn Salmon.

'Disrespectful of his profession and the opposite sex,' was Glyn's comment, 'loathsome,' he paused for a few seconds and then declared: 'should the medical authorities be informed of his behaviour?'

'No, we wait,' Eric said, then: 'Friday morning is crucial to the investigation. We consider, individually, what we've heard today; therefore, I suggest we have a sandwich lunch and afterwards we'll return to CID headquarters.'

Jimmy and Glyn agreed and left.

Eric contacted Iwan Drew on the internal phone, summarised the morning's proceedings and then said, 'If there are no new inspiring outcomes, we'll see you on Thursday morning to check the evidence before we question the Glovers.'

40

On Thursday, high patchy clouds and a weak sun had replaced the dark rain clouds to praise a perky dawn. Despite the pleasing amendments to the weather, an agitated Iwan Drew couldn't relax in his room, checking his wristwatch and the room's wall clock every few minutes while he waited for Eric Bolton and his team to arrive.

Iwan left his office just before eight-fifteen and went into the station's foyer, walked out to the building's entrance and glanced at the car park. No sign of the CID team.'

Seconds after his return into the foyer, he made for the toilet, anxiety affecting his bladder.

Back in the foyer he looked at the duty officer and asked: 'Any sign of the CID officers?'

The tall, young PC, pointing to the forecourt, told Iwan that they had just arrived.

A tense Iwan greeted them.

Eric looked at him: was Iwan perspiring? He looked pale, edgy, toying with his wristwatch, in obvious psychological distress, not like him to be uptight. He asked Iwan: 'What's the problem, Sergeant?'

'I'll tell you in the privacy of the incident room.'

Eric, Jimmy and Glyn followed Iwan inside.

Iwan waited while the officers removed their warm coats and settled in their respective chairs.

Eric looked at a shaking Iwan.

'Sit, Sergeant.'

'Thank you, sir, but I'd rather stand.'

Eric nodded to him and waited.

'It concerns PC Roger Young -'

'Out of town duties, Sergeant?'

Eric looked at Iwan and said, 'I guessed that you and PC Young had a reserved agenda,' a smile, then: 'perhaps concerning this inquiry.' He clasped his hands and told Iwan: 'You and PC Young are commendable professionals. Roger Young, a young member of your team is anxious to make a mark in the force.' Eric sighed, scratched the side of his face, looked at Iwan and said, 'I'm a senior CID officer because I'm a good detective, Sergeant. I knew you had plans, and that you would inform me of their nature eventually. That is why, on Tuesday morning, I didn't pursue your answer to my comment that I hadn't seen PC Young in the station for several days.' He looked at Iwan; waited for a response.

A fretful Iwan was silent.

The perceptive Eric asked him: 'What's happened?'

'It concerns the current whereabouts of PC Roger Young.' Iwan explained: 'Roger was on a clandestine mission, watching the caves in the peninsula on the end of Criccieth's south beach and those beyond that boundary. He has not contacted me for forty-eight hours, and that is unusual.' Iwan drew paper tissues over his forehead as he continued speaking: 'As you are aware, Chief, he's young, lean, strong and fit from playing soccer for a local side. He lives alone in a tiny old stone-built cottage in a village between Madogton and Criccieth His parents live in Harlech; no siblings and he has no girlfriend. Professionally, he's still a sapling, but he's determined to climb up the police ladder. For this venture he drove his own car, a two-year-old red four-door Vauxhall Astra, knew where to park so that it wasn't visible to people walking along the beaches or using the caves.'

A concerned Eric asked Iwan: 'Have you contacted his friends in the soccer club?'

'He's not been there for a practice session, they have phoned him at home and on his mobile, but without a reply.'

'Neighbours?'

'I phoned his next door neighbour and friend, Edgar; he's seventy, a widower, hobby is gardening and he sees to Roger's small back garden. He heard Roger's car leave around seven-thirty on Wednesday morning. It hasn't been back since.' Iwan wiped more perspiration off his brow and face, then looked at Eric and his colleagues.

Eric glanced at the wall clock, then turned to his two expressionless colleagues and said, 'I suggest Sergeant Drew takes us to the caves.'

Both men nodded.

Eric picked up the internal phone and spoke with WPC Helen Manning, explained the impending police action and then told her: 'I want you or Norma to visit Josie Harold's flat, keep all the occupants in conversation for the next two hours, none of them is to see the activity near the Criccieth caves.'

'I'll arrange that now, sir.'

Eric replaced the phone in its cradle and, turning to Iwan, told him: 'Arrange a car to take us there; we'll meet outside in five minutes.'

Iwan nodded then said, 'It's a nippy breezy morning; the beach will be very cold; wear adequate head cover, warm anoraks and, if you have them, protective goggles, blowing sand has no respect for a person's eyes,' and then he left.

An unmarked black purpose-built police SUV, with driver Alan Reed inside, was waiting outside the police station for the officers.

Eric Bolton, Jimmy Elson and Glyn Salmon, all dressed, on Iwan's advice, in warm clothes and carrying small knapsacks containing woollen hats, fleece-lined gloves and goggles, entered the vehicle.

Iwan sat in the front passenger seat and told Alan: 'The caves south of the peninsula, no problem with the tide, neap, very small,' he paused for a few seconds and then said, 'I have a hunch we'll find Roger's car parked near there, hidden byte dunes.'

Alan Reed drove out of the car park.

'How long a journey?' Eric asked Alan Reed.

'Ten minutes,' Alan announced as he drove through the town, 'it's about three miles from here.'

True to his word, Alan arrived at the main entrance to the beach in less than ten minutes, stopped the vehicle, glanced at Iwan Drew and waited for instructions.

Iwan looked out of the window for several moments and then turned to the three CID officers. 'We are at the uppermost point of the foreshore.' He pointed at the sea and said, 'White horses are plentiful in the bay. The peninsula provides protection from this north-westerly wind, hence the water lapping the foreshore is, in comparison with the sea…. tranquil. However, beware swirling sand blowing from the dunes.' He then pointed. 'Note the rocky peninsula at the southern edge of Criccieth beach; it has caves on its north and south-facing inclines.'

Iwan focused on a section of the dunes and, indicating at them with his hand, told Alan: 'Those undulating higher dunes with the tough Marran grass provide the ideal hiding place,' he smiled, 'for example, lovers.'

Alan smiled, didn't respond.

Iwan continued: 'There's an undulating mixed stone and sandy narrow lane a hundred yards to the right of here, take that lane and you'll arrive, eventually, at a wide turning circle; it's a hub for several narrower twisting lanes down to numerous entry points on the foreshore. I guess Roger might have parked near there, out of sight and sheltered from inshore winds, I'll advise you.'

Alan drove slowly along the deserted lane, snaking his way between the sand dunes. The car's wipers, in slow mode action, clearing the screen from drifting sand.

'There it is,' Iwan shouted, pointing and then said, 'to your left, about twenty yards ahead, I can see a car's red roof in between the dunes. I'm certain that's Roger Young's Vauxhall Astra.'

Alan drove to it.

Everyone got out of the vehicle.

The car was empty.

Eric felt its bonnet. 'It's cold.' He looked at the sand-covered uneven narrow lane. 'No sign of any other tyre marks.'

'An eerie locality,' Jimmy commented, cupping his hands to shield his face from the painful drifting sand. He looked at the lively sea, the barren land and the emptiness of the vast beach. Turning his back to the wind he looked at the uninspiring hinterland: just one farm house tucked in an indistinct vale. 'Not my desired scene.'

A shaking Glyn concurred and added: 'especially this time of the year,' a sneer then: 'November's grey and moody ambience.'

'We investigate the caves,' Iwan said. 'Torches please, Alan.'

Alan Reed opened the four-by four's hatch, fished out five powerful torches and handed them to his shivering colleagues.

Iwan Drew said, 'Despite it being the middle of the morning, at this time of the year it's black inside those caves, no sunlight enters them.'

They all entered the vehicle and Iwan pointed. 'A narrow bumpy mixed grass and sand covered lane down there connects with the beach, Alan. Drive around the point to Criccieth beach and its caves. The foreshore has a firm, unbroken sandy surface during small tides; no ruts, no problem driving or parking on it.'

41

Screeching low-flying seagulls signalled the arrival of the SUV, the avian cacophony complaining at the object, seen only rarely on the foreshore at this time of the year. More gulls, responding to their colleagues complaining tuneless chorus announcing the intrusion of their territory, arrived. Seconds later the noise acquired a higher pitch-electric saw-sounding noise overwhelmed the beach's natural sounds.

Alan Reed drove slowly towards the caves, looking for tyre marks on the firm sand before he came to the caves' entrances in the lee of the onshore gusting wind. He looked through the windscreen and the side window, checking the sand for evidence of recent presence of vehicles or people. There was none.

He stepped out of the vehicle and looked at the sandy expanse. This place must have witnessed much activity, good, bad and indifferent over the centuries, embracing copious secrets. He walked along the beach towards the castle, stopping at the stark glass-frontage seashore café with panoramic views that included Criccieth and Harlech castle and the watery expanse of Tremadog Bay. The empty café's windows were boarded up, trading over until March next year. The adjacent ground was dry, unblemished by the small tides and strong north- westerly windy blasts. Relative tranquillity prevailed now, but he imagined the scene during a vicious storm. He shivered at the thought and hurried towards the high dunes to the north, barren hinterland, saw a train travelling towards Criccieth station. To the north of the railway line a solitary cottage was visible at the south entrance to the town. He shook his head, ran back to the SUV and announced: 'No tyre marks or footprints and, no litter; the beach is pristine.'

The five men stepped out of the vehicle to be greeted by another dozen gulls, in apparent grievance at the human presence.

Iwan looked up at them, shivered as he focused on the wailing birds: were their cries depicting despair, intimating death? He decided not to divulge such thoughts to his colleagues. He turned to Alan. 'Rubber gloves please.'

Alan opened the SUV's hatch again, collected several four-pack rubber gloves from one of the many purpose-designed compartments and handed everybody a pack.

Iwan looked up again at the colony of gulls, and then, countering their incessant noise and that of the breeze, shouted: 'This way, try and protect your eyes and mouth from the airborne sand.'

The silent, chilled group followed him to the mouth of the first cave. Sighs from everyone followed as they appreciated the sheltered refuge and its comparative warmth.

Eric chatted with Jimmy and Glyn for a few seconds, then he approached Iwan and told him: 'From now on, you're in charge.'

Iwan asked everyone to switch on their torches and then said, 'We follow the rugged contour of the cave's asymmetrical walls, shine your torches on the sandy floor, look for footprints, careful as to how you walk, you might trip on cans or other debris left by undesirable humans. The only sound you'll hear is water running down the craggy sides and echoes of your breathing; no resonance from the sandy floor.' He directed his torch beam at the cave's roof. 'Please note there will be bats in the rocky inlets.' He smiled and then they left and entered the second cave.

A larger cave, similar contours to the first, had some litter but, otherwise, nil of note. 'No one has been inside either cave recently,' Iwan declared: 'we'll now check the three on the south side of the peninsula.'

They returned to the SUV and Alan drove round the point to the first cave.

A cold and disillusioned Eric asked Iwan: 'What are we looking for?'

Iwan told him: 'I asked PC Roger Young to watch these caves and the immediate sands.'

They all got out of the SUV and entered the eight-foot wide cave.

Iwan sighed, then admitted: 'That's good, glad of the respite from that ever-present face-piercing briny wind. The height of the caves' ceilings varies between seven and eight feet, bats are plentiful.' He guided his torch's beam across and along the craggy roof while his colleagues concentrated on the rugged walls. Iwan said, 'This cave, the smallest of the three is about thirty yards long.' He looked at his colleagues and, his voice bouncing off the unyielding walls, asked: 'Shout if you see anything of note.'

Silence, lasting a few minutes while the cave was searched, was eventually fractured by Alan Reed: 'An occasional bat, but no signs of recent human or vehicular activity, Sarge.'

They left the empty cave.

Outside, Eric raised his eyebrows and then looked at Iwan.

Iwan shrugged his shoulders and, in an energetic voice, proclaimed: 'I've a gut feeling, Chief, that something has happened to Roger,' a pause then, after a long inhalation and exhalation, he gestured with an outstretched arm at the third cave and declared: 'we might find the answer to my ominous vibes in here, sir.'

Iwan directed his torch on the ceiling while his colleagues targeted the floor and the jagged walls.

A few bats flew from their perches in the coarse ceiling as the group walked, slowly towards the back of the cave.'

'Over here,' Alan Reed shouted, aiming his torch on the floor. 'Footprints.' He narrowed the beam, focusing it on the prints. 'Probably from boots, the person was walking towards the back of the cave.' Twenty yards later Alan's torch highlighted a body. It was on the floor, face upwards. They all stopped walking.

'Roger!' Iwan yelled, 'its Roger Young.'

Eric grabbed Iwan's arm. 'Leave this to us,' then he looked at Alan Reed.

Alan Reed held Iwan's shaking arm and told him: 'It's a CID job, we wait.'

Eric, Jimmy and Glyn put on the rubber gloves and approached the body.

Jimmy checked the corpse and said, 'Rigor is present, the body has a blue hue. Mouth and eyes are wide open.' A sigh, then he continued in a slow firm voice: 'A black woollen beanie hat covers his head and upper face; the facial muscles are twisted as if he was frightened, scared of something he might have seen or heard. Clothes are warm casual: a thick woollen polo neck sweater underneath a chunky body warmer and white anorak, thick corduroy trousers and sturdy boots. No evidence of any damage to the clothes. A wallet containing his ID.' He commentated on his cursory examination: 'Few coins in one trouser pocket; mobile phone in the other. Gloves and two sets of keys in the anorak's pockets. Torch in left hand, no beam, probably spent batteries.' Jimmy then checked the face and hands: 'No defensive signs, no sign of a struggle and no marks around the neck. No evidence of violence.'

A stern-faced Eric said, 'Forensics will supply us with an answer, Jimmy,' then he called Iwan over to view the body. 'Can you confirm this man's ID?'

A shaky Iwan walked slowly to the body, nodded and said, 'Yes, sir; it's PC Roger Young.,' he paused, looked at the face for several seconds then, in a quivering voice, said, 'that expression depicts fright; he encountered something in this cave?'

Eric didn't speculate, instead, sympathy commanding his quiet voice, he asked Iwan: 'When was the last time you heard from Roger?'

A trembling Iwan thought for several seconds, then, his voice hesitant, answered: 'Tuesday evening around seven; he said he was cold. I told him to leave the area, resume his surveillance on Wednesday morning and, I repeat, Roger's neighbour heard Roger's car leave the cottage around seven-thirty that morning.'

Eric focused his torch beam on his wristwatch and said, 'It's now eleven-thirty-on Thursday morning; it's approximately thirty-six hours ago since he left his house, so I guess death occurred about thirty hours ago.' He directed his torch beam around the cave and, noticing a pale-faced and shocked Iwan, declared: 'Someone will have to stay here.'

A shocked Iwan coughed, looked at the CID officers and said, 'I'll stay; I was his boss, Chief, I believe it's my duty to be here with him.'

Eric nodded, patted Iwan on his back and told him: 'We'll return to the station; I'll arrange for police presence and the paramedics and forensics.' He looked at Alan Reed. 'You can guide the police officers and paramedic here, then return to the station, wait for forensics to arrive and lead them here.' Eric looked at the sullen Iwan and said, 'Uniform support will be with you soon.'

An unresponsive Iwan watched the SUV leave and then he entered the cave.

42

Eric Bolton, back in the incident room, informed forensics.

Helen Manning brought in mugs of hot coffee for him and his two colleagues.

Eric thanked her, then asked her: 'Where's WPC Taylor?'

'She's visiting Kelly, her husband and Josie Harold.'

'Good,' Eric said then, looking at the wall clock, told Helen: 'Give her another ninety minutes with them, then call her on the radiophone and tell her to return here.' Eric then updated her, and added: 'Iwan Drew needs a flask of sweetened hot coffee.'

A shocked, silent, tearful and shaking Helen looked at him.

Eric told her: 'I'll organise officers and advise them of their visit to the cold and unfriendly beach.'

Helen, wiping away tears from her face, nodded, and left to make the flask of coffee.

Eric, having briefed the uniforms officer, returned to the incident room and phoned the coroner.

Eifion Pask wrote down the details and agreed to a post mortem examination of the body. He'd wait for further details before arranging an inquest.

Eric replaced the receiver in its cradle.

Helen returned to the incident room, told Eric she'd placed the coffee at the station's front desk; uniform would take it to Iwan.

Eric briefed Helen and then ordered her not to divulge the news to anyone. The station's staff would be updated eventually. 'Okay, Helen, you can leave now. See you and Norma Taylor later.'

Alan Reed, the CID officers, plus a paramedic's team arrived at the cave just before two o'clock. Uniform were there already, chatting with the perished, distressed and trembling pale Iwan, who was sheltering at the cave's entrance from the icy breeze.

Eric handed Iwan the flask of coffee, then checked the time and told Alan Reed to return to Madogton police station. 'Forensics will be there soon, they're returning Kelly's black plastic bag with the washing. We'll return it to her eventually.' He updated the uniform officers, then the paramedics and said, 'I'll wait until forensics have examined Roger's car before ordering a low loader to take it to the purpose built forensic garage in Bangor.'

Uniform officers cordoned off the caves and the access lanes to the beach with blue and white tape.

Eric began coughing from inhaling the wafting sand and, shielding his eyes from the briny wind eddying between the peninsula and the high dunes, walked towards Iwan.

Eric cleared his throat then, speaking in a solemn, but determined voice, told Iwan: 'We'll have to view Roger Young's body again,' then, in an understanding tone, added: 'however, I appreciate your distress and, if you believe you can't continue, return to the station. My colleagues and I will brief forensics.'

A sullen Iwan drank the last of the coffee, placed the flask on the sand and, his voice croaking from obvious stress, said, 'I'd rather stay, Chief; I feel that I should remain here while the investigation continues,' a pause, then a tearful addition: 'I'm not abandoning my colleague.'

Eric patted him on the back and told him: 'I'm pleased with your decision.' He picked up the empty flask and, handing it to Jimmy Elson, told him and Glyn Salmon: 'I'll take Iwan into the cave again, I want you to stay here and wait for forensics.'

Torches switched on, Eric and Iwan walked to the body.

Iwan knelt, checked the body once more without touching it and said, 'No evidence that he was killed unlawfully, and I'm certain he was too strong a character to contemplate suicide, his life revolved around police work.'

A thoughtful Eric said, 'From what I know of the way he's helped you in this inquiry, it was a clandestine toil at times. This is a bizarre situation.' He pointed to Roger's face 'That expression represents extreme fright. What did he encounter here? Whatever it was, it had to be considerable. I can't imagine him being frightened; he was strong physically and mentally, portrayed self-assurance.'

'Everything about this inquiry is creepy,' a contemplative Iwan said, 'Unreal, surreal and lacking in evidence. No pattern to what's happened, no clues.' He shook his head. 'A fantasy? I'm struggling with an outlandish thought that Roger's death is, in some way, connected with, what I believe, is an illusory atmosphere pervading through that flat in Criccieth,' a pause, then: 'a possible masquerade?'

'A great deal of what's going on defies logic,' Eric admitted, 'and, as you say, we are nowhere nearing a solution as to how this family ticks; we so need forensics help, a lead from someone, somewhere please -' He stopped speaking; a loud echo was announcing: 'Chief, the forensics team has arrived.'

Iwan, a rash of unruly goose pimples spreading across his trembling body, rose from the cave's floor, sighed and then the two men walked slowly to the entrance.

Alan Reed and a shivering forensics team: Tim Wilding, Edward Brown and Tony Simpson, were standing at the cave's mouth.

They greeted one another in staccato voices, and then Eric advised everybody to enter the cave. 'It's a shelter from the unfriendly incessant wind that's strengthening as if it desires to accelerate nightfall.' He summarised the events up to the present, told the team of the police's initial findings, and then, an appealing tone to his voice, said to the forensics team: 'We need your help, gentlemen.'

Tim asked Eric if the cave's floor was firm enough to take the weight of the paramedics' ambulance. 'I need the vehicle's headlights on to boost the light from our torches.' He added: 'Once we've completed our initial investigation in the cave, we'll check the car before it goes to the garage in Bangor.'

'Understood,' Eric said, then advised Tim: 'the cave has ample headroom and width for the ambulance to drive up to the body.'

Tim and his colleagues entered the forensics van, changed into their uniforms and hurried into the cave.

Eric walked to the paramedics in their ambulance, two men who hadn't, personally, witnessed nature's present harshness. He described the police situation plus Tim Wilding's request and then told them that he and his team, plus Sergeant Drew and PC Alan Reed, would wait in the SUV until forensics had completed their work.

The ambulance, it's headlights on full beam, followed the forensics team into the cave.

Initial forensic e4xamination completed, several bats flew out of the cave as the paramedics' ambulance reappeared onto the beach. A three-point turn and the vehicle approached the police's SUV.

Jim, the burly ambulance driver, jumped out of the cab and told Eric and his colleagues that forensics had completed their preliminary examination and that the body was being transferred to the forensics morgue.

Eric thanked him and the ambulance left.

Alan Reed drove the SUV up to the cave's mouth and waited for Tim Wilding and his team to appear.

'We'll stay inside the cave's entrance,' Eric said to Tim Wilding, 'protection from the screeching gulls and the onshore wind; will allow us to talk here.'

Tim described their findings and that numerous photograms were taken of the body and the inside of the cave. He carried on, his soft Manchester accent highlighting each syllable: 'Preliminary examination shows a cyanotic corpse, rigor mortis is present; there is no obvious cause of death.' He asked Eric: 'When was the last time anyone had contact with PC Young?'

'Sergeant Drew spoke with him a few minutes after seven on Tuesday evening.'

Tim Wilding looked at Iwan.

'That's correct, sir; however, the next door neighbour heard PC Young's car leave early   Wednesday morning.....around seven-thirty.'

Tim squinted at his wristwatch and said, 'It's now just after three, he was alive about thirty hours ago; that helps us to assess the time of death,' he paused for a moment and then said, 'it's very cold inside the cave, temperature at night would be around freezing...... liver probe temperature might help.' He shrugged his shoulders and then said, 'I'll have more news after we've examined him in the lab -'

A fretful Eric cut in: 'Thanks,' then: 'now to the car please, Tim.'

Nil of note was discovered on the initial examination of the vehicle and, thirty minutes later, the car was on a low loader heading for the garage cum vehicle lab in Bangor. The forensics team followed it.

Eric, speaking in a solemn voice, asked Iwan: 'What of Roger's relatives?'

Iwan described Roger's history. 'I knew him well; we were friends. I repeat: he was a fit twenty-seven-year old, played soccer for the village team._An only child and single. Roger lived in a small cottage in a village between Madogton and Criccieth. A non-smoker, he drank lager occasionally. Transport was that two-year-old Vauxhall Astra. Girls were, out of choice, absent from his life; his priority was to reach the top rung of the police ladder.'

Eric asked him: 'What about informing his parents?'

'They live in Harlech,' Iwan said, 'I'll visit them tomorrow, Friday, explain all and stress that the press and media have not been informed of his death.'

43

Eric, his CID colleagues, plus Iwan Drew and Alan Reed, hurried from the cave. Heads bowed, combating the freshening gritty wind, they made for the SUV. All breathless, they appreciated the vehicle's refuge and slumped into their respective seats.

Eric removed his goggles and, after wiping briny sand from around his eyes, looked at everyone and in a candid voice, declared: 'There's nothing more to be done in that cave. Police tapes can be removed; we were fortunate that no member of the public visited the beach. It's possible somebody might have been walking their dog on the top of the promontory or on the other beach. None of our activities, however, suggested our presence was due to suspicious events, hence my reason to depart now -'

'People,' the troubled Iwan interjected, 'do, out of interest, scan the beach with binoculars. They see police activity here occasionally, sometimes a body is found on the foreshore, a rare event,' he looked at Eric and added: 'we have training exercises regularly involving the local lifeboat crew, so the locals accept police presence here.' Iwan sighed, then, despair in his voice said, 'Someone might have seen us and informed the press and media, hence members of those corps might be present when we return to the station.'

'I'll deal with them,' Eric said, 'provide them with a summary of the professional endeavours on the beach.' Shivering, he glanced at his watch and said, 'Okay, Alan, it's getting dark; the location reeks of unfriendliness. Madogton police station next stop.'

'Luck is with us,' Alan shouted as he drove into the station's car park, 'no press or media presence.'

Everyone checked with PC Ken Parry, the duty officer.

There were no phone calls for them.

Eric asked Ken: 'Are WPCs Helen Manning and Norma Taylor here?'

'In their room, sir.'

'Thank you.'

Eric smiled at his colleagues and said, 'Freshen up everybody, my face feels as if it's been rubbed with sandpaper,' and then to Ken: 'please tell WPCs Manning and Taylor to be in the incident room in ten minutes.'

Ken nodded. 'Will do, sir.'

Eric turned to Alan Reed, thanked him for his diligence and then, handing him a twenty-pound note said, 'a request before you join us; snacks from the supermarket for everyone please.'

'Ten minutes, sir,' Alan said and left.

Despite freshening their faces in the restroom, tiredness dominated the CID officers and Iwan's movements as they ambled into the incident room.

They hung their foul weather gear on the back of the chairs and, despite sore eyes and rosy faces, no one spoke as they settled in their seats, relishing the station's tranquillity and its comforting warmth.

Eric said, 'My unremarkable reaction to the events is that we've experienced an eventful few hours. We can't even surmise what happened in that cave,' a pause, then: 'I cannot erase the image of Gareth's face from my mind, elements of surprise and horror were evident.'

The still grief-stricken Iwan described his sensations and emotions when he was alone in the cave while he waited for everyone to return: He trembled as he spoke: 'I must have been hallucinating, visualised colourful beings, couldn't distinguish whether they were man or woman, some were protease figures, tortuous walk, communicating with one another by monosyllabic grunting noises, no capacity for obvious speech. Other figures were sublime female beauties, dressed in skimpy robes and yet, in my eyes, they looked decorous, dancing and singing as they entered the cave.' He rubbed his eyes; exhaled loudly and admitted: 'I'm unable to account for these.....I can only describe what I saw as apparitions -' a knock on the door stopped him speaking. Alan Reed, plus WPCs Helen Manning and Norma Taylor, entered with food and mugs of coffee.

Eric thanked them. 'Please join us.' Eric smiled at Norma and said, 'Update us on your morning's trip to Criccieth while we eat.'

A tense Norma opened her notebook, flicked through a few pages, then looked at Eric and everyone else. Her stomach churning, she felt unreal as she began speaking; 'I was nervous going there. Circumstances surrounding the three people caused me concern, why? I have no idea, a peculiar sense that I was entering an inhospitable environment.' She stopped speaking, walked to the water vending machine and then returned to her chair.

No one spoke, everyone waiting for her to continue.

'A tense Josie Harold answered the door and invited me into the flat. There was no sound, even the radio wasn't on. I felt cold, a rash of goose pimples crossed the back of my neck. I shivered. I was asked to sit and then I explained that I was checking if everything was okay and if any help was required from us or anybody else. An expressionless Josie responded with a cold grunt.

I explained the situation, and then Kelly and Ray walked into the room and sat next to one another on the sofa. They didn't greet me.'

More water, then Norma's voice took on a dutiful tone as she described the scenario: 'Kelly and Ray Glover had no eye contact. However, they both answered in the negative when I asked them if they required anything.' Norma flicked to the next a page, checked what's she'd written and then said, 'Ray Glover looked directly into my eyes and spoke in a soft, soporific voice, a tone that defied my logic, the tone and his stare providing a relaxing mood. I listened to his words, I'm still able to recall each one. He said that he felt well, unperturbed and was looking forward to explaining his actions to the police tomorrow morning.'

Eric thanked her, then told the two WPCs: 'Report for duty tomorrow morning as usual, I want you to be present when we interview Ray and Kelly Glover.........depending on their answers, I might question Josie Harold again.'

The WPCs left.

A weary-looking Eric drank his coffee, then some water and admitted: 'I feel exhausted from the briny bashing.' He looked at his colleagues, then at Iwan Drew and Alan Reed and said, 'before we finish for the day, a question: Has anyone new views on this trio of Ray Glover, his wife and Josie Harold?'

Iwan, having recovered from his initial grief, said, 'Vibes tell me that Ray Glover manipulates people by using his eyes and a specific, well-trained spiel that sends the listener into a form of relating confidence where he or she accepts every word and command he utters.' He turned to Eric, then to Jimmy and Glyn and stated: 'Ray Glover has been interviewed by you three; did you feel at risk, unsettled, suspicious of his answers and body language during these sessions?'

Glyn Salmon nodded his head. 'The man has poise with no fear of being interviewed by the law; he possesses an aura that transferrable to others. Amy Coleman and Josie Harold's descriptions of their contact with him confirms my feelings; he manoeuvred and controlled them.'

Jimmy Elson, rubbing his still sore eyes, said, 'I agree with all that's been said. It has been mooted that this trio are players in a ploy to fool us. Do we believe Kelly's visions and their linkage with Robert Graves's poem? Do the imaginary stanzas control her?' Yes, if you accept that

Ray has complete control over her by his absolute psychological manipulation and,' a short pause as Jimmy considered, then: 'do we believe Josie Harold's account of the troubled ambience within the flat?'

Eric sighed, and then said, 'We are cynical of all the disagreeable situations; if, and I stress *if,* we are witnessing a sophisticated sham, who is in charge? Are the trio working in unison, control freaks?' He looked at Iwan. 'Your opinion?'

A still tense Iwan said, 'The mythological poem has dominated my mind since we discovered Roger Young's body.'

Eric turned to Alan Reed.

'I wasn't present when you interviewed Ray Glover or the others involved in this mystery,' he shrugged his shoulders, 'I'm unable to give you an opinion, sir.'

'Okay, Alan,' Eric said, 'collect Dr and Mrs Glover plus Josie Harold tomorrow morning at ten thirty', then to everybody else: 'we've plenty to occupy our minds. We meet back here at nine in the morning, think of questions for the Glovers.' Then to Iwan. 'Travel to Harlech tomorrow in an unmarked car.'

44

The ambient temperature, highlighted on the console of Eric's car, was eight degrees centigrade when he arrived at Madogton police station at eight-thirty on the crisp and sunny Friday morning.

Everybody, bar Iwan Drew, was present in the incident room at nine o'clock.

Eric waved a hand at the evidence board. 'Up to date, compliments of PC Alan Reed.' He smiled at Alan and then told everyone: 'Concentrate on the board's info for a few minutes, then I'll ask if you've thought of any questions following yesterday's experiences.'

An apprehensive-looking Glyn Salmon said, 'The lack of any physical signs on Roger's body is strange, I cannot dismiss his stricken gaze from my mind, those staring wide-open eyes, maybe clenched teeth -'

Jimmy Elson interjected: 'Forensics might be able to provide you with answers to your queries,' adding: 'the near-freezing condition inside that cave might have influenced our initial screening of the body.'

Eric looked at Glyn Salmon. 'Anything you wish to add?'

A thoughtful Glyn shook he head once and said, 'No, sir; we all saw the same. I hope that forensics can supply key answers to the issues.'

Eric, glancing at the wall clock, looked at the two WPCs. 'I know it's early, but we won't have time for a coffee break later.'

Helen and Norma left the room.

Eric looked at the evidence board again and commented: 'That board lacks helpful clues. I've a gut feeling that forensics will phone while we're drinking our coffee,' he grinned then: 'their preliminary findings will be interesting.'

Helen and Norma, carrying a tray each, arrived with the drinks and a selection of biscuits and placed them on the main desk in front of Eric.

Eric thanked them, described the planned action to them and afterwards, tapping the trays with his pencil, said, 'Everybody help themselves to the drink and food.' He then turned to Alan Reed. 'Leave for Criccieth after this break; I want the Glovers and Josie Harold in the station by eleven. We'll question them, together, in interview room two.'

Alan left the room minutes later.

Eric finished eating his biscuit and drank the remainder of his coffee then, after a squint at the wall clock, said, 'Time is approaching ten; I'm wishing forensics contact us inside the next hour -' the ringing phone interrupted him; he picked it up. 'Chief Bolton -'

'Tim Wilding, sir.'

'Good morning, I hope it is, Tim; my team is present; we're questioning Ray Glover, his wife and her aunt, Josie Harold, at eleven; they are unaware of the policeman's death.'

Tim Wilding spoke in a soft voice: 'The conditions inside the cave required a more perceptive post mortem examination: liver probe did not record a temperature, therefore it's difficult to assess the time of death. We know it was after seven-thirty on Wednesday morning because of his next door neighbour's observation. Rigor mortis was still present when we examined the body in the cave. The near-freezing temperature slowed the progress of rigor, possibly for several hours.'   A short pause and he continued: 'It was nightfall, and after studying the circumstances and factoring in the unusual environs, I've arrived at an approximate time of death, late Wednesday afternoon, six o'clock at the latest. However, in view of the location, it could have been hours earlier.'

Eric asked: 'Any clues as to the cause of death?'

'Photographs taken by Tony Simpson at the scene suggest he'd been in that spot for a considerable time. No petechiae on the eyelids or lips, hence no sudden oxygen deprivation from carotid arteries' occlusions. No sand was found under the nails, in the mouth or on the front of his clothes. No marks on the sandy floor to suggest the body had been moved, or that PC Young had tried to crawl out of the cave. No evidence of trauma, such as penetrating wounds, were found. Stomach contents consisted of the remains of a cooked breakfast; the bowel was empty and the bladder was devoid of urine, suggesting he had nothing to eat or drink for several hours. We're checking bloods; it's possible he developed hypoglycaemia from lack of food. I'll fax you the initials findings soon. Toxicology results and histology finding will be available on Monday.'

'Thanks,' Eric said, then: 'before you go, we've not checked inside Ray Glover's Mercedes car.'

'Examine it,' Tim Wilding said, 'my hunch is that you'll find a laptop, no documents.......that laptop might provide valuable info.'

'Indeed,' Eric said, writing a memo in his desk pad, then: 'I'll be in touch,' and ended the call.

Eric reiterated Tim Wilding's news and then told his colleagues: 'we'll tell Ray Glover we want to look in his car and if he brought a laptop to Criccieth.' A smile, then: 'I expect he did bring one,' then a formidable statement: 'if he's obstinate we'll get a warrant' – the fax machine rumbled into action and dispensed Tim Wilding's report.

Eric printed several copies, handed everyone the two-page document and then, after everyone had read the contents, asked: 'Any questions?'

Helen asked: 'Do you want myself and WPC Taylor to be present during the interviews?'

'Yes; note how each reacts to answers provided by the other members of the trio plus, your female perspectives on Kelly Glover and Josie Harold's body languages will be valuable.' He looked at the wall clock. 'Ten-forty; we'll have a comfort break, then I want the two WPCs to meet the Glovers and Josie Harold in the foyer and escort them to interview room two.'

45

A few minutes before eleven o'clock Alan Reed escorted Kelly Glover, her husband, Ray and Josie Harold into Madogton Police Station.

Helen Manning and Norma Taylor met them and Helen explained the procedures to them before they entered interview room two.

Eric Bolton stood when the trio entered, gestured with a wave of a hand to chairs, waited until everyone was seated and, in a clear voice, informed them: 'My colleagues and I, after intense discussion, advise you that this meeting is essential to the inquiry.' He switched on the tape recorder, looked at the three and, in a stern tone, said, 'None of you is under caution; we are still uncertain as to what happened on the Friday morning; the tape recorder is for evidence.'

A tense Kelly, dressed in warm casual clothes: beige cord trousers and a thigh length grey hooded anorak, and leather ankle boots, wriggled in her chair, squeezing a wad of paper tissues in one hand.

An apparent unconcerned Ray, wearing a thick red and blue check cotton shirt under a red V-neck woollen sweater, navy jeans, black slip-on leather shoes and a heavy white shower-proof anorak, listened to Eric's opening remarks, then leaned back in his chair, folded his arms and gazed at the room's white ceiling.

An unusually nervous-looking Josie Harold guided a twitching forefinger between her grey polo-neck cotton sweater and the back of her perspiration-damp neck. Her other attire was calm seasonal clothes: cream thick crew-neck woollen sweater over the polo-neck cotton garment provided warmth. Substantial beige cord trousers and brown lace-up sturdy leather walking shoes completed her outfit.

Eric, hands clasped while in thought, looked at Jimmy Elson.

Jimmy smiled, acknowledging the unspoken sign, eyed Ray Glover and said, 'Considering the strangeness of the situation, we require further information regarding what happened on that Friday morning, the 27th of October.'

A silent Ray Glover stared at Jimmy for a several seconds.

Jimmy, unsettled by Ray Glover's gaze, looked at his case notes for several seconds and then asked: 'Do you have anything to add to the previous statements you made to the police, Dr Glover?'

A composed Ray Glover, fashioning no discernible body language, remained silent.

Jimmy Elson glanced again at his case notes, then raised his head slowly and, focusing on Ray Glover's eyes, said in a soft, convincing tone: 'Mrs Amy Coleman and,' casting Josie Harold a smile, said, 'she and Mrs Harold have provided us with statements regarding your professional and,' a long pause then, after simulating a cough, continued: 'your association with them.' He stopped speaking again for a couple of seconds then, raising his voice slightly, added: 'in the wide-ranging meaning of association.' He looked at Ray Glover.

No response.

Jimmy glanced at Eric Bolton.

Eric took two documents out of his case file, placed them on his desk, checked the contents and then told Ray Glover: 'Please read these,' he glanced at Josie and Kelly as he handed Ray the papers, 'statements provided by Mrs Coleman and Mrs Harold.' He looked at Ray and said, 'Your comments please, Dr Glover.'

'What they say is true,' an unperturbed Ray Glover said, 'they were two grieving widows, required comfort, emotionally and physically. Neither was a patient, hence no professional advice was given, purely friendship, both women seemed satisfied, they didn't complain.'

Eric looked at Amy and Josie.

Neither spoke.

Eric turned to Ray and alleged: 'You hypnotised both women, took advantage of their vulnerability.'

Ray Glover shook his head. 'No, Chief Inspector; they approached me, wanted my advice.'

'Did you charge them a fee?'

A deadpan Ray said, 'I was rewarded, Chief Inspector.'

A sneering Eric, a hint of annoyance in his voice, chided Ray: 'You exploited their grief in a ruthless fashion.'

Ray Glover, unruffled, answered in a soft voice: 'There was no aggression, mentally or physically.' He spread his hands on his thighs. 'I provided a service, one which both women had sought. Nothing odious took place.'

Eric looked at Kelly Glover and, in a soft voice, asked her: 'Were you aware of your husband's contact with Mrs Coleman and your aunt?'

An ashen-faced Kelly looked at the floor and then, in a quiet, broken voice, said, 'No, Chief Inspector; I took little interest in his work, and had no idea as to what his private practice entailed. Although we were only married for less than twelve months, we went our separate, professional, ways.'

'Were you aware of his expertise in hypnotherapy and hypnosis?'

Kelly nodded, then said, 'I was aware that this can be an additional branch in anaesthesia, albeit an option in the training and the teaching of the speciality, procedures to lessen patients' anxieties before they undergo surgery.'

'Did he hypnotise you?'

'If I became obsessed with poetry, which was often, and especially the poem that depicts phenomena on Criccieth beaches. He tried to obliterate my concept and thoughts,' a short pause, then: 'he didn't succeed.'

Eric checked the time. Five past noon. 'We'll break for lunch. Snacks and hot drinks are available. We meet back here at one-thirty.'

Alan Reed and the two WPCs escorted the interviewees out of the room and then Eric told his colleagues: 'Have some food, try and make sense out of what we've heard and then we meet in the incident room at one o'clock.'

46

'I'm confused,' an exasperated Eric announced as he and his colleagues entered the incident room. He removed his jacket, hung it over the back of his chair, sat and opened his case file.

Jimmy Elson and Glyn Salmon sat opposite their boss, opened their case files and, appreciating his frustration, remained silent.

'It's a bloody circus,' was Eric's further loud remark. He thumped the desk top twice with the side of one hand and then asked aloud: 'Have I, have we, been listening to a load of verbal manure this morning? Do the people we interviewed think they can fool the police?'

Silence followed for a few moments, then Jimmy Elson fractured the tense aura: 'What we heard this morning from the three defies rational human conduct.'

Eric glared at the ceiling, then told Glyn: 'What did we witness? Are we any the wiser as to Kelly Glover's past and present history. We know she's obsessed with this particular poem by Robert Graves and that Ray Glover asserts she's detached from reality.' He leaned back in his chair, looked at Glyn Salmon and asked him: 'Your thoughts?'

A forthright Glyn declared: 'Stage-managed; remember and consider Kelly's interest in amateur dramatics: is she savouring a studied theatrical role?'

Eric then asked him: 'What of Ray Glover?'

'Recollect last Saturday when we questioned Ray Glover: has he practised hypnotherapy on his wife? Is the poem a stimulus for him to control her? Is she deluded?' Glyn gave out a long, deep sigh and then continued in his candid manner: 'She is described as being hallucinated and vulnerable to an intimation by her husband. He has beguiled her emotions and her thoughts, manoeuvred and controlled her compulsion and convictions for particular poetry,' a pause, then: 'are we, as I suggested last Saturday morning, witnessing a well-crafted confidence trick? If that is true, what is the motive or motives for such? I remind myself of the main motives in any crime: love, money, emotional upsets and jealousy. Is Kelly playing the spurned bride or does she have her own agenda?'

Silence followed Glyn's words, his colleagues reflecting on his words.

A tense Eric cracked the hush: 'A complicity -' a knock on the door interrupted him.

'Come in.'

A pale Iwan Drew, head bowed, ambled in.

Eric rose from his chair, helped Iwan to remove his anorak and then guided him to a chair opposite him.

Silence again.

Iwan raised his head slowly, fished his notepad from his jacket's pocket and looked at Eric, then at everyone else. Didn't speak.

'Take your time, Iwan,' Eric said, 'I'm sure it's been a harrowing time for everyone in Harlech.'

Iwan, struggling to speak, described the situation 'Both parents were shocked and distressed; their only son, a devoted police officer and athlete is dead, couldn't believe what's happened. I tried to describe the situation inside the cave, that he'd been dead for possibly thirty-six hours. No sign of violence and that we await reports from the forensics team. I explained that the coroner is aware of the facts and that he'll contact them when he receives further and detailed info. They cried profusely. I explained that, in view of the delicate nature of the death, the police would be grateful if they would not divulge the news to anyone until they heard from us or from the coroner.' He coughed.

Eric fetched him a glass of water.

Iwan gulped it down and then continued speaking in a solemn voice: 'I asked if there were any other relatives; there are none, only the parents and Roger-a tiny family.' He stopped speaking then, a tear appearing in each eye, said, 'You can imagine the psychological turmoil they are experiencing.' Another pause, then Iwan said, 'Before leaving I told them they could contact us if they need help.'

Eric spoke in a sombre voice: 'It was difficult, Iwan, but I thank you. Of course we'll provide all the support they require. There's nothing we can do until we hear from forensics.' He looked at his colleagues.

They agreed with Eric's sentiments.

Eric then told Iwan of the morning's deliberations, that the interviews would resume at one-thirty and added: 'in view of your stressful experience, I suggest you try and get something to eat.' He emphasised: 'Don't mention anything about this to other members of the staff,' then added: 'if you feel up to it, you're welcome to join us in interview room two at one-thirty.'

A silent Iwan rose from of his chair, collected his anorak, thanked everyone and walked slowly out of the room.

Despair filled the incident room for several moments once Iwan had left, then Eric looked at Glyn Salmon and said. 'I asked you, just as Sergeant Drew entered the room, if you believe Ray Glover and the three women are involved in a complicity.'

Glyn nodded and said, 'It's my top option, sir.'

Eric scanned the wall clock and declared: 'One-ten. We'll have a toilet break then meet in interview room two in twenty minutes.'

47

The two WPCs, Alan Reed and the interviewees, were outside interview room two when the three CID officers arrived.

Eric ushered everybody in, gestured to chairs, and then welcomed everybody. Switching on the tape recorder he said, 'The time is approaching one-thirty; we'll now continue the interviews.' He summarised the morning's conversations, then turned to Kelly and said, 'You are now reminded of your answers to my questions; please confirm that you are aware of your husband's expertise in hypnotherapy and hypnosis?'

A tense Kelly threw him a positive nod.

Eric thanked her and then said, 'when I asked you if your husband ever hypnotised you, the answer you gave was that he did if you became obsessed with the poem depicting phenomena on the Criccieth beaches. You were of the opinion that he wanted to obliterate such visions from your mind, but you said he wasn't successful.'

Kelly, remaining silent, nodded in agreement.

Eric noted her reaction, then checked his case file, looked at the two WPCs and, in an understanding voice, asked Kelly: 'Do you still see the activities on the beaches?'

'I do, sir.'

'When was the last time?'

'Two days ago, early morning, I couldn't sleep, so I got up early, went into the kitchen…it was before six; though blurred by the weather, I saw numerous lights on the foreshore.'

A dumfounded silent Eric looked at his colleagues.

Astonishment detailed their facial expressions.

Eric coughed, had a drink of water and then asked Kelly: 'Are you certain? It was still dark.'

'The six o'clock news bulletin came on the radio. I agree, it was black outside, but I saw lights coming down on the beach from the back of the peninsula, presumably the caves on the south beach, not from the Criccieth side. They moved towards the sea, then returned and disappeared at they moved behind the peninsula.'

'Did you mention this to your husband or your aunt?'

'No, they would dismiss it as make-believe.' She stopped speaking, looked at Eric and stressed: 'I did see the lights; they moved between the beach and the sea, then along the beach before disappearing behind the headland. Robert Graves was immersed in mythology, he regarded the sightings as being fascinating and easily misread. He was of the opinion that myths were seldom simple...... and never irresponsible. He reckoned that one function of a myth is to justify an existing social system and account for traditional rites and customs.' She coughed.

Helen handed her a mug of water.

A hyped-up Kelly drank it in two gulps and continued: speaking 'Myths of origin and eventual extinction vary across the world's climatic regions, but even these are altered or discarded. Robert Graves was of the opinion that myth is a dramatic summary of recent invasions, migrations, dynastic changes, admission of foreign cult and social reforms.'

'How long did you look at the beach?'

'About half an hour; my aunt Josie entered the kitchen and asked me if I wanted anything to eat or drink. I wasn't hungry or thirsty. She left.'

Jimmy Elson took over the questioning: 'It was dark everywhere -'

Kelly interjected: 'Just before seven I saw lights again, approaching the beach from the back of the peninsula. Were they welcoming someone, or they were leaving?' She looked at Jimmy. 'I believe you all have a copy of the poem, although the time of the day and the year differ from now, I'll quote the part that alludes to what I saw.'

Eric, Jimmy and Glyn fished out their copies, then Eric said, 'Okay, please quote the relevant passage.'

Kelly's voice, having gained strength and confidence, began: 'This section begins at line thirty-five; it relates to Robert Graves's vision of Harlech's Silver Band playing on the beach. Robert Graves did admit that the poem was intended to be a satire, a pleasing joke that's possibly associating a parable with reality. I now quote:

"Welcoming the things. They came out on the sand,
Not keeping time to the band, moving seaward
Silently at a snail's pace. But at last
The most odd, indescribable thing of all,
Which hardly one man there could see for wonder,
Did something recognizably a something?'
'Well, what?'
      'It made a noise.'
            'A frightening noise?'
'No, no.'
      'A musical noise? A noise of scuffling?'
'No, but a very loud, respectable noise-
Like groaning to oneself on Sunday morning
In Chapel, close before the second psalm.'"

Kelly sighed and, in an emotional voice, admitted: 'I visualised that part of the poem when I was looking at the black expanse.'

Iwan Drew entered the room, sat and nodded to Eric.

Glyn Salmon asked Kelly: 'Did you hear any sounds, screams?'

'No, the flat is situated some distance from the peninsula, Gulls only, although they are not usually present or heard at this time of the morning, especially in the darkness. They were screeching, that also, is unusual for them. Something had disturbed them.'

Eric thanked Kelly, then turned, looked at Ray Glover, then Josie Harold and asked: 'What time did you both enter the kitchen?'

'The eight o'clock news was ending on the radio,' a confident Josie Harold said, 'Kelly was standing at the window looking out over the bay; I asked again if she wanted something to eat or a cup of tea; she had a glass of water.'

'Did she mention anything regarding her experience?'

Ray Glover answered Eric: 'She was quiet, not disturbed; tense, yes, but morose.'

A trembling and unsteady Kelly rose slowly out of her chair.

Helen Manning placed an arm around Kelly's shoulder.

Kelly looked at her husband, at Josie, then the CID and uniform officers and, in a quivering voice, full of anger, said aloud:. 'Not one of you believes me.' Sniffling, she and, in a quiet tone: 'I challenge you to visit the caves next time I see these phenomena; they'll be present again during neap tides. Check the state of the tides during the next few days and weeks.' She looked at Helen.

Helen Manning helped her back into a chair.

Eric wrote several notes and then addressed Kelly: 'You are obviously upset, I suggest you return to the flat with your husband and Mrs Harold.' He gestured with a nod of his head to Alan Reed and the two WPCs, then told Kelly: 'The uniform officers will take you home.' He then said to Ray Glover: 'We want to inspect your car,' he paused then added: 'you can give us permission or we'll obtain -'

'Be my guest,' Ray said and handed Eric the keys, 'there's a laptop in the boot. I couldn't concentrate to use it under the present circumstances.' He then took out a smartphone from the inside pocket of his anorak and handed it to Eric.

Eric thanked him. 'We'll check your car tomorrow; afterwards we'll arrange for an officer to take samples from it. Your laptop and smartphone will be taken to IT forensics in Bangor.' He opened a desk drawer, took out a sheet of blank paper plus a pencil and passed them to Ray.

'Passwords for the laptop and smartphone please, Dr Glover.'

Ray obliged.

Eric thanked him, then advised the group: 'My WPCs will visit you regularly; you remain in Criccieth until our inquiries are complete. I do not anticipate any developments over the weekend.' He turned to Kelly. 'Forensics have returned your bag of washing, Mrs Glover; please collect it on the way out. Towels are missing; discuss that with your husband.'

Eric switched off the tape recorder, then signalled with a wave of a hand to Alan and the two WPCs and told them: 'Report here when you return from Criccieth.'

The three escorted Ray Glover, Kelly and Josie Harold out of the room.

Eric, after thinking in the ensuing silence for several seconds, lifted the phone and called IT forensics, explained the situation and then said, 'PC Reed will deliver all to you tomorrow morning before ten. He then told his colleagues and Iwan Drew: 'We return to the incident room; although the evidence supplied still lacks outline, there's much for us to discuss.'

48

Eric Bolton waited for everybody to settle in their seats in the incident room and then said, 'Okay, gentleman, what are your observations?' 'He looked at Iwan Drew and advised: 'Sergeant Drew came into the room as the interviewing ended, so I'll recap for his and everyone else's benefit.'

Five minutes later Eric looked at his colleagues and asked again: 'Your opinions on the session?'

Jimmy Elson, scratching the side of one temple in thought, said, 'I'm unable to feel any compassion towards any of the interviewees: Ray Glover was unaffected, in fact, looked as if he enjoyed the session, playing with words and emotions. My opinion of him? A callous selfish individual who gains his kicks by his ability to manoeuvre people into his psychologically-orientated lair, an insensitive maze.' Jimmy glanced at his notes and then added: 'Josie Harold lacked emotion and, despite the serious nature of the interrogations, wasn't overwhelmed. She maintained a composed staid attitude most of the time,' a pause of several seconds and then added: 'she required the attention of a younger man, one with power. She enjoyed his company and, as to their carnal relationship. I reckon it remains active.'

No response, everybody waiting for Jimmy to continue.

'As to Kelly Glover? That woman is enigmatic. What are my feelings towards her? I have one concerning her whacky behaviour; I'm inclined to believe her husband; that she is hallucinated -'

'Or she's a clever dame,' an exasperated Glyn Salmon interjected, 'and, depending on tides and their times, I'm interested in viewing inside the caves again,' he grinned, 'to quell Kelly's scrutiny and her interpretation of this particular poem's anatomy. I'm of the opinion that she's visited the beach and caves without her husband or her aunt's knowledge...... she might have seen and spoken with Roger Young; influenced him so that he didn't report back to his colleagues.' A shrug of his shoulders, then: 'I believe that scenario is a possibility, especially with the present small tides.'

Iwan Drew raised his hand to speak.

Eric noticed. 'Your views please, Iwan.'

'Info for DC Salmon; you'll find the tide heights and times for the month in *The Weekly Wanderer*; it's printed on Saturday and is available in all the local newsagents.'

Glyn nodded and gave Iwan a thumbs-up sign.

Iwan acknowledged Glyn's gesture with a smile and then carried on speaking: 'I haven't been privy to all that's been discussed, but I've had time to try and develop an objective attitude towards this weird set-up.' He looked at Eric.

He was answered with a smile for him to continue.

'A question for us to consider,' Iwan said; 'is Kelly, when quoting Robert Graves's poetry, telling us how Ray manipulated women? Were the people in the poem guided into and out of the caves? If so, by whom? Then there is the band music on the beach. Ray Glover factored music into his ruse.'

Jimmy Elson suggested: 'Background music in his consulting room and maybe in women's homes, it'll be interesting to see what music he has on his laptop.'

Glyn said, 'Josie Harold maintained that he played background music while he hypnotised her.' He looked at Iwan and said, 'That might answer your question as to the significance, albeit weird, of the music on the beach.'

Iwan thought for a few seconds, then declared: 'It's feasible.'

Eric said, 'Despite Amy Coleman's absence today, I'd appreciate views on this young widow -'

Jimmy Elson chipped in: 'She's known Ray Glover for years and has remained his friend since her husband died.' A wry grin, then: 'I believe, from what she said when interviewed, it's been more than a friendship for a long time, admitted being hypnotised by Ray Glover and, although they both denied having an intense relationship during the initial interviews……. they had sex. She displayed no remorse, accepted that he had manipulated her, but it seems to me she was a frustrated female and wanted sexual satisfaction. A cold evaluation? Maybe, but she isn't the first one to succumb to amorous advances following a bereavement, and she won't be the last.' He grimaced, then stated: 'Regardless of her statement that the affair had finished, I consider that a pleasure-seeking relationship prevails.'

Eric commented: 'When we first spoke with Ray Glover he was adamant that he wanted refuge that Thursday night in Amy Coleman's flat; denied there was any sexual involvement with her. However, the history, the evidence and human nature being what it is, did anybody believe that?'

Glyn Salmon professed: 'I didn't. An enthusiastic relationship was obvious, thus the reason for his presence there and not with his wife of twelve months. An avid bond with Amy,' Glyn sniggered before adding: 'he's still able to persuade her.'

Eric, looking at his case notes, said, 'According to Amy, Ray Glover realised that, after many sexual encounters, he became remorseful and ended the loving last March when they no longer had the privacy of the quiet beaches they'd had during the previous months. The only people they saw were dishevelled beings entering and leaving the caves, youngsters who were probably high from drugs, alcohol, or both.'

Jimmy Elson piped up: 'Yet, after that passionate affair I wonder if either wanted it to end?'

Eric noted Jimmy's words then said, 'everybody please consider Josie Harold's story: when interviewed she admitted that following hypnosis Ray Glover dictated her emotions and she succumbed to his desires. Later, having insight into and perceiving the state of play, she threatened him: if he didn't stop his activities she'd inform his wife. That, according to her, ended their relationship -'

Glyn voiced aloud: 'I doubt that.'

Eric raised a hand to acknowledged Glyn's thought, then said, 'A forthright Josie said that after she'd threatened him he no longer oversaw her mind and body and admitted that she was relieved that she'd defined and explained Ray Glover's actions. She, as you all heard at the time, described him as being a female predator.' Eric checked his notes once more and said, 'Towards the end of the interview Josie Harold, having reflected on her experience, uttered that she wasn't convinced that Kelly is disturbed psychologically.'

Seconds after Eric had finished speaking Alan Reed and the two WPCs returned.

Eric greeted them, then asked: 'Any problems?'

Alan answered with a definite 'No, sir, they were all subdued, glad to get back to the flat.'

Next from Eric: 'I have additional work for you tomorrow morning, PC Reed.'

A silent Alan looked at him.

'We'll take samples from Ray Glover's car early tomorrow morning and return here. I then want you to deliver the packages, plus the laptop and smartphone to IT forensics in Bangor, to be there by ten o 'clock.'

Alan nodded.

Eric looked at the two PWCs.

Helen said: 'Norma and I decided we'll keep away from the flat over the weekend; I'll call there on Monday morning, didn't specify a time.'

'Good, 'Eric said then, looking directly at the WPCs, mentioned: 'You both noticed Kelly and Josie's facial reactions and body languages when questioned. So, I'm hoping you'll inform me of your feminine perceptions.' He looked at Norma. 'WPC Taylor, your understandings of Kelly Glover's response pleas.'

'Tense, still admits to seeing something on the beaches, says she saw moving lights on Wednesday. Is there any significance in that this was the day before Gareth Young died?' A short pause as she considered her evaluation, then: 'what she describes is, to me, inexplicable. I have neither an association nor a dissociation of her thoughts, sceptical about what she pronounces and her interpretation of such. However, most riddles have a rational explanation.'

Eric thanked her, then he turned to Glyn. 'Please enlighten WPC Taylor of your hypothesis, Glyn.'

Glyn described his views on Kelly's possible meeting or meetings with Roger Young on the beach.

Norma smiled at him. 'We think alike.'

Eric looked at Helen. 'Your observations please, WPC Manning.'

'Considering Kelly's academic history. A senior lecturer in English literature in a college in Manchester, you would think that she is a confident, self-sufficient woman. She has command of her particular subject. Married to a successful anaesthetist, they are financially independent. The marriage is on a rocky course. Do we know why? Diverse professional cultures led them to separate pathways. Is her body language genuine? After all,' a shrug if her shoulders, then a pointed remark: 'she partakes in amateur dramatics. I'll not enlarge on that. Is she a member of a subterfuge, one which we have considered but not tried to analyse? Are her answers to questions, plus her body language, tinged with theatrical melodrama? My jury is still out on that.'

Eric wrote a few notes in his desk pad, then raised his head, sighed and said, 'We'll call it a day. My colleagues and I, plus PC Alan Reed, will be here tomorrow morning. We all meet back in the incident room at nine on Monday.'

49

Ray Glover's Mercedes car was searched and samples taken for forensic analysis before eight-thirty on Saturday morning.

Eric Bolton and his team arrived back in Madogton police station at eight-fifty.

PC Alan Reed was waiting for them.

Five minutes later the samples plus Ray Glover's laptop and smartphone were on their way to IT forensics in Bangor and were delivered at nine-forty five.

Alan Reed's return journey on a cold, dry, part cloudy morning was a leisurely affair He was back at the station at ten-forty.

On entering the station the duty officer told Alan Reed that Chief Inspector Eric Bolton and his colleagues were in the incident room.

Alan reported his morning's work to the CID officers.

Eric thanked him, then: 'check your morning's duties with Iwan Drew,' and added: 'we meet again on Monday morning.'

Alan Reed left.

Eric Bolton looked at the evidence board again, wrote a few notes in his desk pad and then told Jimmy Elson and Glyn Salmon. 'Have a break from this, be back here on Monday morning.'

He then dialled Iwan Drew's number, updated him and added: 'I must make one phone call and then I'll be leaving, see you on Monday morning; thank your team members for their help.'

Eric scribbled notes on a sheet of A4 paper, checked his scribe, then picked up the phone and dialled.

It was answered on the third ring. 'Howard Baker.'

'Good morning, Howard -'

'How are you, Eric? You either have news for me … or you're about to request further investigative work from me.'

Eric chuckled. 'Courtesy call, Howard, to update you.'

'Intriguing,' was Howard's remark after listening to Eric, 'Ray Glover had a satisfying time with the women. You say that the relationships, as far as you are aware, have ended?'

Eric, sensing hesitancy in Howard's speech, said, 'You have a thoughtful pitch in your tone, suggesting disbelief, one that epitomises an investigative journalist. What have you discovered, Howard?'

'I've received interesting info relating to your inquiry, I'm still assimilating it, confirming the facts before I phone you on Monday morning.'

'Howard -'

'A reliable source, Eric, but I'm yet to substantiate what I've been told.'

'Don't trash my weekend, Howard. A police officer is dead and, because the reason for his demise is unestablished, the incident hasn't been reported to the media. I'm desperate for any scrap of info that might prove helpful.'

Howard spoke slowly: 'Kelly Glover, in addition to her hobby of amateur dramatics, embarked, las year, on a course that taught the art of hypnosis. Why?' I assume, from what you've told me, it relates to her husband's private practice. Did Kelly sense something that hinted the marriage had become a non-event. A woman scorned?'

'Hypnosis?' was a bemused Eric's retort. 'Hypnosis? Are you certain, Howard?'

'I'll paraphrase the adage: if you can't beat them, join the gang,' a quietly-spoken Howard said, and then he advised: 'Think about it; figure how this quirky bit of news links up to the story's format.' A cough, then Howard pronounced: 'I'll contact you on Monday morning.'

50

The beginning of November's third week was dry and sunny, but spoilt by a near-freezing temperature, when Iwan Drew stopped at a small general stores-cum-newsagents.

The shop owner told him that tide tables were available on page two of the local newspaper, but if he required the annual tide times, a small booklet was available, price of two pounds.

Iwan bought the small booklet, thanked the owner and continued his journey to Madogton police station, arriving a few minutes before eight-thirty. Iwan handed Alan Reed the thin book. 'Tide details for this year.'

Alan thanked his boss. 'I'll write this month's times on the evidence board.'

Iwan smiled at him and proceeded to his office.

Eric Bolton arrived at the police station at eight-forty and checked with the duty officer at the front desk. There were three letters for him, no phone calls, and then he strode into the incident room.

Alan Reed was updating the evidence board. 'Good morning, sir.'

A shivering Eric, huddled inside a heavy fleece-lined jacket, nodded. 'If you say so, Alan; it's warm in here.' He smiled, then, pointing to the board, asked Alan. 'What are you recording?

Alan explained.

'Good,' Eric said, 'my colleagues will be here shortly.'

Eric removed his jacket, hung it on the back of his chair, sat and then he opened the mail: nil of note. He placed the contents in the out-tray and asked Alan: 'Any news over the weekend?'

'None,' a despondent Alan announced.

Eric scanned the board, wrote a few notes in his desk pad, then rose from his chair and ambled to the board. He stared at it for several moments and then turned to Alan. 'Meticulous,' then: 'you keep this board updated to inform the CID team, yet you haven't been involved in any of the interviews.' Eric, scratching the side of his nose, said, 'You have been paramount in accumulating information appertaining to this inquiry.' He grinned at Alan. 'What are your thoughts on this mystifying situation? I'd value your views.'

'I've reorganised the board, sir, try to make the events easier to understand; I agree that the evidence lacks a sequential pattern.' Alan picked up a marker pen and, following seconds of reflection, said, 'The board has been extended into three sections: names of the main participants are on the first section; the middle segment relates to the happenings starting on the Thursday night and, in the third part, I've tried to relate times with each individual's activities; for example, the time Ray Glover arrived in Amy Coleman's abode and the time Kelly Glover went into the garage that Friday morning and saw her husband on the floor. We know that her story is true because, Huw Davey, a chef in a local hotel was walking to work.' He stopped speaking and looked at Eric.

Eric agreed and then said, 'Josie Harold was in Manchester when all this happened.'

'Correct, sir,' Alan said, adding: 'I'm not certain about Amy Coleman's story; she seems protective of Ray Glover.' A sigh, then: 'Do we believe Ray Glover's stories? Both Josie Harold and Amy Coleman described their thought-provoking contacts with him. What game was he, or perhaps still is, playing with the women, plus his wife?' A short pause, then Alan asked: 'Is he playing each against the other two?'

Eric tapped a pencil on the evidence board. 'I'll note your thoughts, Alan, the problem -' the door opened and DS Elson and DC Salmon entered.

Everyone greeted one another and then Eric summarised his chat with Alan and, flicking a hand at the evidence board, said, 'This is updated including tide times until the end of the month.'

Eric switched on the kettle and said, 'We'll have a hot drink while we consider the evidence.'

A mug of hot coffee was handed to everyone and then Eric said, 'On the evidence collected, which isn't much, it remains that we have no validation of the people's statements.' Irritation in his tone, he conceded: 'I find that remarkable.' He looked at the board again and then said to Glyn Salmon: 'You suggested there could be a ploy, but why and what's the motive, does it involve basic primal emotions?' He shook his head, 'I have a gut feeling, albeit weak, that this is not a hoax; one person has stage-managed this, but irksome questions remain: who it is the instigator and what, actually, is the reason?' He looked at Glyn Salmon and Jimmy Elson and said, 'I asked PC Reed about his interpretation of the events since that initial weekend.' He summarised Alan's assessments, then looking at him, said, 'Finish your reasoning, Alan.'

Alan, speaking in a clear confident tone, explained: 'I've studied the info for a considerable time and considered the paltry evidence: Kelly Glover is the dominant player. She's been painted as being deluded,' a long pause.

Eric stared at him.

Alan continued in an assertive mode: 'She's a clever woman, devious even; although I'm without proof for my thoughts, I reckon she's the prime contributor to,' a snigger, 'taxing domestic settings. She's physically and mentally restless, suffers, maybe, from an unsettling life,' then: 'is her wounding sufficient for her to develop destructive actions?'

Eric looked at his colleagues and asked: 'Any views on what we've heard?'

Neither Glyn nor Jimmy commented.

Eric thanked Alan. 'Finish your drink then report to Sergeant Drew.'

51

Eric Bolton walked to the evidence board, picked up a black marker pen, ticked each person's name and then challenged his two colleagues. 'Your opinions on Alan Reed's summations, please.'

Jimmy Elson and Glyn Salmon agreed that it was a comprehensive look at what appeared to be ongoing disharmony in the Glover household, and then Glyn said, 'Alan's dissection of the situation is interesting, especially his daunting assessment of Kelly Glover's character.'

Eric turned and asked Jimmy Elson 'Has your incisive mind evaluated this bizarre theatre?'

'No player has yet portrayed a dominant role in the story. Each, in his or her own right, controls a particular phase,' he paused to consider and then said, 'it starts with Kelly Glover witnessing the apparent death of her husband, and from there we've accumulated internecine mistrust, a suggestion of deceit and lying witnesses.' Tapping a pencil on his notepad, Jimmy asked: 'Is there a link between each individual, perhaps a conduit regarding their shams as to the motive for their actions? It defies logic at the present moment.'

'Your thoughts, Glyn.'

'I'm sceptical of the obtuse domestic scenario, regarded it as being dysfunctional, but then, that description can apply to many domestic environs in the twenty-first century.'

Eric, unsure of Glyn's opinion, stared at him and said, 'I am also, concerned with each individual. Your views are noted.' A sigh, then: 'Are these people's actions manufactured, illusionary whereby they deceive, play-act to confuse us and,' after exhaling, shook his head several times, ended with: 'although I believe it not to be desultory, it is a harmonising schedule that defies explanation?'

'I'm only repeating what I've always maintained, sir,' Glyn said. He opened his case notes and explained: 'From the outset of this investigation I've voiced my suspicions regarding the sparse evidence. I believe it's a well-rehearsed charade but,' a sneer, then: 'I have no idea as to what they are attempting to achieve; realty related to myth? I'm unable elucidate a motive, not even fantasise one.' He turned over a page of his notes and declared: 'I've followed the events, and more recently the interrelation between the people we've interviewed. We've spent much time trying to ascertain if there is an ongoing connection within the group. Are they misdirecting us? Is there something going on in the caves? We haven't looked at that possibility.' Glyn looked at Eric, sighed and then leaned back in his chair.

A despondent Eric looked at the evidence board once more and admitted: 'We've heard many theories as to what has happened, why people are behaving in a confusing manner and reacting in a particular sequence to various stimuli. None has provided us with a pathway we can follow and,' with conviction in his voice, told Glyn: 'in my experience, there has to be an underlying intention for what has happened and, I believe that personal aims dominate the drama.'

The phone rang.

Eric stopped speaking and lifted it. 'Chief Inspector Bolton -'

'Howard Baker, here, Eric; my return call as promised.'

'And?'

Kelly Glover attended that particular night school for nine months and obtained a diploma and a licence to practise hypnosis in March.'

Silence followed.

'Eric?'

'Sorry, Howard; I'm here, cogitating your news. Interesting; it throws a new aspect on the events here. Thanks, I'll keep you updated.' He ended the call and told his colleagues.

A stern-looking Glyn Salmon remarked: 'A new slant on the story, perhaps we should assess the evidence, view it from Kelly's role in this convoluted tale.'

Jimmy Elson thought aloud: 'Husband and wife with powers to hypnotise? That is interesting, could be important cogs in the mystery.'

Eric wrote a few notes in his desk pad and then said, 'We wait for Helen Manning to return from Criccieth and ask her to collect Kelly tomorrow morning.' He rose from his chair. 'We'll have a toilet break before I update Iwan Drew.'

The phone rang soon after they returned to the incident room. 'Can't even have a break for nature's calling,' was an annoyed Eric's remark.

He lifted the phone. 'Chief Bolton.'

Tim Wilding said, 'We've checked the morbid anatomy again, confirm there is no evidence of violence and no obvious cause for Roger Young's death. Toxicology is negative, but there was a low blood glucose reading, a significant hypoglycaemic level, metabolism was zero. In view of the other negative findings, hypoglycaemia could be the cause of death. No fluids or food, specifically carbohydrates, were found in the stomach; and the bladder was empty. The body lacked fuel for the increased metabolism required to counter the cold conditions inside the cave.'

Eric asked Tim Wilding: 'Are you suggesting he died from exposure in near-freezing conditions?'

'I'm assuming he saw something terrible, an occurrence that shocked him. He fell to the floor. No sign of a skull fracture, but the back of the brain has minimal bruising damage, which you sometimes see in boxers, but not enough to kill. Roger might have been concussed. Loss of consciousness is possible in those conditions. He lay on the cold floor for hours. My cause of death is cessation of body functions caused by prolonged hypothermia and hypoglycaemia.'

Eric thanked him.

'We'll continue to investigate,' Tim said, 'but, my team and I are not confident of detecting any new findings Examination of Roger's car was unhelpful. I'll keep you informed. A fax will follow soon,' and he ended the call.

Eric rose from his chair and said, 'I'll inform the coroner before I update Iwan. Afterwards, we'll check the evidence again while we wait for WPC Helen Manning's return. I expect her to be back around noon.'

The fax machine droned and dispensed several pages.

Eric printed copies of Tim Wilding's report, handed one to each colleagues.

The coroner, Eifion Pask, declared he'd open the inquest into Roger Young's death at ten o'clock next Tuesday in Pwllheli Magistrates' Court and that the body could be released for interment.

Eric then dialled an internal phone, updated Iwan and told him he wanted more help from WPC .Helen Manning.

Iwan said, 'I'll phone Roger's parents, explain the forensics findings and that I'll represent the force at the inquest and the funeral. I'll visit them soon.'

Eric nodded. 'Good man, I appreciate your empathy. Please contact the parents now and then I want you and WPC Norma Taylor to be present here when Helen Manning arrives.'

52

Helen Manning arrived at the flat in Criccieth a few minutes before eleven o'clock on a calm, sunny, but bitterly cold, November morning.

Amy Coleman greeted her.

'Please remove your coat,' Kelly said, 'hang it on the hook in the hall way.''

'Thank you, 'Helen said, removed her black three-quarter-length official police coat and hung it on the peg.

Amy Coleman took her into the lounge and waved to a chair. 'Please sit, PC Manning. Kelly is in the kitchen, she'll join us soon.'

Helen thanked her.

Silence filled the room while they waited for Kelly to return to the lounge. 'Sorry' she said, I was checking the fridge's contents.

Josie Harold and Ray Glover were in the flat. That was odd, Helen thought and then, knowing Ray Glover's history with Josie and Amy, was surprised that Kelly and Amy were together. She thought further for a few seconds and then, in her soft north Wales lilt, told Kelly: 'I'm here as per a directive from Chief Inspector Bolton.' She added: 'We have no further news,' then: 'the mystery remains enigmatic.' She looked at Kelly, noticed her trembling hands and her pale strained face-mental turmoil was evident. 'Any problems, Kelly?'

Kelly, looking at the floor, shook her head once and uttered an unconvincing 'No.'

Helen, determined to get some significant news for Eric Bolton, turned to Amy Coleman. 'How are things here? Please describe the atmosphere; it's important that we have a complete picture of the situation. We, the police, are dealing with a disturbing tale; therefore, we have to explore every avenue.'

'It remains tense,' an uneasy Amy said, slight hesitation in her voice, her slight north-east Wales accent highlighting tension.

Helen Manning asked her. 'Did you stay the night?'

Amy, her brain staggering from the effect of the question's express delivery, stuttered: 'No, Miss Manning, I arrived this morning around ten.'

Helen mulled the situation for a few moments: Why was Amy here? The initial impression she projected was a woman who kept her own counsel, rarely saw her Helen, her landlady 'What was the reason for your visit, Amy?'

'I couldn't sleep last night, thinking about recent events at the police station, how I, together with Josie, Ray and Kelly were, somehow, involved with one another, each contributing to the mystery.' She exhaled loudly, then: 'I heard you leave the house this morning, PC Manning, and then I showered, but I couldn't settle, had a mug of coffee, was anxious to discover the family's present structure, so I came here.'

A succinct: 'And?' from Helen.

'Ray and Josie are taking advantage of the crisp, benign November morning, ideal for walking along the beach.'

''Were you surprised they went out together?'

A pale Amy, one hand clutching a wad of paper tissues, stumbled again through her answer: 'Josie enjoys walking, tries get out every day, weather permitting, so I wasn't surprised she was out. However, as to Ray Glover accompanying her, that did surprise me, especially after his recent testimonies and Chief Inspector Bolton has arranged for a WPC to be present here this morning -'

Helen interjected: 'His absence troubles you, Amy?'

'Unprofessional.'

'It is,' Helen agreed, 'an insult to Chief Bolton's authority.'

Realising that this situation had been simmering for a considerable time, Helen decided to play a waiting game, discuss events that involved Amy and Kelly, reckoned that both had much information to further colour the drama,

How to gain this information was her prime object. She decided to use her power: she looked at Kelly and, in a firm voice, said, 'I'm not receiving any constructive information from you or Mrs Coleman; this morning's conversation is vague so, I'll question you. What time did your husband and your aunt inform you that they were going for a walk along the beach?'

Kelly's response was a quiet: 'A few minutes before ten.'

'What time did they actually leave?'

'Soon after ten.'

'To confirm,' Helen said, 'they left before Mrs Coleman arrived.'

Kelly nodded once. 'Yes, several minutes.'

Helen, glancing at her wristwatch, said, 'It is now eleven-twenty; what time do you expect them to return?'

A bothered Kelly, walked to and forth between kitchen and lounge while she considered her answer, then she looked out of the lounge window and, after studying the weather, said, 'About two hours. Today's weather is ideal for her to stroll along the long foreshore. They should be back around midday.'

'I'll wait,' Helen said. She turned to Amy and asked her: 'Have you any thoughts as to why Josie and Ray went out together?'

'No,' an uneasy Amy said, fidgeting with her trouser belt as she spoke: She shrugged her shoulders, opened her palms and then said, 'I repeat, I was astounded that they had gone and left Kelly, alone, in the flat.'

Helen looked at Kelly and then asked Amy: 'Are you worried about Kelly?'

A perspiring Amy said, 'Four peoples' lives are affected by this unimaginable story: Ray Glover and three women, one his wife. A complicated scenario that describes many undesirable aspects of life that were beyond my norm, in fact frightening. When I look back on how I became involved with Ray Glover; I regard it as been an uncanny experience, possibly the result an immature person. I suspected that Kelly felt isolated. The significant combination that included the general election and the terrorist attacks and other tragedies might have heightened her insecurity, -' she stopped speaking when the door to the flat opened.

'I'll leave my sand covered boots outside,' Josie shouted, then added: 'I'll deposit my hat and anorak in the bedroom and then I'll join you.'

Seconds later, and wearing moccasin-style slippers, a rosy-cheeked and smiling Josie walked into the lounge. Her smile disappeared when she saw Amy and Kelly's demeanour. She stood in the centre of the lounge and pronounced: 'A fine welcome, I must say.' She looked at Helen. 'Good morning, Miss Manning.'

A silent Helen nodded.

An impatient Josie asked: 'Well, is anyone going to speak?'

Helen described the last two hours and then said, 'I waited until you and Dr Glover returned from your walk.'

Josie's impatient gaze became a baffled stare as she asked: 'Is he not back, Miss Manning?'

Silence was Helen's immediate response, then she asked Josie 'Where did you go?'

'Along the foreshore, appreciating the face-tingling November weather. We walked to the peninsula, then Ray said he'd visit the caves again, gave no reason. I told him I'd see him back here and I continued to walk along the beach.'

'How much further did you go along the beach, Mrs Harold?'

'Sorry?'

'Time-wise;' a curt smile, then: 'the remainder of your walk from the peninsula and caves, and then back to your flat?'

'Half an hour's walk beyond the caves then another thirty minutes back and, then about twenty-minute stroll along the foreshore from the peninsular to here.' She frowned then, looking at her wristwatch, said, 'It's eleven forty-five now; my walk took less than two hours.'

'Did you see or hear any activities in or around the caves?'

Josie, scanning the floor for a few seconds, said, 'No,' then she glared at Helen and affirmed: 'I expected Ray to be back here at least half an hour before me.'

Helen, still eyeing Josie, said, 'There's a decent mobile signal near the peninsula, but we are unable to contact Ray-'

A riled Josie interjected: 'Because the police confiscated his phone.'

A thoughtful Helen, refraining from answering Josie's icy retort, looked out of the lounge window at the lengthy sandy expanse and, in a considerate, questioning voice, asked her: 'Any danger or problems from the tide?'

'No, they're still small, you are able walk along the foreshore at any time during the next few days.'

Helen pondered then, looking at her watch, said, 'It's approaching noon; I must report to Chief Inspector Bolton; update him.' A sense of trepidation galloping through her arteries, she looked at Amy, then at Josie and then stated: 'If Dr Glover hasn't returned by one o'clock, please use a payphone to contact me in Madogton police station.' Helen wrote in her notepad, and handed the sheet to Josie. 'This is the police station's phone number.' She thanked Kelly, Amy and Josie and then left.

53

Eric Bolton and his colleagues had just finished their snack lunch when Helen Manning and Norma Taylor entered the incident room. A tense lull, lasting several seconds, followed while both WPCs stood in front of the desk, arms at their sides, awaiting commands. Helen thought: Why such a silent status? What's happened.....or about to transpire?

Eric, a concerned look masking his face, spoke slowly: 'Please relax, ladies,' and pointing to chairs, said, 'please sit. I'll update you,' and then, checking the time, asked the women: 'Have you had lunch, a hot drink?'

Both shook their heads.

Eric dialled a number on the internal phone, explained the women's plight and said, 'ASAP please.'

Both women thanked him.

Eric leaned back in his chair and said, 'Forensics phoned this morning, elucidated their findings following further examination and investigations into Roger Young's death -' the door opened.

Iwan Drew brought meat rolls and two mugs of coffee into the room and placed them on the desk. 'I collected the meals when I saw WPC Manning return.' He smiled. 'Could be called fast food service, prompt sustenance service or cuisine come quickly, then: 'excuse me, I need to collect my notes.' He left the room and returned a minute later.

Iwan, holding an A4 pocket folder, apologised for the delay, the banter and then he took out a typed document from the folder and handed it to Eric. 'My report on my meeting with Roger Young's parents. I told them I'd take them to the inquest.'

'I appreciate your sentiments,' Eric said, 'Thank you. Please sit.'

Eric smiled at Helen and Norma. 'Your lunch, enjoy.'

Eric opened his case file and handed a copy of Tim Wilding's report to everyone. 'On the evidence he has, Tim Wilding believes Roger Young saw something, or an occurrence that shocked him, disbelief and then a severe response: Roger fell on to the floor. He became concussed. Although the skull hadn't been fractured the back of the brain had minimal bruising, damage you sometimes see in boxers. So, loss of consciousness was possible, bearing in mind the conditions inside the cave. Dr Wilding is of the opinion that death was caused by cessation of body functions from prolonged hypothermia and hypoglycaemia.' He looked at everyone. 'Any questions?'

Jimmy Elson spoke: 'We must accept the forensic team's inference. However, the big question is: what happened inside that cave?'

Eric agreed and, in a solemn voice, said, 'If we only had that info.' He turned and looked at Helen Manning, who was munching her tasty meat and tomato roll.

The final piece was swallowed quickly with the help of a swig of coffee. She licked her lips with a fleshy tongue, wiped her mouth with a tissue and then said, 'Sorry, sir.'

Eric smiled, then said, 'Digest the mouth-watering food.'

Helen gulped and then said, 'I'm fine now.'

Eric waited a few seconds and then said to her: 'Describe your morning in Criccieth.'

Helen opened her note pad. 'Unnerving, sir,' and then she stopped speaking -'

Eric, concern in his voice, interjected: 'Please explain.'

A hesitant Helen described the events in full. 'Amy's presence didn't seem to fit into the situation. Why had Ray Glover and Josie Harold gone walking together?' She flipped over a few pages and continued speaking in an emotive voice: 'Conversation with Amy Coleman and Kelly was difficult, an unreal atmosphere percolated throughout the room. I sensed foreboding. Did these two women know of an impending incident, wanted it kept secret?'

A silent Helen looked at Eric, then at Jimmy and Glyn, Norma and Iwan.

Iwan threw her a reassuring smile.

Helen continued in a low voice: 'The menacing vibes increased when Josie Harold returned. The conversation that followed lacked sense and direction.'

Eric threw Helen a rhetorical question: 'You left the flat soon afterwards?'

'Came back here to report.' She checked the time and then said, 'At one o'clock we'll know if Ray Glover has returned to the flat.' She stared at Eric, finished the remainder of her coffee then, after a few seconds' silence, asked him: 'What do we do if Ray Glover hasn't returned?'

Eric didn't answer; scribbled in his note pad and looked at his team members.

Glyn asked Helen: 'What time did Ray Glover and Josie Harold leave the flat to go walking?'

'A few minutes after ten.'

A deliberating Eric said, 'I'll answer your question regarding Ray Glover following the phone call at one o'clock, Miss Manning,' then, an afterthought, he looked at the evidence board and said, 'the tides are increasing during the next few days.'

Iwan agreed: 'until Saturday's new moon, then they begin to drop and continue in this mode for seven days, rising again towards the end of the month.'

Eric thanked him, checked the time, then looked at Helen Manning and said, 'Time for you to inform the front desk about your forthcoming phone call from Criccieth. Ask for it to be transferred here and, handing Helen the phone, told her: 'afterwards, we'll have a break.'

54

A minute after one o'clock the ringing phone fractured the uneasy silence in the incident room.

A discouraged Eric lifted the phone and, handing it to Helen, told her: 'I'll listen on the extension line; don't tell her I'm listening.'

'WPC Manning.'

Josie Harold was on the line.

'Yes, Mrs Harold; I'm with Chief Inspector Bolton.' She wrote notes while listening to Josie Harold's spiel, and then said, 'I'll inform Chief Bolton now, seek his advice and I'll phone you within the next ten minutes; the number please.'

Josie Harold gave it. 'It's a payphone in Criccieth's town centre.'

Helen handed the phone back to Eric Bolton and then he replaced the extension phone in its cradle.

Helen threw him a wanting stare; the last time she expressed such was with a boyfriend several years ago. She suppressed a smile. 'Sir?'

Eric informed every one of the news: 'It's three hours since Ray Glower left the flat; its lunchtime and. despite his physique, he would be keen to return to the warmth of the flat.'

Glyn considered aloud: 'I concur yet, from what I've discerned about Ray Glover, I wouldn't regard the present situation as being unusual. His behaviour and life style are without a pattern, he's devoid of self-regulation, and erratic is an apt adjective.' He gave out a long deep sigh and, looking at his colleagues, proclaimed in a firm voice: 'I suggest we wait until three o'clock then, if he hasn't returned, we comb the dunes, the immediate hinterland and the caves.'

Jimmy Elson agreed. 'No mobile phone, he might have had an accident, unable to walk.'

'A possibility,' Eric said and then he confirmed with Iwan. 'No problem with the tides.'

'High water around three this afternoon, but small tide. The water wouldn't approach the upper regions of the beach, certainly not the caves' entrances.'

A considering Eric, wringing his fingers, said, 'I'll wait until mid-afternoon,' and then he advised Helen: 'ask Mrs Harold to update us at three.'

Everyone agreed.

Eric handed Helen the phone.

'WPC Manning returning your call, Mrs Harold.' She explained the situation. 'The police have considered reasons as to why Dr Glover hasn't returned; please phone me again at three, then we'll decide if the police should become involved.'

Josie agreed; she'd phone the station soon after three.

Helen handed Eric the phone.

Eric replaced the phone in its cradle and, after gazing at everyone, asked: 'If Ray Glover hasn't returned at three do we regard him as being missing?'

Jimmy Elson was positive: 'Glyn suggested earlier that we scour the beach, the dunes and inside the caves. If there's no sign of him, yes is my answer to your question.'

'Glyn?' Eric asked.

'I can't think of anywhere else he would be. Why his absence?'

Eric gazed at Helen Manning. 'Did Amy Coleman mention Ray Glover?'

'No, sir, but wore a permanent frown, and her body language indicating concern. I asked myself: Why did she visit the flat following the recent interviews with their lurid revelations?'

'Feminine intuition, Miss Manning,' Eric said. 'Do we believe that Amy's relationship with Ray Glover is over or -'

'No,' was Glyn Salmon's assured interjection,' and, spreading his arms to gesture disbelief, added: 'a flame continues to flicker between them.'

Eric looked at the wall clock. 'Another hour before we hear from Josie Harold; I suggest we have a break to catch up on any outstanding work.' He turned to Iwan and said, 'Brief PC Reed of this meeting, tell him to organise the SUV. I have a gut feeling we'll be on the beach soon. We all meet back here at two-fifty.'

Iwan nodded and left with Helen Manning and Norma Taylor.

Eric looked at Jimmy Elson, then at Glyn Salmon and, dejection filtering through his voice, announced: 'I wish for the smallest scrap of evidence to fire up my tormented brain. I'm without any direction and thought as to what drives these people's minds.'

'All are concealing some weird secret, maybe secrets,' Glyn proclaimed. 'No one has provided us with a true statement. Instead, we've obtained a maze of stories that are impossible to circumnavigate. A dark veil covers their actions.'

'Jimmy?'

'The convoluted scenarios is beyond a conundrum. I'm without inspiration. Myth and truth seem to be the two main factors in this mystery. Is truth stranger than fiction? Do either conform to a river of life that provides truth and hedonism?'

Eric shook his head. 'The answer lies in how that poem is construed; I'm sure there are many analyses and opinions.' He looked at his colleagues. 'Take a break, see you later.'

55

Everyone was back in the incident room at two-forty-five.

The phone rang at five minutes past three.

Eric picked it up.

The front desk's officer said, 'Call for WPC Manning from a Mrs Harold, sir.'

'Okay, put her through.

Eric handed Helen the phone and then picked up the extension.

Helen listened to Josie, thanked her and said, 'Hold the line, Mrs Harold, Chief Inspector Bolton is here; has listened to your information and he'll advise you of our action.'

'Mrs Harold,' Eric's voice was strong and decisive, 'the situation must be worrying for Kelly and you. Nightfall isn't far away so I've decided to check the beach and surrounding areas, plus the caves, soon. In the meantime, please stay in the flat. We'll inform you of any developments. Either myself or a member of the CID team, plus a WPC, will talk with you this evening.'

Josie thanked him and ended the call.

Eric looked at the two WPCs. 'Stay in the station,' then to Iwan: 'Is the SUV ready?'

'In anticipation, PC Reed is waiting for us at the main entrance,' then Iwan advised: 'he has powerful torches for us, warm clothing plus flasks of coffee. The tide is not a problem for driving along the beach in the gloom.'

It was three-thirty with daylight drawing to a close when Alan Reed drove onto the beach.

Iwan declared: 'We'll be able to check inside the caves before nightfall.'

Eric told Alan Reed: 'Drive up to the mouths of the caves as previously, full beam on as we enter each one.'

Alan Reed handed everyone a powerful torches, gloves, a woollen hat and a heavy fleeced-lined anorak.

The caves on the Criccieth side of the peninsula were empty, no new signs of animal or human life having been inside recently.

On the peninsula's south side, the first two caves were empty, no sound from the tranquil tide, the only noise coming from the officer's echoing conversation.

Half way into the third cave a male body, face upwards, lay on the sandy floor. The officers walked up to the corpse and shone their torches on the man's face. It was Ray Glover.

'Déjà vu,' Eric proclaimed and then hurried back to the four-by-four. 'Radio-phone please, Alan.'

Eric informed Tim Wilding.

The forensics and the paramedics' teams would be there within the hour.

Eric Bolton then phoned Madogton police station, spoke with Helen Manning and Norma Taylor, described the finding and then said, 'Police activity on the beach might prompt members of the public to inform the media and the press. If the units contact the station, fob them off by saying that we are investigating reports of possible drug-related incidents, and that it might be on-going for several hours.' Eric completed the call and then told Alan. 'We'll have that coffee now; keep the vehicle's headlights on full beam.'

Alan Reed handed Eric two flasks.

Eric returned into the cave and informed his colleagues.

Alan followed him carrying two more flasks plus several plastic mugs.

Eric walked around the body as he drank his coffee. 'That look on his face, reminds me of Roger Young's expression.'

Iwan Drew agreed. 'Did Ray Glover witness a frightening incident?'

Jimmy Elson looked at Iwan.

Iwan stooped, looked at the body and, Roger Young's dead image tinting his thoughts, a cold shiver clasped his spine. He said, 'No evidence to suggest he was assaulted; his clothes are undisturbed.'

'Check his pockets,' Eric said.

A gloved Iwan them. 'A few coins, a wallet containing his IDs, plus several twenty and ten-pound notes. No keys.'

Eric nodded once and then looked at Glyn.

'Motive was not robbery,' Glyn said, then finished his coffee, handed Alan the empty mug, knelt onto to the cave's dry sandy floor and looked at Ray Glover's hands. 'No defensive marks to suggest a struggle.'

Jimmy Elson scrutinised Ray Glover's eyes, lips, jaws and then felt the limbs and thought aloud: 'He was last seen by Josie Harold at about eleven o'clock; that is nearly four hours ago. Rigor mortis is present; I believe he died soon after Josie Harold began her return walk to the flat...... about eleven-thirty.'

Jimmy stood, looked at everybody and, pointing at the cave's floor, said, 'Similar situation to when we examined Roger Young's body. Ray Glover hasn't moved from this position. There is no evidence of anybody else having been present.'

'Night has arrived,' Eric said, then told Iwan: 'Contact the station, update the WPCs, one of them will have to accompany me to Criccieth later.'

Iwan hurried to the SUV and notified Helen Manning and Norma Taylor.

Eric walked to the cave's mouth, the moon's weak power unable to modify the beach's blackness. No sign or sound of anyone nearby. He shone the torch's powerful beam into the cave again, walked several yards inside and looked at the craggy walls and ceiling. A sigh, producing a soft echo, prompted a thought: what the hell has caused two deaths here? He surveyed the scene for several minutes. A goose pimple rash crept over his upper body and he shivered. Viewing the cave's structure produced surreal thoughts in him-all lacking constructive ideas for the cavern's recent history. He left.

Outside, he arranged for the entrance to be cordoned off.

The forensic van and the paramedics' ambulance arrived at the cave's entrance at four-forty.

Clad in warm clothes, Tim Wilding's team approached Eric Bolton to be briefed.

The team's members got into their forensic garbs and Tony Simpson, guided by the police's four-by-four and the paramedics' ambulance headlights, walked with Edward Brown towards the body.

Numerous photographs later Tony Simpson left the scene.

Tim Wilding joined Edward Brown, made a cursory examination of the body and said, 'He was alive about eleven this morning, rigor is present,' then checking the temperature inside the cave, declared: 'two degrees; probably hasn't varied since this morning.'

Edward Brown inserted a probe into the liver; removed it several minutes later and checked the temperature. 'Taking the elements into the equation, the approximate time of death is around eleven-thirty.'

Ten minutes later the two forensic scientist emerged from the cave and approached Eric Bolton.

Edward Brown told him: 'The time of death is as DS Elson estimated.'

Tim Wilding gestured with a wave of one arm to the paramedics, told them to remove the body, and then added:

'We'll follow you soon,' and then to Eric Bolton: 'you will need positive ID before you inform the coroner. Kelly Glover will have to travel to our lab in Bangor; should have some news for you by tomorrow afternoon.'

Eric thanked him. 'I'll inform the coroner in the morning,' a deep sigh and then he added: 'I'll break the news to his widow this evening.'

Tim Wilding blinked and nodded once. 'A thankless job, Eric,' then the forensic team removed their garbs and left the scene.

Eric said, 'Arrange overnight duties, Iwan, flasks of hot drinks and a change of watch every four hours. Remove the tape at eight tomorrow morning.' He frowned, and then said, 'I wish to speak with the two WPCs.'

Iwan followed Eric's order and then told Alan Reed: 'Another journey to here later with essential provisions.'

Alan Reed raised his eyebrows, shaped his lips into a suggestion of a grin and then drove the CID officers and Iwan Drew back to Madogton police station.

56

The warmth inside Madogton police station was welcomed by everybody following the last few hours at the beach. The officers removed their warm over coats and entered the incident room.

Mugs of hot coffee on trays, carried by WPCs Helen Manning and Norma Taylor, were placed on the main desk. The recipients smiled.

Eric Bolton, after two sips of his hot drink, thanked the women and gestured with a twist of his shoulder to chairs. 'Please sit; I'll update you.' Afterwards he looked at the two WPCs. 'I need your help.'

Both women agreed to his request.

Eric checked the time. 'It's approaching six.' He buzzed Alan Reed on the internal phone, briefed him and then told him: 'We leave at six-fifteen.'

It was arranged.

Eric told the women: 'Be at the main door in time,' and they left the room.

More mouthfuls of coffee, then Eric swivelled his chair and addressed Iwan Drew: 'Update your staff, remind them not to divulge any of this operation to the media.' Then to Jimmy Elson and Glyn Salmon. 'Once you've finished your drinks, call it a day.' He added: 'My first phone call tomorrow morning is to the coroner; I'll see you here, usual time.'

Both men, glad of the directive, left.

Alone in the incident room, Eric, thinking over the scene inside the cave again, wrote down more memos in his desk pad then pondered: How would Kelly Glover react to the news? It wasn't the first time he'd informed someone of the death of a partner. His mind, still vibrating from the unreal situation, acted as a caution: this particular situation, however, was one he'd not experienced previously. There were many unexplained aspects to the case, hence the inquiry remained open to suggestions, even weird ones. Despite his experience in dealing with macabre circumstances, this was illusory. Unease galloped through his arteries as he considered how he should break the news to the widow. His reverie over, he deliberated and asked himself: Were, are Kelly Glover's actions gambits?

He jotted down more points of interest then, recalling past disagreeable situations, the initial response to his presence at the door was important. The affected person, he or she, knew that his demeanour and dismal expression signalled a disquieting situation. Dark news was forthcoming; the impending meeting with Kelly would be a heartfelt challenge.

Thirty-five minutes later Alan Reed parked the police vehicle at the front of the flat.

Eric and the two WPCs alighted, and then Eric told Alan: 'Leave now,' he checked his watch, 'Be back in thirty minutes.'

Alan Reed left.

Eric switched on his torch and led the way up the iron stairway to the flat's door. He fingered the doorbell.

The door was opened by Kelly. She invited Eric and the two WPCs inside and directed them to the lounge. Josie Harold and Amy Coleman were there.

Kelly, waving to the empty sofa, said to the police officers: 'Please sit,' and then she sat in an armchair.

Eric described the afternoon's events to Kelly, Josie and Amy and, beckoning with a nod of his head for the two WPCs to be near Kelly, said, 'We believe that the dead person is your husband, Dr Ray Glover.' He stopped speaking and waited for a response.

Alarmed, Amy Coleman and Josie Harold, standing near the door, had tense expressions accentuating a wide-eyed pale expanse, their hands covering their mouths to counter nausea and possible vomiting. Trembling and perspiring, they said nothing and stared at the floor.

A pregnant silence dominated the room's tense atmosphere. Kelly got up from her chair, remained unemotional. She looked at the ceiling for several moments, and then she lowered her head slowly, focused her thoughtful eyes on Eric and, in a near-whisper, asked him: 'How, Chief Inspector?'

Eric considered Kelly's actions for a few seconds and then, sympathy in his calm voice, asked her: 'What do you mean, Mrs Glover?'

A short nervous cough and then Kelly raised her voice: 'How did Ray die?'

Eric considered again, decided that this astute female had to be told in definitive words; no further spinning a yarn that provided the same answer. This woman, despite her history of vulnerability, didn't want an experienced police officer showering her with sympathetic words. She desired facts.

'We checked Dr Glover's body for possible evidence as to the cause of his death, no suggestion of physical violence, no marks on his body, robbery was not a motive, his documents and some cash were still inside his wallet -'

A restless Kelly, waving an arm, cut in: 'You say "robbery was not a motive". Are you suggesting he was killed illegally? That cave I know; was in darkness; damp, cold and quiet, no sound of the sea, or any form of nature? Did you see his face?'

Eric, defending this unexpected robust reaction, said, 'We do not know how he died; I'm informing you of our findings. Forensics however, will examine the body. As to the dark cave, nightfall had arrived when we were there. My officers and I checked it with powerful torches. The cavern was wet, cold, temperature only a few degrees above freezing. An unnerving atmosphere saturated the grotto, an uneasy quietness. Your husband's face was taut, wide-open eyes looking upwards. Mouth was open, at the point of shouting -'

Kelly intervened: 'As if scared?'

'That's a possibility, Mrs Glover.'

'And the time of death, Chief Inspector?'

Eric was hesitant, hot under the collar from the transformation in Kelly Glover's manner. His demeanour lacked assertion, his confidence kicked into the long grass. 'Estimated at about eleven-thirty; the time was assessed by a colleague and was confirmed by a forensic pathologist.'

Kelly Glover remained silent.

Eric turned to Josie Harold and Amy Coleman: 'Tomorrow will be a busy day for Mrs Glover. She'll needs support tonight.' He then turned to Kelly and told her: 'We will require you to identify the body.' He described the format, and then said, 'A police car will call for you tomorrow morning at ten-thirty and take you to Bangor.'

A silent Kelly nodded.

Eric gave his two WPCs a side glance and then said, 'We'll leave you now.' He handed Josie a card. 'The incident room's direct phone line.'

Silence prevailed, then Kelly Glover, her voice hardly audible, whispered: 'I wish to see where my husband died.'

Eric agreed to her wish. 'After we return from the forensics department in Bangor, wait until Wednesday afternoon,' and then a frustrated Eric led his WPCs out of the flat to the waiting Alan Reed.

Back in the incident room, Eric told Iwan Drew and the WPCs: 'No further evidence, negative vibes from the women, nothing can be gained by remaining here.' He collected his document case and, weariness in his hoarse voice, thanked the staff and then added: 'we review the situation at nine tomorrow morning.'

57

A clear sunny sky and low temperatures heralded Tuesday's dawn.

Sparkling frost covered the main roads' deep grass verges when Eric Bolton drove the thirty miles to Madogton police station. Warm cloths, advised by his wife, were his wear.

He checked with the station's duty officer at eight-thirty-five.

No calls.

He thanked the young officer, then hurried to the incident room, hung his fleece-lined white anorak on the back of his chair, then sat and dialled the coroner's office.

The strong north Wales voice surprised him. Eifion Pask was in his office at this early hour?'

'Eifion?'

'Eric Bolton.'

Eifion commented: 'It must be serious for you to contact me at this hour.'

Eric described yesterday's events. 'Forensic examination is desirable to establish the cause of death.'

Eifion Pask, speaking in a softer voice, commented: 'Such sad news in that small town during the past few weeks. Autopsy is granted.' Silence flowed down the line for several moments, and then Eifion Pask, now in a self-important sounding deep voice, declared: 'I've checked the diary regarding inquest hearing; I'll arrange for the initial inquiries into Roger Young and this death to be heard on Tuesday morning, ten o'clock in Pwllheli Magistrates building.'

Eric thanked him again, replaced the receiver, then buzzed the main office and asked Iwan Drew to attend the incident room.

Ten minutes later Iwan Drew left the incident room and briefed his staff.

Eric updated the Manchester Police Force and added: 'Initial forensic results should be through this afternoon.'

He then phoned Howard Baker and briefed him. 'That is the present state in this unexplainable sequence of events. Another body awaiting forensics inspection,' a sigh, then: 'no positive findings on superficial examination. Keep digging in Manchester.' He placed the receiver in its cradle and looked at the wall clock. Eight forty-eight.

Eric checked the updated evidence board, then he opened and read his case file while he waited for his colleagues.

All members of the team were present before nine.

A short greeting to the team followed and then, in a subdued voice, Eric said, 'I shall not remind everyone of the mystery, a wry grin, then: 'I'm assuming that you are, as I am, weary of the fragmentary situation. I apologise for my negative attitude, but the more I delve into this challenge, the more my confusion increases and an inference seems miles away.' He had a drink of water and then said, 'The coroner has been informed, an autopsy on Ray Glover's body will take place and there will be inquests into the two deaths next Tuesday morning. I've briefed Sergeant Drew. A media and press blackout continues. Manchester police have been updated, also. I'm waiting for news from forensics.' He waved a hand at the evidence board. 'Alan Red has amended it, please read it, try and determine a pattern.'

No one could.

'We have a busy day ahead,' Eric said, 'Kelly Glover will identify her husband's body today.' He buzzed the main desk. 'Ask PC Reed to come in please.'

Eric checked the time, then told a restive Alan Reed: 'Time we collected Mrs Glover,' He looked at the two WPCs. 'Your female presence please.'

The four left Madogton police station and collected Kelly Glover.

Formal identification of Ray Glover's body was completed by ten-fifteen in Bangor and the two WPCs escorted Kelly Glover to the SUV.

Eric, on leaving the forensic department, was anxious for any little helpful information. He asked Tim Wilding as to how soon results would be available.

'I'll contact you around three o'clock this afternoon.'

Eric Bolton and Alan Reed stayed in the police vehicle as the two WPCs escorted Kelly back to the flat.

Helen Manning described the meeting in Bangor and then told a tearful Josie Harold and a frowning pale Amy Coleman: 'Kelly is distraught; please continue to support her. We'll call for her tomorrow afternoon at two o'clock, take her to visit the cave where her husband's body was found.'

The two officers were thanked by Josie Harold and Amy Coleman. They left the flat and Alan Reed drove everyone back to the police station.

The time was approaching eleven-forty when they returned to the incident room.

Eric made everyone a mug of hot coffee.

Leaning back in his chair, Eric, after sipping his coffee for several seconds, said, 'I'm glad this one exercise, not one I was relishing, is over.' He stopped speaking for a few seconds and then added: 'It went well, no histrionics from Kelly.'

The two WPCs smiled in silent agreement.

After another drink of his coffee, a contemplating Eric looked at the evidence board once more and admitted: 'I've scrutinised the data, attempted to fathom out a story that is believable,' he hesitated, then: 'no, apart from forensics evidence, I don't believe the participants' tales.' He emptied the mug then, in a firm voice; declared: 'Kelly Glover remains a perplexity.' He looked at his colleagues. 'Does anybody disagree?'

Norma Taylor raised her arm. 'Perplexity, sir? She's a clever woman, I describe her as being adept at manoeuvring and transferring her ideas and philosophies to many members of present-day society,' a grin, then; 'she has acquired specific, maybe deadly, skills. Trying to make sense of what her visions mean, a study of her peers and its corrupting complexions, remain beyond my logic.' She stopped speaking, collected a wad of paper tissues from a box on the desk top, wiped her forehand , face and hands and was about to continue speaking when Eric, realising Norma's determination intervened: 'Relax; we are listening.'

Norma thanked him, wiped her forehead again and resumed her thoughts: 'Is the poet, Robert Graves, predicting a controlled self-destruction of the human race? After all, the human animal is the most efficient self-destruct machine; is it playing a unique genre inside the poet's mind? Is what he sees a crude copy of a unique zombie sect?'

Eric, needing time to digest Norma's words, checked the time and announced: 'We'll break for lunch, weather's cold but sunny. Have a healthy walk up town. I'm expecting a phone call from Tim Wilding this afternoon; I'll contact you via the station's operational room after I've received it.'

58

Eric received Dr Tim Wilding's call a few minutes after three.

Eric asked him to wait a few minutes: 'while I contact my colleagues to attend and hear your news.' He picked up the internal phone and dialled the operational room. His colleagues arrived within a minute.

'Sorry about that, Tim; all team members are now present. I'll put my phone into hand-free and voice-amplifier modes; everyone can then listen to your news.'

Tim Wilding declared: 'High-tech communication, Eric. I have the initial report for you. The various departments fast-tracked my requests,' a pause and then, his north Manchester accent flowing through his gentle voice, asked: 'Is it OK for me to continue?'

'We're listening,' Eric said.

Tim spoke slowly in a precise, controlled voice 'We know the history prior to the discovery of the body. On our general post mortem examination we found no evidence of physical assault,' a short pause, then he continued: 'stomach had remains of bacon and other breakfast foods; the bladder was empty. Heart and lungs showed no sign of macro disease. No evidence of petechiae, that is, small pinpoint haemorrhages, on the lips and eyelids, negated asphyxia as being linked to his death. There was, however, a small haemorrhage at the rear of the brain, he'd fallen backwards, similar to our findings in Gareth Young's autopsy and, Ray had remained in that position until found. The large time difference in the two deaths, and the pathological changes will vary. Comparing the findings was difficult because those in Ray Glover's body will differ from the ones found in Roger Young's -'

Eric intervened: 'Are you saying, Tim, that after considering the different circumstances, the autopsy findings in both bodies are not dissimilar?'

'Indeed. I stress that we only have basic findings; toxicology and histological results will follow soon.'

'Thank you.'

Tim Wilding propelled his report in an unyielding manner. 'I am convinced that hypoglycaemia, from the lack of food, plus hypothermia contributed to Gareth Young's death. Tony Simpson's photographs taken in Gareth and Ray Glover's deaths revealed only one set of footprints on the cave's sandy floor. The rugged walls and ceiling reveal nothing and, using our strong torches, have confirmed that there is only one entrance into the cave. As to the cause of Ray Glover's death?' A sigh, then a second-long pause before Tim continued: 'Hypoglycaemia won't be a factor in this fit, strong and active young man,' another pause, then: 'possibilities as to the cause of his death? Hypothesis only: sudden death in such a person can be the result of a cardiovascular problem, known as a vasovagal syndrome. This happens when the nervous system that regulates the heart rate and the blood pressure malfunctions. Causes for such are numerous but, in this case, I think it happened following sudden fright or the fear of bodily injury problem. Other explanations are a plug of mucous in the airways, infection, a foreign body blocking air entry, aspiration of food or vomit and an acute allergy, but none of these has been established -'

Eric cut in again: 'An unexplained death?'

Tim Wilding exhaled loudly and then carried on speaking in a subdued voice: 'I repeat, Eric, my findings lead to suppositions. Roger Young and Ray Glover's faces had similar expressions; their facial muscles frozen from witnessing a possible alarming situation, visual or auditory, maybe something that might be associated with that cave. Hallucinations are possible in a claustrophobic atmosphere. The body reacts to such, often, grotesque, visions with, what we term the fight or flight reaction; that is, you either stay to fight the agitator, or you flee the scene. Both men didn't fight and, whatever terrorised them, neither attempted to flee from the scene. They died where they were found. Such a terrifying experience produces an excess flow of adrenaline, causing the vasovagal attack. Loss of consciousness follows the drop in blood pressure. In that cave, considering the conditions and near-zero temperatures, loss of consciousness would lead to death. We'll have more news for you by mid-morning tomorrow following microscopic analyses of the heart,' another pause then: 'I must advise you that microscopic examination of organs doesn't always provide an answer. The toxicology results might prove helpful.' Tim hesitated, then said, 'An important question for you to consider, Eric.'

'Explain.'

'What prompted the two men to go into the cave?'

'Indeed, Tim, the answer to that question could be crucial.' Eric thanked him and replaced the phone in its cradle.

A confused Eric spent several seconds considering Tim's words and then, a disconsolate tone shrouding his voice, admitted to his colleagues: 'The investigation continues to pose problems,' then he asked them: 'your reaction to Tim Wilding's news.'

Glyn Salmon, shrugging his broad shoulders, said, 'We are without a motive for each of the deaths, and that hurts my ego.' His north Wales accent became more pronounced as he added: 'basically, although findings follow numerous hours' difference between the discoveries of the bodies; the pathological verdicts are similar: no definitive cause for either death.'

Jimmy said, 'Negative outcomes, and a suggestion that both men died from a sudden death, we have to wait for the results of Tim Wilding's further investigations. As to why they entered that cave?' A shrug of his shoulders.

Eric agreed, then said, 'stating the obvious, whatever caused their demise was triggered inside the cave and,' he hesitated for a moment, and then said, 'Kelly Glover wishes to visit it.' He looked at Glyn Salmon. 'I want you and the two WPCs, plus Sergeant Drew, to escort her.' He lifted the internal phone and asked Iwan Drew to join him.

Eric updated him, told him about Wednesday's programme, and then said, 'your knowledge of the local history and the area's myths could be valuable.'

Iwan nodded.

'Kelly Glover's reaction when she enters the cave might be pivotal. Any views, Sergeant Drew?'

Iwan spoke in a measured tone: 'I've struggled to evaluate the history and evidence surrounding her attitude towards this area. She is obsessed with its myths. There is an abundance in Gwynedd; one of the best known involves the mountain range, *Cadair Idris,* at the southern end of the Snowdonia National Park. Its English translation is *Idris's Chair,* a bowl-shaped depression in the mountain formed by glacial movements many centuries past. Nearby lakes are deemed to be bottomless and were inspirational to local poets. The mountain's name refers to Idris, the mythological stargazing giant, who was considered to be a poet, astrologer and philosopher.' He sighed and then, in a considerate voice, suggested: 'It's possible that she interrelates the myth of Cadair Idris with what Robert Graves observed on the beaches.' He carried on, a trace of scepticism in his slow, considered monotone: 'there have been incidents that persons, fascinated and inculcated by the inexplicable aspect of Wales's mythology, became hallucinated when they enter caves and mountains' tunnels. Some described images of an avatar constructed from their double inside terrifying incarnate hybrid forms.'

Eric smiled and, zipping a side glance at Iwan, told him: 'You might wish to discuss the local myths with Kelly tomorrow afternoon before you enter the cave.'

An expressionless Iwan remained silent.

Eric looked at the wall clock and said, 'We've had enough for today. Everybody back here at nine tomorrow morning.'

59

Early on Wednesday morning, Eric Bolton and Iwan Drew were in the incident room discussing the evidence. The rest of the team, all dressed in warm gear, arrived a few minutes before nine.

'A frosty sunny November day again,' a smiling Eric said, 'unusual. As far as I can recall this month's mornings are dark and depressing.' Eric asked: 'Anyone with news since yesterday, my pigeonhole and the email section were empty.'

No one had.

Eric ambled to the evidence board and said, 'Checked by the meticulous PC Alan Reed despite the absence of new info.' He returned to his desk, drank some water and then said, 'We'll discuss any queries before I open the official meeting.'

There were no queries.

A solemn tone shaded Eric's voice as he spoke: 'Knowledge of the circumstances at this stage takes on a greater importance. I remind you to think back to the Friday that prompted this inquiry,' a pause why he dwelt on the history, then: 'a complex trail, the weird events have led us nowhere. I ask you to consider the evidence again; try to gauge the offbeat situations.' Eric shivered, then said, 'a foreboding collection of evil and uncertainty, numbing.'

Silence filled the room.

Eric asked: 'What did Robert Graves observe all those years past? What did he hear?' He threw everyone a short wry smile and declared: 'Whatever it was, he kept it a secret, playing with the reader.'

Glyn Salmon quipped: 'That last remark applies to me.'

Eric changed tack. 'The weather was foul throughout the days and nights when Kelly saw people on the beach. What did she actually observe in those atrocious conditions? The continuing severe weather foiled Halloween and Guy Fawkes parties on the beaches. Weird. We report our lack of findings to Kelly. We've interviewed her, plus her departed husband and Josie Harold.' A sigh, then he asked: 'Where does Amy Coleman fit in all this? Is she connected in some way to the present problem because of her relationship with Ray Glover?' He stopped speaking and waited for a response.

Silence prevailed.

Eric opened his case file, put on his reading glasses, checked over a few pages and then, in a determined voice, said, 'Try and view Kelly's request to visit the cave from her point of view,' a wry smile, then: 'our attitude to the problem needs to be delicate, but forthright.'

Jimmy Elson asked: 'Who will accompany her?'

'My decision is for discussion,' Eric said, 'This is it: DS Elson and I stay here; less police presence is desired, hence I suggest DC Glyn Salmon, Sergeant Drew and WPC Helen Manning, people who are acquainted with this area, will witness the event.' He cast Norma a knowing smile and said, 'I need WPC Norma Taylor to remain in the station, backup if necessary.'

Eric looked at everyone he'd mentioned and then said, 'PC Alan Reed will use the large unmarked police vehicle; collect Kelly at two o'clock and then drive you and her to the beach. The weather forecast is reasonable, the tides are small, and a slight north-easterly cold breeze will keep everybody alert.' He looked at everybody, waited for a reaction.

Glyn Salmon asked: 'How long do we allow her to remain inside the cave?'

'When you believe she has seen enough.' He took typed A4 sheets of paper from his case, handed one to everyone, and then said, 'Please read the detailed m.o. for this afternoon, to be discussed now.'

Silence lasted until the m.o. was read and then he said, 'Early afternoon, when you take Kelly Glover to the cave, the temperature inside it will be near freezing. Wear appropriate clothes, including woollen beanies. When you enter the cave drag them over your ears, muffle the echoes inside the cave when you're in conversation. Every police officer to possess a powerful torch, a radiophone and a mobile phone. Mobile signal should be good on the beach. Once you enter the cave, Alan Reed returns to the station. Phone the station as necessary; he'll collect you as per plan.' A sigh, then: 'Any questions?'

Iwan Drew asked: 'A journey into the unknown, any back-up if we encounter problems?'

'A contingency strategy exists,' Eric said, 'several officers will be on standby and will be transported there if the situation requires such.'

Iwan nodded.

'Anymore?'

There was none.

The phone rang. Tim Wilding was on the line. He said in a solemn voice: 'No helpful info, Eric: no evidence of drugs or alcohol or any other noxious substances in the body, and no pathological cause for the death,' then he apologised: 'sorry, Eric, but we are unable to supply you with a cause for Ray Glover's death.'

Eric thanked him, replaced the receiver slowly into its cradle, told his colleagues, grimaced and then said, 'Finish any outstanding work you have. Meet back here at one o'clock.'

At one o'clock everyone was back in the incident room.

'Everybody up to date with their work?' Eric asked.

An orchestrated 'Yes' was the answer.

'Check you have everything,' then looking at the wall clock, Eric said, 'Time to meet up with Alan Reed at the main entrance. Good luck.'

The group arrived in Criccieth soon after one-thirty.

Glyn Salmon, Iwan Drew and Helen Manning got out of the unmarked car and climbed up the iron stairway to the flat.

Glyn knocked on the door.

Kelly shouted: 'Come in.'

60

Kelly greeted everyone.

'It's very cold, despite the sunshine,' a shivering Iwan remarked. He looked at Kelly. 'You're wearing sensible clothes and footwear for the beach, warmth is a must.' He added: 'We suggest a woollen beanie also, worn over your ears, stifles echoes inside the cave, won't hinder conversation to any extent.'

Helen Manning looked at Josie Harold and Amy Coleman. 'Good, you both are geared for the cold: warm gloves and sturdy walking boots are essential -'

A jittery Kelly interjected: 'We've had an intense chat, my aunt and Amy Coleman wish to join me.' She looked at Glyn. 'If that's all right with you.'

Glyn looked at Iwan and his female colleague.

Helen Manning told him: 'Check with the Chief.'

Glyn used his radiophone.

Eric had no objection, then said, 'Phone the station immediately the women leave the cave.'

Glyn told the three women of the procedures, then pointed to the flat's door and said, 'When you're ready, ladies.'

Five minutes later, Alan Reed drove them to the beach, parked outside the cave a few minutes before two and helped everyone out of the vehicle.

The three police officers checked for a mobile phone signals; a strong one was present.

Alan told Glyn Salmon: 'Hear from you in about an hour.' He left the beach and briefed Eric Bolton when he returned to Madogton police station.

Glyn Salmon and Iwan asked Helen Manning to accompany the three women as they entered the cave.

Glyn Salmon then said, 'Sergeant Drew knows the area well, he will be in charge while we're inside.'

A surprised Iwan nodded and then explained what the conditions inside the cave would be: 'blackness throughout; once we enter we pull the woollen beanie hats over our ears.'

Glyn Salmon then said to the three women: 'WPCs Manning, Sergeant Drew and I have powerful torches, we'll guide you to the spot where Dr Glover's body was found.'

Iwan led the way, shining his torch on the dry sandy floor and declared: 'No animal or human footprints, not even the weather's been affecting the geology.'

An emotional fifteen minutes followed while Iwan described the findings. He looked at a weeping Kelly and, his muffled voice penetrated Kelly's woollen beanie, asked her: 'Any questions?'

A bemused Kelly looked at him.

Had she heard his question? He repeated it in a raised voice.

'You say the expression on Ray's face suggested he might have been frightened.'

'Correct.'

A shivering Kelly, her speech a nervous stutter, said, 'Sh..shine your torch on the c..ceiling and the wall please, Sergeant.'

Iwan obliged, then waved to Glyn and Helen Manning to do likewise.

The powerful beams scanned the farthest point of the cave and its bleak, craggy multi-coloured rock-strewn ceilings and walls that were home to bats.

Kelly looked directly at all the police officers for several seconds and then, in a resolved voice, said, 'I've seen enough, Sergeant; there is nothing here that would have caused Ray to be alarmed,' and then she directed a hand in the direction of the cave's entrance.

The group walked slowly out of the cave's blackness, shielding their eyes from the glare of the low setting sun.

Kelly looked at Iwan Drew and said, 'This mid-November evening is quiet, not the often dark, bleak and stormy ones. They can be depressing.' She smiled at Josie and Amy, and then, gesturing with the wave of a hand at the two women, told Iwan 'We three will walk along the foreshore to the flat, we'll be there before darkness falls.' She focused her eyes once more on Glyn Salmon, Iwan Drew and Helen Manning and then, a degree of confidence trawling through her voice, insisted: 'We'll be fine, please look inside the cave again, final check, before you leave.'

The three women shook the officers' hands, and then they ambled along the foreshore towards Criccieth castle and the flat.

The police officers watched the three women stroll along the seashore, then Iwan asked his colleagues: 'What did you make of the visitation?'

Glyn Salmon, still disbelieving Kelly's actions, said, 'A charade, Iwan, not quite a melodrama, but her reaction to the event lacked sincerity.'

Iwan asked Helen Manning. 'Any views?'

Helen Manning, her gentle north Wales lilt flowing through each syllable, agreed with Glyn Salmon and added: 'Kelly portrayed a cool, calculating woman; no warmth or compassion in her body language or voice.' She raised her eyebrows, flashed her eyes and added: 'Kelly is an annoyed woman.'

Iwan, noting Helen's concern, said, 'Please continue, Helen.''

'A devious woman,' a sigh then: 'the other women's reactions were bland, neither showing emotion; they were present because Kelly had summoned them to attend. Both lacked interest, seemed oblivious to what was happening,' a pause, then: 'I found their attitude towards a delicate situation difficult to ascertain.'

Iwan said, 'We all agree with what is, yet again, another bizarre episode shadowing this investigation.' He checked the time. 'Two-fifty.' He gestured with an outstretched arm to the cave and said, 'We'll honour Kelly Glover's request that we check inside it once more before we leave the area.'

They walked towards the mouth, then Iwan raised his hands. 'Stop; please. Listen. Did anyone hear a sound?'

No one answered.

Glyn Salmon said, 'The wind, even a slight breeze, blowing from a particular direction through the undulating deep dunes and their grass, produces weird sounds at times.'

Several bats flew out of the cave.

Iwan smiled and commented: 'Our presence has disturbed the small roosting mammals. Dusk is approaching, their active period is about to start.'

The group waited for five minutes, and then, when no more bats flew out of the cavern, Iwan said, 'We check the ceiling and the walls while we walk to the end of the cave and then again on the way back, and afterwards, I'll phone Alan Reed for our lift back to the station.'

Iwan Drew, Glyn Salmon and Helen Manning entered the cave.

61

Eric Bolton and Jimmy Elson, experiencing an intense and thought-provoking mental exercise, focused on the direct, indirect, plus the anecdotal evidence collected on Kelly Glover. They collated the information and produced a written report, a comprehensible account on what they deemed lacked concrete evidence, unrewarding. Yet, Eric Bolton's professional experience reminded him that an investigation always had an interlocking pattern, identifying this one was a challenging problem. A knock on the door interrupted his deliberations.

'Come in.'

PC Alan Reed entered.

'Yes, Alan?'

'It's just gone three o'clock, Chief; have you heard anything?'

Eric shaking his head, looked at the wall clock. 'Is it that time? No, Alan. I've not had news from the beach. Give them another fifteen minutes,' he hesitated and then, while struggling to control a nervous smile, said, 'no news is usually good news.'

'Yes, sir,' and Alan left.

Eric Bolton was thinking about the silence from the beach when the internal phone buzzed.

He lifted it. 'Chief Bolton.'

It was Alan Reed. 'It's after three-fifteen, sir; any news?'

Concerned by Alan Reed's question, an anxious Eric looked at the computer's monitor and said, 'No, they should have completed their viewing of the cave by now, should be back on the beach, ready to leave.' A grunt, then: 'Try and contact the officers on their radiophones and mobiles, then report back to me.'

'Yes, sir.'

Eric looked at Jimmy Elson.

'Worrying,' was Jimmy's answer.

Ten minutes later, Eric Bolton's phone rang again and Alan Reed told him that he was unable to contact any of the police officers. 'No one answered their radiophone or their mobile phones, sir.'

'It'll be dark soon,' Eric remarked, and then, in a commanding voice, told Alan: 'I'll be with you in a few minutes, get the four-by-four -'

'The vehicle is ready to go,' Alan announced, 'I'll be outside the main entrance,' and ended the call.

A thoughtful Eric told Jimmy Elson: 'Please stay, the phone might ring while we're travelling.'

'What the hell is going on?' a disgruntled-sounding Eric cried out as he jumped into the vehicle.

Alan shook his head, drove out of the station's forecourt and declared: 'Strange that no one answered my calls. Do you want the blue light flashing?'

Eric, shaking his head, said, 'We don't want to alarm people or invite the media to question our haste, drive at a sensible speed.' He picked up the vehicle's radio phone and contacted Norma Taylor, described the situation and said, 'We might need your help.'

It was three thirty-five, and night imminent, when Alan Reed drove onto the beach.

Eric said to him: 'Turn the vehicle full circle;' then: 'direct full beam headlights at the cave.'

Alan completed two full circles, the beach was empty: no one walking their animals, seagulls were non-existent, only noise was from the swaying Marran grass on the large and tall dunes.

'No sign of any kind of life,' Eric said, 'drive up to the cave.'

Alan did as ordered.

Eric thanked him, then told him: 'Wear warm gear, beanie hat and gloves; it's going to be very cold. Grab a camera, then check your torch, radiophone and mobile and leave the headlights on; it's a new moon tonight so the beach will be in total darkness. I might need photos of the area.'

Suitably clad, they left the vehicle, shivered momentarily as the cold breeze greeted them and then Eric asked: 'Can you hear anything, Alan?'

Alan shook his head. 'I can only hear the flooding neap tide's waves lapping the sandy shore.'

Eric activated his torch and directed the beam onto the nearby sand. 'Look, Alan, footprints into and out of the cave.'

Alan Reed took photographs and they entered the cave.

Eric then focused the beam at the cave's floor and said, 'Note the many footprints.'

Alan photographed them.

'Let's look on the beach,' Eric said and stepped out of the cave. He directed the torch's beam down the beach to the foreshore and declared: 'Several footprints visible,' then, pointing at them, said, 'several people have walked towards Criccieth.'

More photos were taken.

A nervous Eric said, 'Time we explored inside the cave.'

They walked inside, the vehicles headlights and the hand torches illuminating their short journey.

Footprints were visible on the dry floor and then the two men stopped.

Eric looked at Alan, said nothing and pointed.

Several yards ahead, three people were huddled on the floor, silent, bland expressions, unmindful of the surroundings and unresponsive when Eric and Alan approached them.

Alan took numerous shots of the group and then, his body shaking, announced: 'Our colleagues.'

A grief-stricken Eric looked at Helen Manning, Iwan Drew and Glyn Salmon.

The three officers, staring at one another, remained motionless, their eyes wide-open, each unaware of their comrades' presence.

Eric shouted: 'Hello.' His voice, and the ensuing reverberating loud echo produced no reaction from any of the group's member. Several bats flew from their roost and out of the cave, disappearing into the blackness.

Eric repeated his loud greeting; no response. He then walked up to a sitting Glyn Salmon. 'Glyn, this is Eric Bolton.'

No response, and the other officers remained motionless, unresponsive.

Eric told Alan. 'Shine your torch on their faces.'

A distressed, trembling Alan, used both hands to direct the beam.

Eric studied their faces, each had a similar expression. His immediate thought was: had they been terrified? He raised his hands, turned to Alan and told him: 'Get the paramedics and the police back up teams here a.s.a.p., no flashing lights or sirens.'

Alan, his heart thumping against his sternum, perspiration trickling down his face, hurried to the four-by-four and contacted both teams.

Both arrived ten minutes later.

62

Eric Bolton provided Jeff Granger, the tall and strong paramedics' team leader, with the nub of the complex story, then briefed the back-up police officers and told them: 'Cordon off the cave's entrance and check the immediate area.' He then joined Alan Reed in the four-by-four while the paramedics' team assessed the three non-communicative police officers inside the cave.

Ten minutes later, Jeff Granger reappeared.

Eric and Alan left their vehicle and walked towards him.

'We've checked the situation,' Jeff said, his strong local accent bounding in each syllable, 'no obvious physical injuries, pulses and bold pressures are normal. They can stand and walk. However, there was no verbal response to our questions.' He shrugged his broad shoulders and said, 'They look to be in mental shock,' then added: 'my colleagues and I scanned the whole of the cave with powerful torches and, apart from several fleeing bats, we saw nothing. The bitterly cold cave and its quietness initiated uncanny imaginations and thoughts amongst my colleagues.' He offered a wry apologetic smile and then said, 'I'll reverse the ambulance into the cave; the reversing lights, plus your vehicle's headlights, will provide a helpful guide for us collect the officers. They'll be taken to Bangor Hospital. You'll be informed.'

The paramedics helped the officers into the ambulance.

A pale, shivering Eric looked at the cave's entrance for several seconds, then asked the police backup team: 'Anyone on the beach?'

No one was in the vicinity.

A thoughtful Eric said, 'Okay. We leave no evidence of police activity. See you back in the station, do not mention this to your colleagues. I'll brief them when necessary.' He then turned to Alan. 'Nothing more for us to do here. No officers to be deployed. We'll return to the station. Media will not be privy to these events.'

Back at the station, a tense Eric told Alan Reed to print the photos and then he walked to the incident room.'

Jimmy Elson greeted him, then a frank: 'you look terrible, sir.'

Eric described the afternoon's uncanny events and then said, 'I'll inform the staff, then we wait for news from the hospital,' he stopped speaking and, following a short thought, said, 'we should visit Kelly Glover in Criccieth this evening.'

Jimmy endorsed Eric's suggestion, adding: 'and with a WPC's presence.'

Eric took his copy of Robert Graves's poem from his case file, read it several times, checked the quotations he'd heard and read, then, using a pencil, underlined the remaining, unquoted, lines. He returned the poem into his case file, then picked up the internal phone and asked WPC Norma Taylor to join him and Jimmy Elson.

Five minutes later, Norma Taylor, sitting in a chair opposite Eric and Jimmy, spoke in a quiet, regulated voice as she portrayed the afternoon's events: 'When Glyn Salmon, Iwan Drew and Helen left in the ambulance they were physically sound.

Eric described the scene inside the cave; 'the three were unaware of their surroundings or the people attending to them. A psychological abyss? Their faces were expressionless and the paramedics had no problem persuading them to enter the ambulance.'

WPC Norma Taylor, the ever-professional WPC, asked in her strong local accent: 'Considering the numerous vagaries that have coloured or tinted this inquiry, is it possible that our colleagues were hypnotised, responding to instructions?'

Eric, caution in his tone, said, 'A possibility? Yes.'

Norma's accent softened, skating across her words, as she asked: 'If we believe that to be the case, how is the hypnotic spell broken?'

Jimmy Elson answered her: 'Chief Bolton and I have discussed the situation; we've decided to visit, unannounced, Kelly Glover this evening at six o'clock. We want you to accompany us.'

Norma agreed, looked at the wall clock and said. 'Ample time for me to complete my report and change into warm clothes -' the internal phone rang.

Eric Bolton picked it up.

Alan Reed had printed the photos.

'That's quick work, Alan; bring them in now, I'll show them to DS Elson and WPC Taylor,' and then he added: 'keep this evening free; short notice for which I apologise. I need you to drive my colleagues and myself to Criccieth; I'll explain when you arrive.'

Eric replaced the receiver and, while he waited for Alan to arrive, told Jimmy and Norma: 'I'll lose another few stripes tonight,' a smile, then: 'I feel as if I'm living in a bed and breakfast establishment, can't recall what my wife looks like.'

Seconds later the door opened and Alan Reed, carrying an A4 pocket folder, walked in. He acknowledged everybody and handed Eric the folder. 'These are the shots I took. I've also enclosed a memory stick, easier for you and the team to view the images on the computer's screen.'

Eric thanked him, then explained the m.o. for the remainder of the day. 'Please stay while I show our colleagues the photos.'

Eric described the photographic sequence, then inserted the memory stick into the computer and opened the machine's document file. He checked the time, then said, 'This will take about ten minutes, and afterwards, we'll prepare to leave for Criccieth.'

Apart from the ghastly expressions on the officers' faces and, despite careful scrutiny of each shot, nil else was noted.

Eric switched off the computer and, looking at his colleagues, asked: 'Any comments?'

Norma Taylor, hands clenched, shaken by what she'd witnessed, said in an unfamiliar quiet voice: 'The photos appear unreal, like something out a horror movie, a weird scenario. Yet, whatever was inside the cave, it had a profound effect on them, all seemed to be in a controlled impassive state.'

'Indeed,' was Eric's assertive response then, waves of frustration and rage travelling through his mind, he said, 'that is why we're interviewing Kelly Glover this evening.'

Eric handed Alan a bunch if keys, 'Josie Harold provided us with a duplicate set for the flat, I had three more made.' He then stressed: 'Get more copies made please, Alan; I believe we all might need access to that flat.' He tossed Alan a wry grin and then said, 'Get the vehicle ready and the radiophones charged up.'

Alan acknowledged and left.

Eric turned to his colleagues. 'It's a bitterly cold night, so everybody in warm gear. We meet at the front entrance in fifteen minutes and,' picking up the main phone said, 'before we leave I'll inform Tim Wilding in forensics of today's experiences and ask him, out of courtesy, to inform his boss, Dr Lucy Grange in Forensics HQ.'

63

Alan Reed arrived in Criccieth a few minutes after six and parked the SUV near the dark narrow street's single lamp, a few yards down from the flat.

Eric Bolton told him: 'Don't stay here in the vehicle, the night's getting colder. Return in an hour,' then: 'I'll phone if I need you earlier,' and then he, Jimmy Elson and Norma Taylor got out of the vehicle.

Alan drove away.

Eric Bolton activated his powerful torch and led Jimmy Elson and Norma Taylor up the iron staircase to the flat's door. He knocked on it a few times. Seconds later it opened.

Despite the police presence, Kelly Glover, holding a gin and tonic in one hand, was sanguine. She greeted the group, invited them inside and, in a composed voice, said, 'This is not unexpected; take off your anoraks,' and, pointing to the warm lounge, said, 'please go inside, sit on the sofa.'

'I hear music,' Eric said, 'it's a song I know.'

Kelly said, 'It's a Chris Rea CD; the song, *On The Beach.*' She pointed to the stereo music centre. 'I play this when I'm in Criccieth; the lyrics define my attitude. I play it often.' She walked to the stereo equipment, switched it off, placed her drink on the coffee table and hung the officers' anoraks in the hall's coat closet.

Seconds later, Kelly returned to the lounge, picked up her drink and sat in the armchair. A few sip of her drink and, portraying a picture of confidence and an inconsequential attitude, asked Eric: 'Yes, Chief Inspector?'

A cogent mental vortex from increasing infuriation with Kelly's offhand attitude rattled Eric's dark mind. Irked by her disdainful manner and glibness, he decided that preliminaries were not on his immediate agenda, his interview and questioning required firm tactics: 'Three hours ago you, your aunt and Amy Coleman, accompanied by Sergeant Iwan Drew, DC Salmon and WPC Manning, visited the cave where your husband's body was found.' He stopped speaking, stared at her, baiting her to react.

Kelly had another sip of her drink and, maintaining a relaxed disposition, remained silent.

Eric thought: she was not displaying the demeanour of a person who had witnessed a seminal, personal, experience. Aware of the absence of any other person in the flat, he winged Norma Taylor a knowing glance.

Norma, raising her eyebrows in a positive response, directed a white-tooth thin smile at Kelly and, her local accent now softened and evident in a comforting tone, asked: 'Are you alone, Mrs Glover?'

Kelly finished her drink, placed the glass on the coffee table and, rising from the armchair, said, 'Yes.'

Norma looked at her.

Kelly picked up the tumbler, ambled to the drinks' cabinet, poured out another gin and tonic, returned to the armchair, had a mouthful of the mixture and then told Norma: 'I'd seen enough inside the cave, then I asked the three officers to check inside it once more and then my aunt and Amy accompanied me back here.'

Norma squinted at Eric.

Eric asked Kelly: 'Why did you ask the officers to check the cave again?'

'For my personal satisfaction, Chief Inspector.'

A frowning Eric said, 'There's no sign of your aunt or Amy Coleman in the flat now.'

An unperturbed Kelly said, 'They left together, about an hour ago, didn't say where they were going.'

Norma stared at her, then asked: 'What time did you get back to the flat this afternoon, Mrs Glover?'

Kelly glared at Norma, a defensive expression masking her pale face. She coughed and, confidence ebbing from her previously poised disposition and her focused mental spirit, said, 'It was getting dark and a cold easterly breeze was freshening. A few people, walking their dogs, were hurrying back to their cars parked on the promenade. We rushed back to the flat, arrived before four o'clock.'

'We'll check the area,' Eric said, then a gut feeling prompted him to tell Kelly: 'Some members of my team have heard and read quotations from Robert Graves's poem.'

Kelly sipped her drink, didn't respond.

'Enlighten us please, Kelly,' Eric said in a gentle, persuasive voice. 'I have read the complete poem; I need it to be explained to me.'

Kelly threw him a side glance: 'Do you have a copy of the poem?'

Eric nodded, collected the document from his case file, handed it to Kelly and told her: 'The quoted parts are underlined with red ink, the unquoted parts are underlined in pencil.'

She glanced at it, then returned it to Eric. 'I can quote all sections, each is central to my thinking. Please follow my recitation.'

Eric put on his reading glasses.

Her body language, accentuating enthusiasm and a tang of satisfaction in her voice, Kelly declared: 'The people that came out of the caves are described by the poet; I presume he is conversation with someone, but don't know who. Is it possible that he might be experiencing ghostly flashbacks of agonising events he witnessed during the Great War? I quote: **"Tell me, had they legs?'**

'Not a leg nor foot among them that I saw.'

'But did these things come out in any order?

What o'clock was it? What was the day of the week?

Who else was present? How was the weather?'

'I was coming to that. It was half-past three

On Easter Tuesday last. The sun was shining.

**The Harlech Silver Band played *Marchog Jesu*
On thirty-seven shimmering instruments
Collecting for Caernarvon's (Fever) Hospital Fund.
The populations of Pwllheli, Criccieth,
Portmadoc, Borth, Tremadog. Penrhyndeudraeth,
Were all assembled. Criccieth's mayor addressed
them
First in good Welsh and then in fluent English,
Twisting his fingers in his chain of office.
Welcoming the things. They came out on the sand,
Not keeping time to the band, moving seaward
Silently at a snail's pace.'"**

A confused Eric looked at Kelly.

She had further sips of the gin and tonic.

Eric said, 'We've heard other quotations,' then: 'please analyse the last two lines of the poem for me and my team.'

Kelly cast him a wry smile. 'Interesting; perhaps I should have told you that the artist Diego Velasquez and the poet and playwright Euripides also, interest me, as does Greek mythology, especially that relating to the river Styx. It is a deity and forms the boundary between Earth and the Underworld. Styx had miraculous powers, produced invulnerability in someone who had succumbed to their individual problems, people who questioned whether they had a solitary existence in the future, one that was open to being fractured.'

Eric looked at her. 'We are aware of your interest in poetry, mythology and that particular artist……. but Euripides?'

'He was a Greek playwright and poet who lived in the fourth century BC. A prolific writer, he became the cornerstone of ancient literary education.' Kelly poured herself another gin and tonic then, looking at Eric, said, 'Chief Inspector, you've asked me as to why I was interested in this man? My answer: he was a pioneer, evolved theatre to modern times. He represented mythical heroes as ordinary folk trapped in exceptional situations. I can relate his philosophy to that of Robert Graves's poetry. Euripides had a sequence of literary periods: an early period of high tragedy, followed by a patriotic stage relating to a war, then a phase concerning its senseless nature. What followed concentrated on post-war romantic intrigue and then, a final chapter that might have been influenced by despair and tragedy.' She threw Eric a wide grin and had another mouthful of her drink.

Eric sighed and threw Norma a questioning gaze.

She acknowledged Eric's implicit hint, then looked at Kelly and fired a symbolic question at her: 'When we came here, I noticed that Mrs Harold's car is still parked near the lifeboat station, but Amy Coleman's white Mini has gone. Where are the two women?'

Kelly shrugged her shoulders, didn't answer.

Jimmy Elson took over the questioning and, an unyielding dark tone to his voice, said, 'We rescued our colleagues from the cave soon after you, your aunt and Amy Coleman left. They required immediate paramedic attention and are in hospital.'

A few more sips of her drink, then Kelly looked at her wristwatch and, her confidence now returned, declared: 'They'll be awake by nine o'clock,' a snigger, then she added: 'six hours under a hypnotic spell is sufficient. I didn't want them to suffer.'

'Excuse me,' Eric said, lifting the radio phone from his anorak's pocket, 'I'll go outside, should have a good signal there.'

He dialled the hospital, informed the staff of his rank and he was then updated by the attending doctor. He then phoned Madogton police station told Alan Reed of the situation and added: 'I sense problems about the state of affairs here; arrange two back-up teams.' He ended the call and returned to the lounge. 'Jobs done.'

280

Kelly lobbed Eric a thin gleaming smile and then, self-assurance gripping her every word, said, 'I confirm your colleagues aren't harmed.'

Norma, fighting to control her emotions, asked Kelly: 'I ask you again: have you any idea as where Mrs Harold and Mrs Coleman might be?'

'I've been victimised,' was Kelly's self-protecting response, vitriol tinting her tone, 'did my husband convey any loyalty towards me? No, he thought he could brainwash me, convert me to being a cloned entity by commands, using certain sounds or particular music to activate certain thoughts or actions in me. I identified his ploy, played the susceptible individual and then, after attending an accredited training college, I also, became skilled in hypnosis and hypnotherapy.'

Kelly walked to the lounge window, looked out, smiled and described the scene: 'Soft lights from nearby dwellings; no human beings in the area, just an eerie silence.' A shake of her head, then: 'Even the sea is quiet, only a slight breeze now crafting crests on tiny waves as they kiss the foreshore.' She turned away from the window, looked at Norma Taylor and, in a firm voice, said, 'What of my aunt and Amy Coleman? Both betrayed me; consider the beginning of the sequence of the troublesome events, Miss Taylor,' a snigger, then: 'and now my ability to hypnotise'. A grin followed. 'Where do you think they are?'

Norma looked at Eric.

Despite his team members' speculations, Eric concluded that the remarkable events of the past few weeks were not a planned collective ploy. Determination commanding his voice, he declared: 'We'll discuss this further in Madogton police station, Mrs Glover.'

'Agreed,' Kelly said. She finished her drink, placed the crystal glass tumbler on the coffee table and addressed Eric: 'Chief Inspector, you asked me about the last two lines of the poem.'

'I did.'

A grinning Kelly ambled around the lounge then, staring at Eric, said, 'Chief Inspector, do you recall the part of the poem appertaining to the silver band playing on the beach, which was then followed by an address by Criccieth's mayor?'

Eric nodded.

'That recitation was therapeutic,' Kelly said.

Eric remained silent, waited for the enthusiastic Kelly's analysis of this section of the poem.

Kelly, after shaping a controlled smile, stood in the centre of the room and declared: 'I can relate to the mayor, Chief Inspector. I will quote you the last two lines of the poem; they describe possible mythical persons who are oblivious to their surroundings when they come onto the beach: **"What did the mayor do?'**

'I was coming to that"'.

A short cynical smile followed, then a confident Kelly declared: 'I stress, Chief Inspector, that Harlech and Criccieth castles' legacies are significant factors in my recent personal history.'

64

PC Alan Reed, after choosing his two back-up teams, informed the two-man units of the phone call from Eric Bolton, then outlined the present set up, briefed them of the future m.o. and, looking at the wall clock, advised: 'PC Sion Parry, who knows the locality well, will be in charge of the first team and liaise with me.' He stressed: 'The flat is without a landline; the mobile signal is poor, verging on absent, so check your radio phones. The narrow streets around there lack efficient light. Ensure your powerful torches are fully-charged. An unmarked car is available for you outside the station's main entrance. I'll be in the SUV; follow me. Wear warm gear and take flasks of hot drinks; it's bloody cold out there.'

Alan then told the second team: 'PC Martin Ford, also familiar with the area, will also, liaise with me. Similar cold weather gear and hot drinks. In the meantime his team will remain here and await a call from me.' He looked at Martin and said, 'Another unmarked car, for your use, is parked at the side of the main entrance.' He then handed Sion and Martin each a set of keys. 'To access Kelly Glover's flat and garage if necessary.'

Alan Reed parked the SUV outside the flat at ten minutes after seven.

Two minutes later, Sion Parry and his colleague, Mark Lloyd, arrived.

Alan Reed, pointing to the iron stairway, told them: 'Follow me. Quietly.'

He switched on his torch and, the three men, grabbing the stairway's wet and cold handrail tightly, climbed slowly up to the flat's door.

The hallway light was on.

Alan inserted the key into the door's lock and opened the door slowly. The three men entered the hallway. Sion closed the door quietly and then they made for the brightly-lit kitchen.

Kelly Glover was there.

The open-mouthed, alarmed woman, stared at the men for a few seconds, then exhaled and shouted: 'Police?'

Alan nodded.

'What do you want?'

Alan showed her his ID card, introduced Sion and Mark to her and then said, 'My colleagues and I are here to take Chief Inspector Bolton and his team back to Madogton police station.'

'Why so many of you?'

Alan smiled at her, didn't answer.

Kelly gestured with a wave of her trembling hand: 'They are in the lounge; follow me.'

Eric Bolton, Jimmy Elson and Norma Taylor, all expressionless, were sitting on the sofa, oblivious to their colleagues' presence.

Alan Reed and his team walked towards them.

They received no response.

Alan shouted: 'Eric, Jimmy, Norma.'

No reaction.

Alan asked Kelly: 'Hypnotised?'

Kelly gave a firm 'Yes,' and then, glancing at the wall clock, declared: 'They'll exit their trances at midnight, physically well and they might even appreciate their unplanned snooze.'

Alan, recalling Chief Bolton's phone call, asked Kelly: 'Where are Mrs Harold and Mrs Coleman?'

She didn't answer, but whispered: 'Do you recall a passage from the poem describing intense colourful things coming out from Criccieth's caves one afternoon and moving seawards?'

A confused, silent Alan stared at her.

Kelly grinned, looked at Alan and said, 'I do not know where my aunt and Amy went.'

Alan remained silent, looked at his alarmed team and then he asked Kelly: 'What time did the women leave?'

Kelly, speaking in a clear-cut voice, said, 'Amy and my aunt left the flat together before six o'clock.' She threw Alan a short arrogant smile and, Glee in her eyes, then a cynical smirk and, with vitriol streaking through her voice, said, 'I'm pleased, satisfied that I've avenged my husband's infidelity with those two women.' Suspiration, then she added: 'I've gleaned that neither woman needed much encouragement to have amorous assignations with my husband.' Pointing to a bedroom, she said, 'I keep a diary when I'm in north Wales, update it daily. It's in the top drawer of the bedside cabinet.' She smiled, then threw her head back, laughed aloud and then, smiling at Alan, declared aloud: 'I've obtained psychological and financial satisfaction, plus improvement in my general health.' Flamboyance in her tone, she boasted: 'My words will interest you when you discover what's happened to Josie Harold and Amy Coleman.' She leered, then: 'I've undergone personal torment, especially a conscience-sapping period, during most of the past twelve months.' Her demeanour altered as she changed tack: 'Are the police or forensics able to explain the deaths, including what happened to PC Gareth Young? I was informed by friends that PC Young was checking on my activities in Manchester and then I discovered he was following me when I was on the Criccieth and the other beaches. I confronted him on the beach, told him that he had pried into my private life in both places and that it had annoyed me. Despite my disdain, he continued his clandestine activities. I caught up with him and dictated his actions on the day he died.' She looked at Alan, and the said to him: 'I apologise for my attitude towards my aunt and Amy Coleman; you wish to know their whereabouts.'

Alan nodded, waited.

A sniggering Kelly said in a slow monotone: 'Are the police or forensics capable of determining who, if anyone, is responsible for what's happened these past few weeks?'

A shrug of one shoulder, then she stared at Alan and, in a teasing voice, declared: 'A labyrinthine journey for the services, PC Reed. As far as I was concerned, gilding the lily wasn't considered.'

Alan, deciding not to pursue Kelly's mischievous words, told her: 'My colleagues will take you to the station later.' He looked at Sion Parry and Mark Lloyd for several seconds, received no reaction from them. He turned away and, in a solemn tone, said, 'I'll arrange for paramedics to take the officers to hospital and afterwards I'll inform the duty officer; I need to liaise with the station's staff.'

Alan went outside, managed to contact the emergency service and the hospital, and then he phoned Madogton police station.

Alan thanked the duty officer, then he radio phoned Martin Ford, updated him, and then told him: 'Josie Harold and Amy Coleman left the flat between five-thirty and six this evening.' He explained his gut feeling: 'I'll meet you and your colleague at the largest cave in ten to fifteen minutes.' He returned into the flat and told Sion Parry: 'The paramedics will be here in ten minutes.'

'Okay.'

Alan nodded to Kelly and said, 'I'll leave now.'

Kelly, a bemused veil covering her face, asked in a melancholic tone: 'Why leave, PC Reed? Please explain.'

'I'm meeting another paramedic crew and a police back up team.'

'I might not be here, PC Reed.'

Alan frowned. 'Pardon?'

Kelly smiled, then chuckled, didn't explain.

Alan noted this, didn't react and then he told Sion Parry of his conversations with Martin, and added: 'I'll contact the North Wales Police HQ and seek their guidance. I'll call you afterwards; in the meantime wait here with Mark; phone me or the station if you encounter any hitches.''

Sion, captivated by this unusual professional experience, straightened his slim but muscular six-foot frame and, his marked north Wales accent flowing through his self-assured strong voice, said. 'There shouldn't be any problem, Alan.'

65

Alan Reed arrived at the beach just before six-forty.

Martin Ford and his colleague, Jeff Arnold, plus a paramedics' team, were there, their vehicles' headlights focusing on the cave's entrance. Amy Coleman's white Mini was parked near the entrance.

Alan zipped up his heavy fleece-lined navy anorak, put on his cap and fleece-lined gloves, jumped out of his vehicle and greeted his colleagues and the paramedics' team. He briefed them and then said, 'The SUV's headlights can stay on full beam.' He walked to Amy Coleman's car: the driver's door was unlocked and the keys were in the ignition. He closed the door, placed his hand on the bonnet; it was warm. He told Martin Ford and then said, 'I'll enter the cave alone.'

No one questioned him.

'Thank you.' He switched on his torch, focused the strong beam on the cave's sandy floor and followed the only set of footprints. Half way into the cavern his foreboding was realised.

Five minutes later he came out and phoned Tim Wilding. 'I'm at Criccieth beach; a dead female, who could be Amy Coleman, is inside the cave where the other bodies were discovered. My colleagues and a paramedics' crew are here.'

Tim and his team would be there in approximately forty minutes.

'OK.' Alan said, 'I'll brief everybody.'

Alan told everyone, then informed Martin Ford of the situation in the flat in Criccieth and then told him: 'I'm returning there now, shouldn't be long gone. In the meantime, if you encounter any problems contact me on the radio phone and update the duty officer in Madogton.'

While walking towards his vehicle Alan recalled what he'd told Eric Bolton and colleagues regarding his opinion on the people involved. While exploring the info and the evidence, he was of the opinion that Kelly Glover was the dominant player in the incredible drama and the scheming advocate in the apparent domestic strife. Was she tormented by an unsettling life? If so, was the personal wounding sufficient to cause her abundant mental unrest to become destructive? Yes was Alan's unequivocal conclusion. A pause, then he thought: but how do I prove it?

Shaking his head and scowling, Alan opened the vehicle's door, sat in the driver's seat, radio phoned Sion Parry, described the beach's scenario and then said, 'I can hear music. Sion; I recognise it; it's *Ebb Tide* by Matt Monro, apt for the circumstances?'

'Kelly Glover's playing a CD,' Sion Parry said, and then commented: 'Anti-climax?'

'Might be,' Alan said and, adrenaline stimulating his thinking, told Sion: 'This chilling story began in Josie Harold's property.' His breathing and heart rate increasing, he added: 'Check inside the garage,' a short pause, then: 'I'll be with you in about fifteen minutes; I have more questions for Kelly. Don't mention to her what I've discovered.' He ended the call and drove away.

66

Vital thoughts captivated Alan Reed's attention as he drove from the beach to Criccieth: is it possible that human behaviour can be afforded from inculcated aspects of literature, generating manipulative power by proxy to vulnerable individuals? Intimidating emotional mechanisms beyond logic had dominated this inquiry, and the oblique mystery continues. He'd phone the North Wales Police from Criccieth.'

The street was quiet. Icy cold rain, driven by a light wind, attacked the SUV's windscreen as he parked the vehicle outside the flat's garage.

After a short, sharp intake of breath, Alan phoned the North Wales Police HQ in Conwy County. He explained the situation to a senior officer, that he updated the inquiry evidence board daily, but had failed to determine a pattern to or piece together any of the activities. Concrete evidence to charge any person or persons involved was absent.

The senior officer, appreciating the seriousness of the baffling events, told Alan to continue his present action, inform the coroner and forensics. He added that he would phone the hospital to confirm the officers' arrival, and then he'd inform their relatives and reassure them. He then said that officers from adjacent divisions would be deployed if help was required, he'd inform WPC Manning to this effect, and then he emphasised that media reporting of the incidents would be blocked until further notice.

Alan thanked him, ended the call and sighed from satisfaction. He added a long blue woollen scarf to his weather-beating outfit, got out the SUV and, teeth chattering, walked to the garage.

It was locked.

He thumped the garage's main door with the side of his gloved fist.

No answer.

He listened.

No sounds from inside.

Alan shook his head and walked to the garage's small side window.

No light on. Weird.

He knocked on the garage's side door.

No response.

He tuned the torch's beam to maximum intensity and walked in the driving wintry rain across an empty parking area at the rear of the garage to the track that ran along the garage's side wall. Kelly's white Vauxhall Astra was parked there, facing the main road. Odd.

He radio phoned Martin and updated him.

Alan approached the wet iron stairway and looked up at the flat.

The light above the main door wasn't on, strange; he'd alerted Sion Parry of his visit.

He shivered; felt his body was caught inside an icy straightjacket, as he climbed to the flat's door.

He looked at a windows while he regained his breath- no lights on in this particular division of the flat.....the place lacked affection. Perspiring, heart pounding rapidly, nervous and hesitant, he knocked on the door.

Seconds later, the outside light came on and the door opened.

Kelly had changed her beach-walking look and gear: her hair was groomed and her clothes consisted of a red cotton polo shirt under a cream V-neck woollen sweater, grey jeans and black loafers. She looked relaxed. A thin smile lurking between plain lips appeared as she greeted him: 'Hello again, PC Reed, your colleague told me you'd be revisiting me. Please come inside from the nasty weather.'

'Thank you.' Alan switched off his torch, pocketed it, and then asked her: 'Has my colleague, PC Parry, been to the garage?'

'Immediately after your call, Constable Reed.'

'Did he comment on his visit when he returned to the flat?'

Kelly shook her head. 'No, said he was waiting for you to return.'

'Where is he now?'

'In the front room with his colleague; no point having lights on in any other.' She grinned and then told Alan: 'Remove your wet anorak and cap, hang them on the hall's hooks and then follow me.'

Concerned that his colleagues hadn't greeted him, a worried Alan followed an impetuous Kelly into the room.

Sion Parry and his colleague were sitting in the three-seater sofa, staring at the wall, oblivious to Kelly and Alan's presence.

The startled Alan walked over to them. 'Hello, chaps.'

No reply, each man wedged inside a controlled poise.

A bemused, speechless Alan looked at Kelly.

'Hypnotised. PC Reed. Both will be out of the trance in two hours,' and then, following a theatrical gesture with a wave of her hand at the sofa, she said, 'Please join them.'

67

The slim, six-two tall, thirty-year-old Martin Ford and the paramedics' crew greeted Tim Wilding and his team when they arrived at the breezy, icy cold, rainy beach at seven-forty-five.

Martin explained the situation. 'Another complex story, Dr Wilding. The woman was last seen alive just before six this evening.'

Tim Wilding looked at him, didn't comment, and then asked: 'Where is the body, Martin?'

'The police car and the paramedics' ambulance headlights are focused on the cave's entrance. The body is about thirty yards inside.'

Tim Wilding and his team donned their forensic garb and then Tim told his photographer, Tony Simpson. 'Usual photos please.'

Tony Simpson, Tim Wilding and the third member of the team, Edward Brown entered the cave, torches in full beam mode and, helped by the vehicles' headlights, they walked slowly along the uneven sandy floor. The clothed woman was lying on her back.

Photographs were taken.

A shivering Tim Wilding made a cursory examination of the body and then looked at Edward Brown. 'Judge the scene and findings please, Ed.'

'The temperature inside the cave is touching freezing,' a cold, quivering Edward Brown said, 'rigor has started in the eyes and the upper facial muscles; the face has the classical grimacing look. Rigor mortis will not be complete for numerous hours. I'll check the liver temperature,' a shrug of his shoulders, then he said, 'the cave's conditions will be factored into my assessment as to the time of death.' He read the liver temperature probe and then, pointing to the lower part of the body's trunk, said, 'The presence of lividity here suggests she hasn't been moved so, from the history, the present findings and the near-freezing conditions, I estimate death occurred an hour ago.........maybe fifteen minutes each side.'

Tim Wilding nodded.

The forensic team left the cave and then Tim advised the paramedics to take the body to the lab in Bangor.

Tim Wilding, and his colleagues, now wearing their cold weather clothes and woollen beanie hats, approached Martin Ford and said, 'Remind me of the history again.'

'Confusing events and acts have dominated today,' Martin said after he'd described the timetable of events leading up to the discovery of the body. He added: 'PC Alan Reed is in charge; senior officers in the North Wales Police HQ are advising him.'

Tim thanked him, then said. 'Nothing more for my team to do here,' then, shivering, added: 'I'll be glad to leave this intensely cold, wet and breezy blackness.'

Martin thanked him, then said, 'No more work for the police here either; I'll inform PC Reed; he'll contact the coroner.'

Tim nodded.

The forensic team entered their van and left.

Martin informed his colleague, Jeff of the situation, and then said, 'We can pack up now.'

They entered the car and Martin said, 'I'll arrange for Amy Coleman's car to be taken to the police car compound in Madogton before I update Alan.'

The car would be collected within fifteen minutes.

Martin told Jeff: 'Have some of your hot drink while I speak with Alan.' He hit four digits on his radiophone and waited.

No answer.

Martin hit the digits again.

No answer. Uncanny.

'I'll phone Mark Lloyd.'

Martin waited ten seconds, twenty seconds, and then, in a strong voice, told Jeff Arnold: 'Speed to the flat in Criccieth.'

68

Jeff parked the SUV outside the flat's garage.

Both men got out, walked briskly to the iron staircase, and then Martin stopped, considered what Alan had told him and, pointing, said, 'Jeff, check if there's a car parked on the other side of the garage.'

Seconds later, Jeff, exhaling white plumes as he returned, announced: 'No car there, Martin.'

Martin said, 'Upstairs; careful, steps are wet, may be icy.'

A light was on in the flat's hall.

Martin knocked the door.

No answer.

Using his well-padded elbow he thumped it three times.

No response.

He unlocked the door with the duplicate key Alan had provided; they entered the hall and Jeff shut the door quietly.

Martin placed an index finger against his closed lips. No noise was heard inside the flat.

Martin then called out: 'Kelly,' and then his colleagues' names.

No reply.

A shivering Martin told Jeff. 'Check the rooms at the front of the flat, I'll inspect the others.'

A moment later Jeff shouted: 'In the front lounge.'

Alan Reed, Sion Parry and Mark Lloyd were sitting on the sofa, bland faces, and their wide-open eyes staring at the opposite wall.

Martin and Jeff walked towards them.

No response from the three.

'Hypnotised?' an anxious Martin suggested, then to Jeff: 'We'll look inside the garage.'

They left the flat, descended the iron stairway slowly and Martin opened the garage side door. He shone his torch on the wall, found the light switch. A woman's body was on the floor.

'I'll phone HQ and then update Madogton police,' a tense and perspiring Martin said, taking the radio phone out of his jacket.

He was about to dial when his radio phone buzzed. A police constable was on the line, said he was at the cave and then asked Martin: 'Did you say there was only one car, a white Mini, to be collected?'

'Correct. Why?'

The constable answered in a quiet voice: 'An unoccupied white Vauxhall Astra is parked next to it. The driver's door is unlocked and the keys are in the ignition.'

Lightning Source UK Ltd.
Milton Keynes UK
UKOW01f1428190218
318127UK00001B/80/P